Dear Reader,

There's a place where life moves a little slower, where a neighborly smile and a friendly hello can still be heard. Where news of a wedding or a baby on the way is a reason to celebrate—and gossip travels faster than a telegram! Where hope lives in the heart, and love's promises last a lifetime.

The year is 1874, and the place is Harmony, Kansas...

A TOWN CALLED HARMONY
PLAYING CUPID

She owns the town dress shop, but Jane Carson's one true love is medicine—and she happily fills in for the local doctor in a pinch...

Years ago, Alexander Evans came to Harmony to start his own newspaper—and to forget the pain of being abandoned by his wife...

When the newsman's arm is badly injured while working his press, he rushes next door to the boardinghouse for help—and unwittingly steps into the latest matchmaking schemes of Maisie Hastings and Minnie Parker! Calling on Jane Carson to set Alex's broken arm, Maisie ponders what Jane's tender care might do for his lonely heart. Not to be outdone at playing cupid, Minnie comes up with her own perfect match for the fiercely independent Jane. But no one, not even the meddlesome twins, can predict the magic moment when Jane realizes that time does indeed heal all wounds—and that the love of her life is right by her side...

*Turn the page to meet
the folks of Harmony, Kansas...*

Welcome to A TOWN CALLED HARMONY . . .

MAISIE HASTINGS & MINNIE PARKER, *proprietors of the boardinghouse . . . These lively ladies, twins who are both widowed, are competitive to a fault—who bakes the lightest biscuits? Whose husband was worse? Who can say the most eloquent and (to their boarders' chagrin) the longest grace? And who is the better matchmaker? They'll do almost anything to outdo each other—and absolutely everything to bring loving hearts together!*

JAKE SUTHERLAND, *the blacksmith . . . Amidst the workings of his livery stable, he feels right at home. But when it comes to talking to a lady, Jake is awkward, tongue-tied . . . and positively timid!*

JANE CARSON, *the dressmaker . . . She wanted to be a doctor like her grandfather. But the eccentric old man decided that wasn't a ladylike career—and bought her a dress shop. Jane named it in his honor: You Sew and Sew. She can sew anything, but she'd rather stitch a wound than a hem.*

ALEXANDER EVANS, *the newspaperman . . . He runs The Harmony Sentinel with his daughter, Samantha. But something is missing from his rather solitary newsman's life—and a good and caring woman is about to make all the difference . . .*

JAMES AND LILLIAN TAYLOR, *owners of the mercantile and post office* ... With their six children, they're Harmony's wealthiest and most prolific family. It was Lillie, as a member of the Beautification Committee, who acquired the paints that brightened the town.

"LUSCIOUS" LOTTIE McGEE, *owner of the First Resort* ... Lottie's girls sing and dance and even entertain upstairs ... but Lottie herself is the main attraction at her enticing saloon. And when it comes to taking care of her own cousin, this enchanting madam is all maternal instinct.

CORD SPENCER, *owner of the Last Resort* ... Things sometimes get out of hand at Spencer's rowdy tavern, but he's mostly a good-natured scoundrel who doesn't mean any harm. And when push comes to shove, he'd be the first to put his life on the line for a friend.

SHERIFF TRAVIS MILLER, *the lawman* ... The townsfolk don't always like the way he bends the law a bit when the saloons need a little straightening up. But Travis Miller listens to only one thing when it comes to deciding on the law: his conscience.

ZEKE GALLAGHER, *the barber and the dentist* ... When he doesn't have his nose in a dime Western, the white-whiskered, blue-eyed Zeke is probably making up stories of his own—or flirting with the ladies. But not all his tales are just talk—once he really *was* a notorious gunfighter ...

Diamond Books by Donna Fletcher

REBELLIOUS BRIDE
PLAYING CUPID

A TOWN CALLED
HARMONY

PLAYING CUPID

Donna Fletcher

DIAMOND BOOKS, NEW YORK

If you purchased this book without a cover, you should be aware that this book is stolen property. It was reported as "unsold and destroyed" to the publisher, and neither the author nor the publisher has received any payment for this "stripped book."

This book is a Diamond original edition,
and has never been previously published.

PLAYING CUPID

A Diamond Book / published by arrangement with
the author

PRINTING HISTORY
Diamond edition / November 1994

All rights reserved.
Copyright © 1994 by Charter Communications, Inc.
This book may not be reproduced in whole or in part,
by mimeograph or any other means, without permission.
For information address: The Berkley Publishing Group,
200 Madison Avenue, New York, NY 10016.

ISBN: 0-7865-0056-5

Diamond Books are published by The Berkley Publishing Group,
200 Madison Avenue, New York, NY 10016.
DIAMOND and the "D" design
are trademarks belonging to Charter Communications, Inc.

PRINTED IN THE UNITED STATES OF AMERICA

10 9 8 7 6 5 4 3 2 1

To my nephew Frank Pizzuta, Jr.
Without his computer genius this
book would have never been finished.
Thank you and much happiness and love
on your marriage to Karen.

and

To Diana Jones
a woman whose own life would make
a page-turning book.
Thank you for being such a good friend.

One

"Damn!" Alexander Evans shouted, his strong voice a lonely echo in the empty office.

Alex glared at the offensive printing press. The object that banged and clattered day after day, sometimes late into the night, bringing to life his newspaper, the *Harmony Sentinel*.

Twenty years of experience he had running the press—twenty years! He shook his head in disgust. Since the age of nineteen he had run a press and without one accident. Now suddenly he had an accident a first-year apprentice would suffer.

A sharp pain shot through his right hand and arm that he held cradled in his left, reminding him the sturdy press wasn't responsible. He was.

Alex sat down on a nearby chair, a wave of dizziness rushing over him. It was all his own fault. He had pushed himself to the limit all night, working straight through till morning and drinking nothing but lukewarm coffee.

He leaned his head back against the wall and squeezed his eyes shut, attempting to concentrate on anything but the infernal pain.

He could use a cigar right now, the thin cheroots he derived such pleasure from and a glass of good whiskey. The kind that burned going down and soon after dulled the senses.

Opening his eyes, he focused on the metal monster that had half chewed his arm. How was he going to get his paper out now? Or for that matter, how would he tend to all the other work that was necessary in producing the *Sentinel*?

Another stabbing pain reminded him those problems could be settled later. Right now he had to get some help. He eased himself to the edge of the chair, cushioning his injured arm against his stomach and continuing to cradle it in his left hand. He stood slowly, wavered a moment, then took a few tentative steps.

The dizziness subsided and he felt more in control. Knowing his arm needed immediate attention, he decided it would be wise to go next door to the boardinghouse. Minnie Parker and Maisie Hastings, the twin widowed sisters that ran it, would be up and about by now. They would probably be in the kitchen in the back of the house attending to breakfast for their boarders.

He gave a quick glance around his office, deciding on which route would be the shortest and least painful for him to take. Taking the front entrance from his office would mean a walk past the worktable and the now silent printing press. He'd have to pass the two desks facing the two large windows that proudly proclaimed in bold black letters that the building was the *Sentinel* and that it was owned and operated by Alexander Evans. And though it was early morning, there were bound to be curious townsfolk about on Main Street who would converge on him with offers of assistance.

He turned his attention to the door that led from the office into the kitchen. When he had purchased the building, he'd had one big kitchen built, moving the sitting room upstairs to join the bedrooms. He had wanted easy access from the kitchen to the garden and the woodpile in the backyard and he didn't want to go all the way upstairs when he worked late and wanted another cup of coffee. Fortunately, it also provided accessibility to next-door neighbors' yards and back doors.

He could make it next door to the boardinghouse without being seen and with as little, and he hoped as painless, an effort as possible.

He walked steadily toward the back door and with a troubled shake of his head stared at the handle. This was just the beginning, he thought. With his right hand and arm possibly broken, how many things would he find himself incapable of doing?

It took more than just a bit of an effort to open the door and walk the few steps next door to the boardinghouse. By the time Alex was ready to knock on the back door, his forehead was damp with perspiration from the exerted effort and pain.

He heard the distinct clang of pots and pains mingled with argumentative voices. He shook his head. Minnie and Maisie were at it again. They agreed on nothing. They probably wouldn't even agree that his arm was broken.

He gave thought to the idea of seeking help elsewhere and was about to turn away when the door swung open.

"Golden brown," Minnie said, her attention directed at her sister standing next to the black cookstove that spewed a steady stream of smoke from its oven. "Golden brown, not burnt," Minnie stressed once again and fanned the door to chase the smoke from the kitchen.

Alex coughed, more to draw her attention than from the smoke that barely made its way out the door. It lingered in the room probably too intimidated to pass by the tall gray-haired woman.

"My goodness, Alexander, why didn't you announce yourself?" Minnie berated and motioned him in with a wave of her hand, never even noticing he needed assistance. "Don't mind the smoke. Maisie's attempting to bake her biscuits again."

"And someone sabotaged my batch," Maisie said, looking her sister directly in the eye.

Affronted, Minnie grabbed her chest dramatically. "Are you accusing me?"

Before matters got completely out of hand and before he collapsed from the pain, Alex interrupted. "I need help ladies."

His words were like a bucket of water poured on a raging fire. Their tempers cooled and they both immediately turned their full attention on him.

"What's the problem?" Minnie asked, wiping her hands clean on a nearby towel.

Maisie wiped her hands on her white apron tied snugly around her waist and shook her head. "It seems obvious. Your arm," she said confidently and walked over to him. She gently pushed him to sit down in the chair next to the worktable covered with bowls, utensils, and flour, and with one quick look she announced, "It's broken."

"Let me see," Minnie demanded and marched over to Alex to inspect his arm, brushing her sister aside.

Alex stiffened, prepared for some rough handling from Minnie, but surprisingly she gave him a quick look, as her sister had, and reached the same conclusion. "It's broken."

Maisie shook her head and irritably confirmed her previous statement. "I said that."

"Just making certain, dear," Minnie said and with a no nonsense tone added, "We best fetch Dr. Tanner."

Maisie, in a flurry of motion, rushed to untie her apron strings. "I'll go fetch help."

Minnie, notably pleased by her sister's unusual compliance, turned her attention to Alex. "Let's see if we can make you more comfortable while we wait for Dr. Tanner."

Alex didn't want Minnie moving his arm in hopes of "making him comfortable." "A cup of that delicious-smelling coffee sure would help."

"Why, certainly," Minnie said with a satisfied smile. "You know the boarders always remark on how tasty

PLAYING CUPID

my coffee is. They much prefer it to Maisie's strong brew. She tends to—"

Alex watched as Minnie paused and cast an uncertain glance at the back door. "Something wrong?"

"Not at all," Minnie assured him, but her wrinkled brow registered otherwise.

Alex wondered what was going on. Maisie had rushed out of there awfully fast in request to her sister's suggestion of fetching Dr. Tanner. Now Minnie seemed terribly concerned about something and he was sure it involved Maisie.

Minnie placed the filled coffee cup on the table in front of him just as the back door opened, admitting Maisie and Jane Carson.

The shocked and annoyed expression on Minnie's face would have been almost laughable if Alex wasn't so concerned with his arm. Jane Carson owned the local dressmaker's shop, and besides being experienced with a needle and thread she was also schooled in some areas of medicine. Most of the townsfolk had relied on her to tend them until the new doctor had arrived in Harmony. But with the doctor's arrival, Jane Carson's status had changed.

"Where's Dr. Tanner?" Minnie asked bluntly.

Jane ignored both women's bickering nature and walked directly over to Alex. "Mind if I look at your arm?"

Maisie hurried over herself, ignoring her sister's question and her accusatory stare. "It's broken and he appeared in such pain that I thought it best to fetch you, being you're right across the street."

"Mind?" Jane repeated, focusing her attention on Alex.

Alex shrugged. "Don't mind as long as it gets fixed right." He hadn't taken much notice of Jane Carson. And he didn't take notice of her now except to watch her long graceful fingers gently press along his arm. Her hands were cool, her examination thoughtful. Though she caused him pain, he didn't seem to mind. It wasn't intentional, and she certainly appeared knowledgeable. She worked her way down to his hand. He squeezed his eyes shut for a moment against the pain that shot up his arm when she probed his thumb area.

"Broken in several places," she announced. "You're not going to be able to use that hand and arm for a good six weeks, maybe longer."

"What?" Alex yelled and jumped out of his seat only to realize that he was unbearably dizzy.

With his complexion paling to milky white, Jane eased him back into his seat. "Longer if you continue to make such stupid moves."

Alex's eyes narrowed and his reproachful remark was meant to irritate. "Are you certain you know what you're doing?"

Minnie interfered, and too pleasantly to Alex's way of thinking. "I'm sure Jane is perfectly correct in her suggestion, but why don't I go fetch Dr. Tanner just to make certain?" Minnie didn't wait for anyone to agree. She was out the door, her apron deposited with a careless toss to a nearby chair.

Maisie gave an anxious glance to the back door before singing Jane's praises. "Jane studied medicine with her grandfather. He was a prominent physician with a large mining company. She spent near her entire childhood watching and learning as he tended to ill and injured people."

Alex couldn't help but be impressed by her background. He didn't doubt that she probably possessed the same amount of medical knowledge as the doctor. The townsfolk spoke highly of her, and she was well-respected in Harmony. She dressed fashionably, though her brown hair was cut short, hugging in curls about her face, an unusual style since most women wore their hair long and done up. She had big brown eyes that stared at you from a round face, which was precisely what she was doing now. Staring at him.

She was waiting for him to speak. She had no intention of defending herself. She actually looked as though she deemed it unnecessary. Her confidence in herself was obviously secure, and it annoyed him. "How am I suppose to tend to my newspaper?"

"You'll need to find help," she answered and held her hand out, waiting for his acceptance of her capability.

More reluctant about his circumstances than her treatment, he frowned and carefully offered her his arm. "Don't know how I'm going to get the newspaper out."

"Your daughter can help you," Jane said, her fingers probing the bones in his arm after cautiously resting it on the table that Maisie had considerately cleared off.

Maisie responded to Jane's suggestion, surprisingly issuing the same remark he himself would have made. "Samantha's newly married. She doesn't have time to help."

"Then Billy Taylor can help," Jane said, her fingers applying more pressure.

Alex tried to object. "He's not—"

"I don't have time to argue with you," Jane said. "I need to set these bones. Now hold still, this is going to hurt."

Alex braced himself just in time. The pain nearly sent him into a dead faint. He felt nauseated, and his head dropped forward, his chin nearly touching his chest.

A gentle pressure at his shoulder and a soothing voice kept him in touch with reality.

"The worst is over. Just relax."

Alex found himself taking the softly spoken advice. His head lolled to the side, resting against a pillowy softness and a smell so fresh and sweet he thought for an instant he had stumbled upon a flower garden in his mist of unreality.

"The pain will pass in a few moments, then I can put on the splints and wrap you up."

Alex lifted his head to address the voice and looked straight up into Jane Carson's large brown eyes. Silky brown lashes framed them and added to their charm.

Her look was one of warmth, tenderness, and a spot of vulnerability that tempted his heart.

With a sudden awareness that came like the dousing of cold water, Alex realized his head was cushioned to Jane's midriff and his thoughts were far from appropriate. Why, she was twenty-eight and he thirty-nine. Besides, he had no interest in a relationship. One disastrous marriage was enough.

He straightened in his seat, away from her sweet-smelling body, carefully so as not to disturb his set arm. He intended to remain in control of his senses. And his senses at the moment were concerned with how easily he had relied on her. He wasn't accustomed to relying on anyone. He had always managed to look after himself and his daughter. But now with his arm incapacitated, what was he to do?

"Will I have any mobility in my fingers?" he asked as Jane stepped around the table away from him to continue working on him.

"Afraid not," she answered honestly. "Your bones need to mend and that means no movement. The broken bones in your arm and hand need splints and wrapping to keep them in place."

Alex mumbled beneath his breath, growing more annoyed over the simple necessities he wouldn't be able to perform for himself. Fastening a shirt. Pulling on his boots. Shaving. "Damn!"

Jane grinned in understanding. "Just realized what you did to yourself?"

"What I *did*," he emphasized, "was work too hard."

"An excuse," Jane accused. "You're old enough to be responsible for your actions."

With his temper steadily climbing, Alex attempted to remain in control. Especially since she was right, though he wouldn't openly admit it. "I am responsible, Miss Carson, that's why I intend to see to my own care once you manage to put me together."

"I'll *put* you together, Mr. Evans, but managing to care for yourself is another matter."

"Think me incapable?" he challenged.

"Not incapable—idiotic if you try." Jane held her hand up, preventing his response. "If you want the breaks to heal properly and quickly, you need to keep your arm immobile."

Alex's question held an edge of sarcasm. "And how do you propose I shave?"

"Grow a beard," Jane said.

"And cook?"

Jane rolled her eyes heavenward. "Goodness gracious, Mr. Evans, do you really think the good ladies of Harmony would let you starve?"

Maisie found this the perfect opportunity to interfere and to put her matchmaking abilities to work. "Alexander has a point, Jane. You yourself stressed his need of help. His hasty and sufficient recovery really depends on live-in help to see him through."

Live-in? Alex gave the idea thought, but only momentarily. He was finally on his own, Samantha married and gone. He enjoyed the solitude, the ease with which he could smoke a cigar and have a drink without his daughter reminding him that too many whiskeys were no good for him and the cigar smoke lingered too long, staling the air. He loved his daughter, but she was married and had a husband of her own to fuss over. And now it was time for him to enjoy his independence. Live-in help sounded not at all appealing.

Jane agreed to his displeasure. "A good idea, Maisie. If he can find someone to tend to things for him on an everyday basis, he'll heal faster."

"Exactly," Maisie said, her mind working wildly.

"I don't know about that, ladies." Alex attempted to interfere, but to no avail. The two women went right on talking and planning.

"I could ask around and see if anyone would be interested," Jane offered.

Maisie smiled sweetly. "Oh, I know the perfect person."

"You do?" Jane and Alex sang in unison.

Maisie nodded, her smile even wider. "She's perfect. A good cook. An excellent housekeeper. Pleasant personality."

"Grab the woman before she gets away," Jane said, looking to Alex with those wide eyes that challenged and cajoled all at once.

Maisie felt victory close at hand and proceeded to secure her win. "Sound advice, Alexander. You should listen to Jane; she does know best."

Alex grumbled. He knew they were right. If he had help, he'd heal faster and once again would be independent. He supposed a bit of help for a few hours a day would be all right. "If you think she would be agreeable, I could use her assistance a few hours a day."

Maisie's mind turned like the wheels of a runaway wagon. "Goodness, Alexander. You need live-in help, not part-time. You will need constant supervision, being your right hand and arm are useless. Why, she'd have to cook and clean, wash your clothes, help you shave, and—"

"Now, just a minute," Alex protested strongly. He wanted no woman tending to him so intimately. "That doesn't sound proper."

"He's got you there, Maisie," Jane said with a wink.

Maisie returned her wink with confidence. "But the woman I have in mind would be acceptable to you and the townsfolk."

She peeked both their curiosities. "Who?" They once again sang out together.

Minnie interfered with Maisie's answer as she hurried through the door. "The doctor's here to take care of everything."

Maisie smiled broadly, her posture straightening tall and proudly. "He's really not needed. Jane has seen to Alexander's arm *and*," she emphasized dramatically, "Jane is going to move in with Alexander and tend to his needs while he recovers."

Two

"Absolutely not!" two voices rang out simultaneously.

"But both of your favored the idea," Maisie reminded them, her confidence still noticeable in her rigid stance.

"It's nonsense," Minnie interfered, giving Dr. Tanner a nudge toward Jane.

Jacob Tanner, a soft-spoken man, ran a slow hand through his graying black hair while he cast a studious glance over Alex's injured arm and added his opinion. "It may not be nonsense. From the look of things, I'd say Alex will be on the mend for at least six weeks."

Maisie seized the opportunity. "See, Alex, Jane's diagnosis was correct. Her talent regarding medical matters would certainly help you throughout your recovery and her stay in your home would not be considered improper, since she has nursed many a man and woman in their homes before."

Jacob probed Alex's arm carefully. "All set to splint and wrap. You did an excellent job, Miss Carson. Where did you acquire such skills?"

"My grandfather was a doctor. He taught me," Jane answered, eager to change the subject. She wanted no part of playing nursemaid to Alexander Evans. She hardly knew him. She was aware that he owned and operated the Harmony *Sentinel* and that young, fourteen-year-old Billy Taylor helped him out. His daughter, Samantha, had recently wed Cord Spencer. And now all the eligible women of Harmony were staking their claims for Alex. Husband-hungry they were.

But not Jane Carson. She relished her independence and intended to keep it. Besides, she had her own shop—You Sew and Sew—to look after. Her business occupied a good portion of her time. Where would she find the time to care for Alex? Though she reluctantly admitted to herself that Alex was a good-looking man as men go. His brown hair waved and skimmed his shirt collar. The faint lines around his soft blue eyes added character to his strong features and alerted her to the fact that he wasn't a man who did much frowning. He appeared to have aged nicely for his almost forty years. No fat or bulges, just firm muscle tone from what she could see, and what she couldn't, she imagined.

Jane chastised herself for such foolish wanderings. Alexander Evans's attributes were best left for someone else to favor. Jane Carson intended to remain independent and free.

Minnie's praising remark caught her attention and pleased her.

"With more professional nurturing, Jane would make an excellent physician herself."

Maisie stepped forward. "The matter at hand is Alexander's need of help."

"I agree," Dr. Tanner said. "He will require assistance."

Maisie set her sights on Jane and with a deadly sweet smile charged in for the final assault. "Men are such helpless creatures, dear. Women need to do everything for them. Why, poor Alexander won't even be able to button his own shirt. And feed himself?" Maisie shook her head, her smile fading to a frown. "Just think of the problems he will face alone and helpless."

Alex had heard enough. *Helpless* was not a word he

associated with himself. "I'll manage just fine, and if not, I'll find someone who can lend a hand."

Maisie intended victory at all costs. "Jane won't hear of it?"

Jane didn't want to hear anymore. It was obvious Maisie and Minnie were up to their old matchmaking schemes. Maisie was out to snare Alex as a husband for Jane and Minnie intended Jacob as her victim for Jane. Both women were in for a big surprise.

Maisie continued as if speaking for Jane. "Why, no decent lady would forsake an upstanding gentleman like yourself in such a time of need. Jane is too kind-hearted and caring to refuse to tend you. Right, Jane?"

All eyes focused on Jane.

Jane stood looking first to Maisie and then to Alex. She could easily refuse to help him. It would not bother her in the least. But this little game between Minnie and Maisie intrigued her. She also had the distinct feeling that Alex didn't want any part of her intruding in his life. And part of her, the part that loved to tease, pushed her to answer, "You're absolutely right, Maisie. I'll move into Alex's home today and take care of him."

Alex almost leaped out of his chair, but his wiser side kept him planted to the seat. Jane Carson wore a teasing grin he intended to wipe off—and enjoy doing so in the process. With charm and a thoughtful smile Alex said, "Thank you, Jane, I appreciate your help."

Minnie sought to champion her own choice in this matchmaking war. "Jacob, wouldn't this be the perfect opportunity for you to take Jane on as an apprentice?"

Jane felt her breath catch. She had always wanted to further her studies in medicine. Her grandfather had taught her much, but new procedures and cures were constantly being discovered, and she wanted to learn all she could.

"I could use an assistant," Jacob answered anxiously. "Harmony certainly does have its fair share of ailments and accidents, and Jane certainly has adequate knowledge."

Encouraged by his response, Minnie urged, "Just imagine, Jacob, helping a woman to study medicine. You would be a pioneer, a leader in your field with the fortitude to make a difference."

Jacob's chest expanded considerably. "The idea does sound appealing. I have heard of a few brave women attempting to enter medicine—and so they should. Jane, I would be delighted to take you on as my apprentice if you so desire."

Jane almost found herself speechless, but her excitement rattled forth her appreciation and acceptance. "I would be honored to apprentice with you. I have so wanted to study medicine further. But my grandfather felt I should have a respectable profession for a woman, and so he bought me the dressmaker's shop."

"Times are changing slowly, but they are changing," Jacob said. "Shall we both finish seeing to Alex's arm, if he doesn't object?"

Alex shook his head. "I have no objections." *Why should I? No one would listen.* His busy thoughts cluttered his brain. How the devil did he get into this mess? He didn't want a houseguest. A nursemaid. A woman telling him what to do in his own home. He didn't want six weeks of pure hell, and that was what he was facing. He was sentenced to a torturous six-week punishment for being such a fool. How the devil would he survive?

"Let me help you get your shirt off," Jane said and reached for the buttons at his chest.

His good hand grabbed her wrist. Iron-clad like a band of steel, his fingers wrapped around her, causing Jane's eyes to widen in surprise. "I can do that."

Jane nodded and backed away. "Suit yourself."

Alex fought with the buttons, popping two off to ping against the cookstove.

Jane stood, her arms crossed over her chest, watching.

Alex grumbled beneath his breath. He wanted to strangle Jane. Mainly because she had been right about him not being able to help himself, and because she stood there no doubt enjoying his foolish actions.

"Shall I help you slip it off?"

Alex looked up at Jane. Her expression was nonjudgmental. The decision was strictly his. He wondered how the hell she did that. Look so innocent and wide-eyed as though she couldn't care less. It irritated the hell out of him. "Sure, why not? Isn't that what you're suppose to be doing anyway?"

"If you would let me," Jane answered pleasantly.

"Fine," he grumbled and leaned forward away from the back of the chair.

Jane stepped close in front of him. His face almost touched the white cotton of her starched blouse. The stiff material fanned his cheek, his stubble of a near day's growth of beard scratching against it. The abrasive sound set his nerves on end and attuned his emotions to a fine high.

He warned himself to back away and was about to do so when her scent assaulted him. An intoxicating combination of fresh flowers and all woman drifted around him. With his emotions already on edge the alluring aroma stung his senses. He wanted desperately to wrap his arms around her waist, draw her close, and bury his face against her middle.

Jane's hand to his shoulder shocked his senses back to present matters. He reminded himself that he sat in Maisie and Minnie's kitchen and not a brothel. Jane Carson wasn't there for his pleasure. A sudden thought interrupted all others—had Jane ever known pleasure with a man?

"No."

Alex reared his head to look up at her, surprised by her response to his unspoken question.

"No," she repeated and shook her head, confirming her own thought. "I don't think this sleeve of yours is worth saving. The material is too torn to repair. I can cut this one right off—so we don't disturb your arm—and I can sew a replacement on tonight or tomorrow. Is that all right with you?"

Alex gave a quick nod of approval, finding himself speechless and his thoughts still focused on his silent query.

Jane's fingers worked like magic removing his shirt. He felt no physical discomfort, yet when her fingers brushed his flesh, his emotions set goose bumps scurrying across his exposed skin and embarrassment rushing to his cheeks.

He berated himself silently for the hundredth time, feeling more like a young schoolboy, fantasizing about his pretty schoolteacher. *Pretty?* Is that how he viewed Jane Carson?

He refused to look up at her and confirm his own suspicions, or display his own discomfort. He kept his eyes fixed steadily on the floor and attempted to concentrate on the pain in his arm, which he wished was all-consuming instead of bearable.

Jane and Jacob worked well together patching up Alex's arm. Jane's skillful manner aided by Jacob's suggestions made for little discomfort or pain for the patient.

Minnie and Maisie fluttered in and out of the room, busy tending to their boarders' breakfast.

Maisie, a platter of hot scrambled eggs firmly in hand, addressed Jane. "Poor Alexander looks exhausted from his ordeal. You should take him home and settle him down to rest."

Before Alex could protest, having hoped to sneak off alone, Dr. Tanner agreed.

"He could definitely use with some rest."

Jane draped his shirt over his shoulders, her hands remaining there to rest upon him. The warmth of her palms drifted into him, racing down his arms, tingling his flesh and making him feel good. Too good.

"I'll help you home and get you settled before I go collect my things," Jane said, her voice steady and professional.

Alex grew irritated over his reaction to her. She obviously felt nothing when she touched him. Why the hell did he?

Gruffly, and more at odds with himself than with Jane, he responded. "I can see myself home."

"Don't make my position any more difficult, Alex," she warned like a nurse chastising an ill-behaved patient. "Either I help you or I *don't*."

She had issued him an ultimatum. Either he agreed to her help or he didn't, plain and simple. He had no doubt if he answered no, she would waltz right out the door without a second thought. And for some strange and annoying reason, he didn't want her to. "Like I said before, I appreciate your help."

Maisie's smile was broad as she practically danced her way through the door to the dining room.

Minnie clattered dishes in annoyance, but her tone was pleasant as she suggested, "Perhaps you should help Jane, Jacob, just in case she has any questions to Alex's care."

Jacob Tanner continued packing his black bag as he answered, "Not necessary, Minnie. I'm confident Jane knows what she's doing and I'll stop by later this evening to see how Alex is feeling."

Jane smiled more in amusement at Minnie's failed attempt to have Jacob spend more time with her than with Jacob's words of confidence. Maisie definitely scored favorably in this matchmaking war. It was a shame both ladies faced defeat, but then the battle was half the fun.

Jane fashioned a sling out of the white cloth Minnie provided her with and gently, easing Alex's arm, she slipped it beneath and drew it up near his chest, securing it around his neck. "Ready to go?" she asked, noticing his complexion had paled.

The ordeal had caught up with him; so had the night without sleep. He wanted nothing more than his bed and oblivion. "All set."

Jane watched him stand, and when he wavered slightly, she slipped up beside him and wrapped her arm around his waist. "Come on, let's get you to bed. You look as though you're half asleep already."

Minnie grumbled and Jacob called out to her that he'd stop by after supper as she headed out the door with her patient firmly in hand.

Once Jane got Alex inside the office of the Harmony *Sentinel*, she sat him down in the first available chair.

"It's all caught up with you, hasn't it?"

Alex looked up at her. Her concern was evident in her tone and her expression. She actually cared how he felt. Her sincere concern pleased and relaxed him. "It sure has. I was stupid for working that press all night."

Jane offered her support. "We all do stupid things some time or another. We're entitled to—we're not perfect."

He smiled his appreciation, too tired to speak.

"You need rest. Do you think you can make the steps?"

Alex sighed. "They're awfully narrow. You won't be able to support me, but if I take them slow, I think I can make it."

Jane nodded, knowing she needed to get him upstairs, but worried he wouldn't make it. She assisted him to the steps. He was right, the passageway was narrow. "Take your time. I'll be right behind you."

Alex eyed her skeptically. "And if I fall, you go with me."

Jane laughed. "Nursing has its drawbacks."

Alex didn't want to see her hurt, especially by his hands, or body, or however he might land on top of her. "Wait at the bottom until I get upstairs."

Jane shook her head emphatically. "Absolutely not. We go together, or you don't go at all."

Alex attempted to protest.

Jane raised her hand. "Don't bother. You agreed to my help; let's not waste time."

"Stubborn female," Alex grumbled but with a smile.

"One of my better traits," Jane teased and waved him up the stairs.

She stayed behind him all the way. Her hands went to the curve of his back when the steps took a sharp winding turn. She felt him weaken, and she shoved as gently, but firmly as she could. "Come on, just a bit more."

"Slave driver," he softly protested.

"You're lucky I forgot my whip."

"Believe me, I've felt your sting. You don't need a whip."

"Thank you for the compliment," Jane said and stepped into the room behind him at the top of the steps. The parlor was neat and sparsely furnished. It was the books and papers and framed portraits of a little girl in various stages of childhood cluttered on the tables that gave the room a distinct comfort, a feeling of it being a home.

"Bedroom?" she asked, realizing Alex had braced himself against the wall with his eyes closed.

He raised his free hand and pointed. "Down that horribly long hallway."

Jane turned her amused smile away from him. The hallway wasn't long. His condition was the culprit. She laughed when she said the words that were certain to get him moving. "Where's your stamina, Alexander?"

Alex opened one eye and moaned before answering. "Probably at the bottom of the steps."

Jane laughed harder. He certainly could be amusing, even when in pain. "Come on, I'll help you." She eased his good arm over her shoulder, tucking herself in the crook of his arm for support. "Sort of like the three-legged race on the Fourth of July, only this one is the three-armed one of May."

Alex grinned. "Just hang on to me, and I'll make sure we take first place."

"And the prize?"

"The bed."

Jane's eyes flashed wide for one moment before catching her surprise. "What are we waiting for?"

"You."

His response had been whisper slow, and it sent the shivers through Jane. She didn't, actually couldn't, respond with any funny or lighthearted quip. She was too unnerved. She got her legs moving and with a minimal of effort made it the short distance to the room.

Jane almost went down on the bed with him as she deposited him on the faded blue quilt. She pulled the draped shirt off his shoulders and then bent in front of him to remove his boots.

"I'd like to say I'll take care of that myself, but I can't," Alex said, feeling miserably sorry for himself.

"That's what I'm here for," Jane reminded. In minutes she had his scuffed black boots off and him tucked beneath the quilt he had been sitting on. "Get some rest. I won't be long."

Her words weren't necessary. Alex's eyes had drifted closed as soon as his head landed on the pillow.

Jane cast a quick, surveying glance around the small room. A chest of drawers, a pitcher and washbowl stand, a brass bed, and a well-worn rocking chair with a table and lamp beside it.

Sparse but again that feeling of comfort caused by the hairbrush set, shaving set, and aftershave bottles arranged neatly on the beige crocheted scarf that ran over the chest of drawers. And then there was the shaded blue lap blanket draped over the arm of the rocker and the framed ink sketches of the Smoky Hill River that ran behind the Kansas Pacific Railroad tracks.

The room dripped of comfort, and the surprised emotion it stirred in Jane brought her glance down to the sleeping man in the bed.

She shook her head. "Alex," she whispered, as if testing his name on her lips. She hadn't expected his shoulders to be so broad when she had removed his shirt, or for his arms to possess such muscle texture, or his hands to have such determined strength.

Jane rubbed her wrist. She recalled the steel grip of his hand on her and the soft, yet decisive blue of his eyes when he looked at her. Even his hair held her fancy. It was the color of rich chocolate. The length was a bit long, he could use a trim. She could do that for him and shave him. And of course he probably would be hungry when he woke.

She shook her head again. This tending to his needs was one thing, but this preoccupation with his looks was another. She had to keep her senses about her. She wasn't in the market for a husband. Her grandfather had reminded her often enough that a woman with too much intelligence tended to remain an old maid. Old maid was not quite how she thought of herself. Free was.

And losing her head—or heart, as most women claimed—over a man wasn't on her list of accomplishments. Becoming a respected physician was, and she wasn't about to upset her chances with Dr. Tanner by involving herself with her patient.

"Stare all you want," Jane whispered to herself, "but remember the *study* of his anatomy is all you're interested in.

"You have work to do," she quietly reminded herself, forcing her thoughts to more important matters. She would see if the women she employed to help out at her dress shop could handle most of the work while she saw to Alex. Orders needed attending, supplies needed purchasing, and new patterns needed discussing.

"Get your business in order, Jane," she scolded herself, having always been organized and intending to make certain she remained so. Her seamstress shop, You Sew and Sew, was a thriving and lucrative business that she was proud of and allowed her to live independently. She didn't wish to give that advantage up, so she worked hard to maintain her shop's success.

She walked to the door ready to attend to business when she stopped and turned to look at Alex. He was quite a specimen of a man.

Study. The little voice reminded her. *Only study his anatomy.* She smiled, shook her head, and strolled out the door.

Three

ALEX moaned. His eyes remained closed, refusing to open. Almost every joint and muscle in his body ached. And his arm? Damn, was it stiff.

He attempted to straighten it when he felt the tug at his neck. His memory quickly caught up with his sleepy thoughts.

"Broken," he mumbled, and his eyes drifted open, a wide yawn accompanying them. The sunlight flooded through the lone window, and he realized it was early morning. His hand rubbed at his chin, the thick growth of stubble added to his observation that he had slept since yesterday morning.

And then of course there was that faint enticing smell that drifted from somewhere in the distance. He sniffed the air and was reminded of eggs, bacon, freshly baked biscuits, and coffee. Hot and strong, he hoped.

The door opened briskly, and the mouthwatering scent followed Jane Carson into the room with a flourish. "Good morning."

She stood in the doorway, a wide smile accenting her red cheeks and a white apron protecting her apricot day dress. Her brown short hair curled delightfully around her face, and her pleasant smile gave thought of a promising day.

"I slept all through yesterday and last night?" He

sought confirmation of a question he had already determined.

"That you did, and by the look of you, I'd say the much needed rest did you good."

Alex's eyes suddenly widened. "My newspaper!" He ripped the covers off himself and would have torn from the bed if it wasn't for Jane's hard shove to his chest.

"No sudden moves," she warned. "Your arm doesn't need any unnecessary jolting. It's just beginning to heal. And as for your newspaper, Billy Taylor and your daughter have seen to everything. I told Samantha to stop by sometime this afternoon to visit with you. Billy is busy downstairs with the press and will come up to talk with you when you're ready."

"I'd better see to—"

"A shave and breakfast. Which one first?"

Alex was about to argue when he caught another whiff of the eggs and bacon and the coffee—God could he use a cup of coffee. "Breakfast," he said without hesitation.

"I'll be right back up with it."

"I can go—"

"Over in that rocker by the window and wait," she finished, removing her hand from his chest to emphasize her order with a pointed finger in that direction.

He raised one brow. "Not until I wash up first and see to putting on a shirt."

"I'll bring some hot water up for you before I bring your breakfast tray, but the shaving you'll leave to me," she cautioned, fixing a steady stare on him while waiting for his objection.

"Much experience, dare I hope?" he asked in a teasing but apprehensive tone.

"Many years of shaving a cantankerous old gentleman," she confirmed with a nod and smiled.

"You've got the job."

"Never doubted I would," she said and waltzed out of the room.

Alex found himself grinning after her. Jane had lightened his usual ponderous morning mood considerably. Why hadn't he noticed his morning grouchiness until now? And how was it that Jane managed to bring a smile to his lips so easily? Her independent nature and forward manner weren't exactly desirable traits in a woman, yet he found her interesting.

In minutes she returned with the promised pitcher of water and filled the bowl for him.

Alex had managed to change into clean black pants, though getting on clean socks single-handedly was another matter.

Jane, after finishing her task and thinking nothing of her actions, dropped to her knees in front of him where he sat on the edge of the bed, and slipped, with great skill, his socks on his feet.

"Want your boots on?"

"They can wait," Alex said, recovering from the gooseflesh that ran up his leg when her fingers brushed his ankles, and the way her fingers sensitively slipped over his foot to make certain his sock fit snug and comfortable.

"I'll get your tray." With a vigorous bounce she got to her feet and took off once again.

She certainly had energy, Alex decided and made his way to the rocker. He stopped a few feet from it. And she certainly had a way of making him follow her commands. He enjoyed breakfast downstairs in the kitchen, yet he had allowed her to dictate to him. He was letting his emotions rule. Damn emotions he had kept locked away for so long that they had finally protested by breaking free and tormenting him.

"Sit down."

Startled by the voice behind him, he turned suddenly and almost collided with Jane and the breakfast tray she held.

"For goodness' sake, sit down!"

Alex remained standing in front of her. "I much prefer my breakfast downstairs in my kitchen."

Jane bit her lower lip for a brief second as though holding back her response, then she calmly explained. "With the set of your arm so fresh I thought it best you moved around as little as possible today. Especially taking those stairs too often, you would only unnecessarily jostle your arm."

Alex was properly and pleasantly chastised. "You do think of everything, don't you?"

"I try. Now, will you sit or continue to play the dominant, overbearing male?"

"I am not dominant and have never been overbearing," he snapped.

"Then sit down!"

Alex took a deep breath, ready for attack, when the smell of freshly baked biscuits and hot coffee rushed to his nostrils. Arguing on an empty stomach lost its appeal and without further comment he sat down.

Jane placed the tray on the table beside him, having cleared it off earlier so it would be ready for him. She sighed and rubbed her arm as she straightened up. "I understand how difficult this must be for you."

Alex settled back in the rocker; it swayed gently with his weight. "I doubt that. *You* have full use of your arms and hands."

Jane hitched her hands to her hips. "I suppose if you intend to remain cantankerous, I'll just have to deal with you that way."

"I am not cantankerous," he argued and reached for the coffeepot with his good hand to pour himself a cup.

She slapped his hand away and saw to the task herself. "If not cantankerous, then what would you call your grouchy manner?"

He gave the question serious thought. Perhaps it had been preoccupation with his work that had set him on edge lately. He had felt irritable—*cantankerous*—more so now with Samantha gone than before. He had attempted to convince himself it was his hectic work schedule that had him feeling so tautly strung. But if he admitted the truth to himself, it was the fact that he was now alone that had caused him such distress these last few days.

Jane rested her hand on his shoulder, offering him her comfort and concern.

Alex immediately became defensive. He didn't need, nor wanted her sympathy. "My cantankerous mood can be attributed to my nurse."

Jane's hand slipped from his shoulder. "How's that?"

Alex deliberately saw to adding his own cream and sugar to his coffee, making it clear by his actions, though clumsy, that there were things he could see to himself. "She thinks me an invalid, or worse, a child."

"Clearly understood." Jane walked toward the door to Alex's utter surprise. Halfway out the door she paused and turned. "I'll keep your place clean and see to your clothes and meals. If you want anything else from me, you need only to ask. Otherwise I'll stay out of your way." She walked out the door without even a backward glance.

Alex suddenly lost his ravenous appetite. She was a damn stubborn woman. Not like any he had ever known. Nothing like Liza. Liza wanted things he couldn't provide for her. She hadn't been happy with him or their little girl. And certainly not with their simple life. She wanted wealth and luxury and cared nothing for love. She finally found it with a wealthy banker from Philadelphia. After she had abandoned him and Samantha, Alex decided to pick up stakes and move west. To start life over. He had never regretted his decision, though he had never found love with another woman. He had had his work and his daughter, but what now?

He shook his head, after taking a drink of his coffee. He had thought he would enjoy his time alone after Samantha married, and he had for a short time. But then the rooms became too silent, the lone ticking of the clock too loud, his meals too lonely, and his solitary nights too long. That was why he had taken on extra printing work, to keep his hands and mind busy.

Now? Now because of his own making he was unable to tend to himself, and he was saddled with a woman who clearly spoke her mind and did as she pleased.

"Damnation," he muttered and reached for a biscuit, no longer hot, but warm enough to melt in his mouth. "She would have to be a good cook." He greedily finished the biscuit and, having faced his irate thoughts, found his stomach once again hungry.

Alex ate with a flourish, deciding that if Jane Carson provided him with sustenance and kept his place clean, there would be nothing else he needed from her.

An hour later he was cursing his own decision. After having finished his meal, he had decided to see to a shave and getting dressed so he could go downstairs and get back to work.

He had gotten his face lathered, but shaving himself was a different matter. He required two capable hands, not one. And besides that his injured arm had begun to throb unmercifully.

Jane waltzed into the room, humming a lively tune, and went directly to the table to fetch the tray. She spoke not a single word to him; she just hummed.

Alex stared at his lathered face in the mirror. His eyes, usually a soft blue, were stormy and his hand gripped his straight-edge razor too tightly.

Jane, tray in hand, wound her way past the foot of the bed and Alex.

"Jane."

She stopped near the door and turned, her humming ceased.

Alex outwardly remained calm, though the forced control in his tone signaled otherwise. "Shaving is difficult."

"I would assume so."

His nostrils flared. She wouldn't offer her help. She intended to make him ask for her assistance. He grew more irritated. "Two hands are necessary."

Her response was casual. "So they are."

He should have grown a beard. He shouldn't have attempted to shave. Now he was stuck standing here in front of her appearing the fool with lather all over himself and razor in hand, and no way of completing his task. And he could have sworn an I-told-you-so look was written on her face.

She remained silent, waiting.

He felt his pride swallow with the lump in his throat. "Could you give me a hand?"

"Certainly," she said with a smile and returned the tray to the table. "All you needed was to ask."

He had the distinct feeling that she intended for him to ask for anything he needed. Perhaps the day would come that she would need something from him. Then the tables would be reversed. Would he oblige her?

Jane took the ladder-back chair from beside his bureau and placed it in front of the washbowl. She motioned for him to sit.

He did, though her silent instructions irritated him.

"Is your razor sharpened?" she asked, plucking the straight-edge from his hand and giving it a quick glance.

He wondered if she intentionally intended to irritate him, for if she did, she was doing an excellent job. "Extremely sharp, so see that you are careful."

That shining little glint that caught in her deep brown eyes when she loved to tease surfaced. And her smile widened much too pleasantly. "No need to worry. I know *exactly* what I'm doing."

Alex didn't care for the way she emphasized *exactly*. He had no chance to protest his concern; her orders were direct and her hands swift.

She lifted his chin. "Don't talk, or I might accidently cut your throat."

He remained silent and perfectly still as she inched in

closer to him and worked the razor up his chin. Her strokes were smooth and accurate. She didn't nick or pull; she glided the razor with skill.

Alex attempted to keep his breath steady. A difficult task. And it wasn't worry that caused his uneasiness. Jane had gently nudged his legs apart to step between them and move in close to him. Her legs were sandwiched between his. She was almost flat up against him. The scent of her, a touch of fresh flowers mingling with biscuits and bacon, stung his nostrils. She smelled temptingly delicious. Then of course there were her breasts sitting just below his chin almost rubbing against him, but not quite. Tormenting him in their nearness and—he shut his eyes against his thoughts and Jane.

He had to stop these sensual wanderings about her. One minute she irritated him; the next he found himself thinking of rushing her off to his bed.

"Tighten up," she ordered.

Her words caught him off guard. He looked up at her blankly.

"Your lip—tighten your upper lip so I can shave it," she explained.

Alex blinked briefly, helping to restore himself to reality. He tightened his lip and concentrated on her face. What danger could there be in studying her face? Plenty. Her brown eyes were wildly inquisitive and beautifully shaped. Their size surprisingly appropriate for her strong facial structure. Her nose was narrow, her lips, pink and plump, moist and meaty, probably full to the taste.

Damnation! He jerked his head with the thought.

"Keep still!" Jane yelled. "I don't want to have to stitch you up."

He obliged her and closed his eyes until she finished, focusing his musings on the newspaper and the work that needed to be done on it.

A few more strokes of the razor and Jane was soon cleaning his face of the remaining lather. She wiped her hands on her apron. "Aftershave balm?"

"The bureau." He heard the tremble in his voice. He hoped she hadn't.

Jane pulled out the stopper and deposited a small amount in her hands. She brought the lotion to his face and patted, gently blowing a soothing breath to his skin to ease the sting.

Mint. Her breath smelled of freshly cut mint, he thought. A most delectable scent and taste.

"I always cooled my grandfather's face this way when I applied his balm," she said in way of an explanation of her actions.

"It works." Alex's response was simple since he found he could say no more. His throat felt too tight, among other areas of his anatomy that were experiencing the same tightness.

They both studied each other for a moment, not sure of what the other one saw, but both feeling that strange tug deep down in their tummies. It lingered, fluttering and teasing and promising of things to come.

Jane turned away, fussing as she cleaned up.

Alex cleared his throat, not really wanting to ask her for more, but needing her assistance for one last task. "My shirt, could you help me on with it?"

"Certainly," Jane said, not turning to look at him. She hurried over to the wardrobe and took a white one from inside.

Alex stood as Jane approached.

Her smile was quick and faded just as quickly as she eased his arm from the sling and helped him into the shirt. She buttoned it, her fingers moving swiftly in their eagerness to finish.

When she was done she gathered the tray and headed for the door.

"Jane." His voice was like a roaring echo in the confined room.

She turned, a tentative smile on her lips.

"Thank you. I appreciate your help."

"As I said, all you need to do is ask."

"I'll remember that."

Jane hurried out of the room and down the stairs to the kitchen. She deposited the tray on the table and took a deep reaching breath, drawing in as much air as she could.

It didn't work; his scent still lingered in her nostrils. A combination of fresh soap and lemon balm with a touch of male that completely devastated her senses.

Her reaction had startled her. She had tended to male patients before and never felt this way. She was having a decidedly alarming reaction to him and it puzzled her.

She sat down at the wooden table and pondered her predicament. She was twenty-eight years old and had never known a man's touch. Oh, the usual kiss here or there she had suffered through. But a heart-wrenching kiss or an intimate caress was foreign to her. She had simply never concerned herself with such things. She had never met anyone who had interested her. So why now? Why Alexander Evans?

He was certainly attractive. His skin had felt so smooth when she had finished shaving him. Her hands had tingled when she had run them across his face, wiping him clean of the lather. And his chest, certainly not shabby for a man of almost forty. Hard muscles, a mat of dark hair in an almost perfect V shape that disappeared beneath his belt to—

Her face rushed with heat, turning her cheeks a furious red. Heavens, what had she gotten herself into? She hadn't expected this turn of events, but then, she had control of the circumstances. She would keep her straying thoughts to herself. Keep her duties on an impersonal level. Do what she must until this job was complete. Six weeks, that was all. She could do it. It would be easy. Alex had made it clear that he really didn't want her help. A bit of assistance here and there and—

"Jane!" Alex yelled down. "Could you help me button my pants?"

Four

By evening Jane found herself frazzled. She had spent a good portion of the morning moving her clothes and personal items into Samantha's old room, settling herself in for the duration. Billy Taylor had been in and out most of the day, getting instructions from Alex. Then Samantha had visited, issuing her father orders to see that he took care of himself and not to worry, then leaving in the same whirlwind flourish with which she had arrived.

Alex, having first decided her assistance was unnecessary, now seemed to find it *most* necessary, summoning her for almost any minor matter.

Her legs were weary from her constant flights up the steps. Her arms ached from the trays of food and pots of coffee she had carted up to him. And she was bone tired from only having had four hours of sleep the night before.

She moaned when Alex called down to her, "Jane, could you bring me another pot of coffee? And maybe some of that apple cake."

He had just eaten an hour ago. She wondered where he put it all and still managed to stay so trim and fit. "I'll bring it right up."

Jane took the stairs slowly, her tired feet protesting each steep step. Once at the top she pushed at the partially open door with her hip. Alex sat on the sofa with his papers spread out beside him and across his lap. Jane placed the tray on the table in front of him.

"Thanks, I really appreciate your help." He was sincere in his gratitude, though he didn't look up from his papers. "I'm looking over this newspaper article about Harmony's beautification project." His glance moved from the paper to her. "What do you think of it?"

Jane couldn't hide her smile. "There is no other word to describe it except *eye-catching*."

Alex laughed and nodded. "My thoughts exactly. I think Lillie Taylor got a bit carried away with the colors."

Jane shrugged. "That's what she gets for insisting her husband send away for paint to spruce up the town. Now you've got a purple building and I've got a green building and the other colors?" Jane gave a dismissive wave. "No one passing through Harmony will likely forget such a cacophony of colors."

Alex laughed again and in a quick glance took note of the way Jane arched her back and rolled her neck from side to side. She was tired. "Why don't you sit awhile?" He gathered his papers up and patted the seat beside him.

She didn't hesitate. She plopped down with a yawn.

"I'll take my meals downstairs tomorrow." His comment was issued with enough authority to suggest he expected no opposition. "My arm may be broken, but my legs aren't."

Jane nodded, feeling after the day's rest he had gotten that the stairs wouldn't cause his arm that much exertion, but she sought confirmation anyway. "Your arm feeling better?"

Alex surprisingly realized it did. "It doesn't pain me much at all. A little discomfort and plenty of annoyance with it cradled in this sling, but otherwise it's fine."

Another yawn attacked Jane.

"Tired, aren't you?" Alex asked, concern clearly audible in his voice.

"It's been a long day."

"Why don't you turn in?"

Jane shook her head. "Not until I'm sure you're settled in for the night."

"I can manage to settle myself."

Jane raised a brow. "How will you unbutton your shirt? Take off your boots? Undo your pants?"

That last question disturbed them both. Their thoughts instantly fled to that morning when Jane had returned upstairs and helped him to hitch his obstinate trouser button. She had had to hook her fingers down his pants and fight with the dumb button. It was a snug fit, and the feel of his warm skin and the tickle of curly hairs only managed to send her emotions swirling out of control. *Way* out of control.

Alex finally answered. "I suppose I do need you."

"That's what I'm here for." Jane tried for a lighthearted tone, but instead it sounded shaky.

"I could turn in now." He felt guilty keeping her up when she was obviously so tired.

"Nonsense," she insisted. "I'll have a cup of coffee with you. That should put the zip back into me." She poured herself a cup and took a sip.

Alex watched her. Her large eyes drooped slightly in fatigue and her shoulders slumped a little, but her spirit? Her spirit was as bright as ever. He suddenly had the urge to learn more about her. "Tell me about yourself, Jane."

She eased back against the sofa, letting her tired muscles relax. "What do you want to know?"

Alex leaned back himself, feeling his own body begin to slow its pace. "Anything you want to tell me."

Jane liked his response. He all but told her he was prepared to listen to whatever she had to say. She chose her favorite subject. "I've always been interested in medicine."

"Even when you were young?"

"Even then." She nodded and took another sip of coffee. "It was really Grandfather's fault. He was a doctor in a mining town—that's were I grew up. As far back as I can remember I watched my grandfather tend to the miners, their wives, and their children. I learned at an early age to set a bone, stitch a cut, birth a baby, and pray over those who couldn't be helped. And as strange as it may sound, I loved every minute of it."

"Yet you ended up owning a dressmaking shop."

"Again my grandfather's fault. He determined that it wasn't proper for a young lady to live in a mining town and tend the sick. He felt too many lecherous looks were being sent my way. So he up and retired, nearly breaking my heart, and moved me to Harmony, buying the dress shop for me. He insisted it was a more respectable position for a woman and pointed out the fact that I had a talent for sewing."

"But you missed the doctoring."

Jane sighed. "More than ever. Mending clothes and such relaxes me, but mending people brings me a sense of deep satisfaction. It could be the simplest ailment or a serious injury, or just someone who needs an understanding ear to bend. Though I must admit my grandfather provided well for me by purchasing the dress shop. It does allow me the independence to pursue other interests."

"Then this opportunity to apprentice with Dr. Tanner must be exciting for you."

Jane's eyes lit with enthusiasm. "I can't begin to tell you how thrilled I am. I never imagined he would agree to apprentice me."

"He made a wise choice."

Jane thanked him for the sincere compliment with a smile and a nod. "And what about you?"

"Me?" he asked curiously.

Jane returned her empty cup to the tray. "It's only

fair, Alex, that if I relate my past to you, you do likewise."

Alex grinned at her reasoning and found he was only too glad to part with some information about himself. It had been a long time since he had sat and conversed so easily with a woman, and enjoyed doing so. "Samantha and I were on our own."

Jane raised a brow as if in question.

Alex clarified. "My wife Liza took off with a banker and filed for divorce. She wanted no part of me or Samantha. I thought it best that Samantha and I begin a new life elsewhere."

"Wise choice," Jane agreed.

"Yes, it was a wise choice. I wasn't certain at first. I had doubted my decision, but looking back, I think it was the wisest decision I have ever made."

"Why did you decide to settle in Harmony?"

Alex's expression grew serious, though a humorous smile tugged at the corners of his mouth. "I assure you my reason was most logical."

"And was?" She waited.

"The name."

"The name?" Jane repeated and yawned.

Alex regretted having kept her up. She looked even more tired now. Her wide eyes fought to remain open. She needed rest. He answered quickly. "I liked the name. It sounded like a place where one could get along."

Jane gave a tender laugh and leaned her head back on the sofa.

A faint spot of flour rested on her cheek, and Alex unmindfully reached out and dusted it off. His fingers found her skin flushed warm and petal soft. He would have explored further if she hadn't nervously snapped her head away from him.

"I am rather tired."

"I find myself feeling exactly the same way."

Jane fussed with the cups on the tray, focusing on the

inert objects while addressing Alex. "Then I'd better settle you for the night."

"By all means settle me."

A cup slipped from Jane's hands and fell to the floor, landing on the beige wool rug and miraculously not breaking. She scurried to pick it up, chasing the low throaty sound of Alex's reply from her thoughts.

"Leave that, Jane. We're both tired." Alex issued his command like a general intent on obedience.

Jane stood straight and tall, her nervous tremors gone. "I should warn you I don't take orders well."

"Neither do I."

"Is this going to be a standoff?" she asked in her usual independent stance of her hands planted firmly on her hips.

Alex stood in a slow, thoughtful stretch. "Not at all."

"Good." She assumed her response clarified the matter, so she bent to clean up the mess.

"I said leave that be." His tone rang of authority.

Jane righted herself slowly, calming her irritation. "I am—"

"My nurse," he completed. "Therefore you will follow my instructions."

"Don't you have that a bit confused?" Her question was sharp in tone and direct in manner.

"I'm not at all confused." He hesitated and when he spoke it was with a strange calmness. "Your are here to see to my *needs*, aren't you?"

She nodded, her voice suddenly stuck in her throat. He made his need for her sound far from medicinal.

"Good. Then you can see to settling me and then getting some rest for yourself. This tray can wait until morning."

Jane nodded again, only this time with a smile. Why argue the point? She would do as she wished anyway and clean it up after she had seen to him.

She followed him down the hall to his bedroom, a wide yawn traveling along with her.

Alex had the buttons to his shirt undone before he entered the bedroom. He was unfastening his belt buckle with his good hand when he stopped beside the bed and turned.

Jane was just finishing her yawn as she walked up to him.

"You've worked yourself too hard today."

Jane seized the opportunity. "My patient is demanding."

His belt fell open. "Really?"

"Really," she repeated and took over, pushing his hands away. She eased his broken arm out of the sling and ever so gently removed his shirt, draping it over the nearby chair. Her fingers went to his trouser button without thought. Her fingers dipped between warm flesh and rough material.

Fool. The word echoed through her head as she continued to work on the stubborn button. She felt the curly hairs just below his navel brush her suddenly sensitive fingers, and her own flesh warmed considerably.

She cautioned herself to be quick, but in her haste and fumbling her fingers slipped, dropping down further into his trousers. She froze.

Alex's body sprung to life, and he squeezed his eyes shut against the exquisite yet torturous ache.

The room grew heavy in silence. Jane barely breathed. Alex dared not move.

Finally coming to her senses, Jane forced her fingers into action and struggled with the button until it finally popped free.

Alex dropped to the bed and ran his hand through his hair several times, before chancing to speak. "Go to bed, Jane."

"But—"

"Go to bed!" he snapped irritably. His head remained bent, his eyes focused on the floor.

She was no fool; she knew all too well the results of their close encounter. He wasn't the only one feeling hot and bothered. She left the room, pausing at the door, and without a backward glance offered, "If you need me, just call."

"Go to bed," his voice cautioned, and Jane obeyed, slipping quietly from the room.

Alex remained as he was, his stare fixed on the floor, and his hand cradling his forehead. He ached in many ways, not only physically, but emotionally. He had forgotten the closeness a man and woman could share. He had been quickly reminded of it this day. Jane had tended to him with a tender patience and a sincere caring. She had helped him, fussed over him, and seen to almost his every need.

He raised his head and released a frustrated sigh. Their intimate scene a few moments before only reminded him of the benefits of marriage. If Jane were his wife, they would be in this bed at this very moment sharing sensual intimacies.

The lonely years had a tendency to make one forget, or perhaps one forgot in order to ease the hurt.

He moaned and dropped back on the bed, wincing at the pain in his arm. Jane Carson was a free-spirited woman intent on her independence and becoming a respected healer. He, himself, looked forward to his own independent lifestyle. They were no match for each other. They both were moving in opposite directions.

He dropped his good arm over his eyes, shutting out the light from the lamp, shutting away his ache, shutting out the nagging voice in his head that reminded him of how much love could hurt ... and how much love could heal.

Jane ran the brush through her short crop of curls for the tenth time and sighed for the tenth time. "You are a fool." She sat in front of the vanity table and spoke to her reflection in the mirror.

"You have the opportunity of a lifetime," she warned

herself. "You'll never get it again, and you chance tossing it away for a man?"

Jane placed the silver brush on the glass tray and rested her chin in her hand, staring into the mirror. "It's because he's your patient and you feel obligated to care for him in every way. That's where these strange emotions are coming from, from a sense of obligation."

She smiled at herself, though it was a weary, cautious smile as though she distrusted her own conclusions, yet needed to accept an explanation whether sensible or not.

She had seen Alex numerous times at social functions and town meetings and had even passed by him on the street. He had always extended a polite greeting. She had never fancied him, nor given consideration to becoming better acquainted with him. He had not in the least interested her in that particular way.

"So why the tingles when you touch him?" She stared at herself, waiting for an answer. "Have you given thought to the wide set of his shoulders or the muscles in his arms, or that mat of hair that forms so perfectly on his broad chest? Then there are his eyes, soft blue, and so often busy in thought. And his lips, luscious and ripe—"

Jane groaned and covered her eyes, blocking out her image. "You fool," she mumbled. Whatever was wrong with her? She was no tender young schoolgirl looking for a beau. She was a grown woman ready to make a difference in the world. Ready to study medicine, to learn, to earn respect for herself in a field controlled entirely by men.

Would she allow a moment of sensual flight erase all that? She stood and made her way to the single bed, the pink counterpane pulled down in readiness for her. She extinguished the lamp by the bed before slipping beneath the quilt.

Once upon a time she had dreamed of marrying and raising a family. Once upon a time many, many years ago. But when her interest in medicine began to take root, she had realized a normal lifestyle wasn't what she sought. And that if she married it would take a very special man to accept her work. She doubted that man existed and still did.

Jane turned over, burying her face in the soft pillow. She would not throw away this chance to learn more about medicine. She would not think of Alex in such an intimate nature. She would not!

She closed her eyes and forced herself to sleep. Her last thoughts were of Alex's broad chest and how his soft mat of hair would make an irresistible and comfortable pillow.

Five

Flapjacks. Their delicious scent filled the air, drifting beneath Alex's nose and rousing him from his sleep. He smiled, yawned, and stretched himself awake. He could almost taste their rich flavor—the creamy butter, the thick syrup. He licked his lips in anticipation.

He was about to spring from the bed, dress, and rush downstairs to the kitchen to attack a stack when the door swung open.

"Good morning," Jane sang out in a cheery note.

Alex remained where he was, the covers firmly entrenched over his half-naked body. "How many times have I told you to knock first?"

She turned after placing the pitcher of hot water next to the bowl in the washstand. "How many times have I reaffirmed my position as your nurse?"

"A week," he said with a shake of his head. "You've been tending to me for a week and we still can't settle this matter?"

"It's settled." She intended to argue no more and proceeded to turn her attention to gathering his clothes that needed washing.

Alex ran his hand over his face in frustration. It seemed he had been doing that a lot lately. Though polite and civil to each other, there was a tension between them and it seemed to spark disagreements. It was as though they waged a small private war, to what end it would serve a purpose proved difficult to say.

"I am entitled to privacy in my own home," he argued.

"I am your nurse." Her statement was meant to clarify her response.

Alex thought otherwise. "That doesn't mean you can enter my room at your whim."

Jane straightened slowly from picking up his soiled white shirt off the floor. "My whim?"

Alex attempted to pull himself up to a sitting position, but with his injured arm that proved impossible. "Correct. Your whim," he restated.

Jane walked over to his bed, leaned over him, and braced her hand beneath his armpit. "Raise your knees and push when I pull."

Alex did as she directed, feeling inadequate in dealing with her in this vulnerable, flat-on-his-back position.

"Now," she ordered, and with her pull and his push he was sitting up in a flash. Jane tucked a pillow behind his back and adjusted the covers over his lap. "As for my whim, if you took notice of my visits to your room, you would see for yourself that they are timed accordingly."

"Timed accordingly?"

"Accordingly," she repeated, as if he were hard of hearing and needed it reiterated. "In the morning I make certain I see to your shave and help you dress before breakfast. Late morning I see to the cleaning of your room. Early evening I see to arranging your bed for the evening, and finally at bedtime I see to settling you."

Her words drifted off to a whisper.

He understood why. Her settling him for the evening had become an extremely unsettling time for them both. He didn't care to think of it and sought another avenue to vent his irritation.

"My arm feels better. You don't need to tend me as vigilantly as you do."

"Your arm may feel better, but it hasn't mended yet. Until that splint comes off you're stuck with me and my tending ways. And let us not forget you agreed to my help."

"You need to remind me?" Alex shook his head, regretting the day he had agreed to such a foolish decision. His life had been turned upside down and pulled inside out. "I protest the agreement on grounds that you did not inform me of your one grievous fault."

Jane wore a broad smile and her brown eyes were wide in their merriment. "Fault you say? And what fault might that be?"

"Stubborn." Alex issued his pronouncement with satisfaction.

"I, my dear Alex," Jane said calmly and walked toward the door, "have always considered being stubborn one of my better qualities."

Alex opened his mouth to correct her assumption when he was interrupted by a high-pitched—

"Hello up there, anybody home?"

Jane and Alex sighed simultaneously. "Maisie."

"I'll not have her up here while I am in such a state of undress."

"Of course not," Jane agreed, as though he were daft for even considering she would allow it.

Alex caught the incredulous tone in her voice. "Yet you feel marching into my room whenever it pleases you acceptable?"

Jane sent him a scathing look. "Let's be sensible. I am your nurse, and I don't enter your room whenever it pleases me."

"Good morning up there," Maisie called out again and with a bit more energy.

"Good morning, Maisie, I'll be right down," Jane called back.

"Take your time," Maisie answered. "I know you have a patient to tend to."

"Not this morning," Jane returned but only loud enough for Alex to hear. "Since you feel I am invading your privacy, why don't you tend to yourself this morning."

Alex heard the challenge in her voice and without hesitation accepted it. "I'll do just that."

"Good and we'll see just how you'll do," Jane said with a wide grin and sailed out of the room.

Jane and Maisie were seated at the round wooden table neatly set for breakfast when Alex entered the kitchen fifteen minutes later.

Maisie took one look at him and whispered, "Oh, dear."

Jane chose silence. A wise decision, especially with the way Alex's eyes accosted her. *Murderous.* He looked as though he would love to murder her. Of course he would have to blame *her* for his unsettled appearance. He would shoulder no fault for his own stubborn nature.

Maisie interrupted the silent skirmish between the couple. "Dear, you really should be a bit more attentive to your patient."

Jane ran a slow glance up and down Alex. His white shirt was buttoned wrong, looking lopsided as it hung partially out of his black trousers, the other part being tucked in haphazardly. His face showed signs of an attempted shave with bloody nicks and partial stubble attesting to his failed effort. And his sling was upside down, the knot insufficiently cradling his arm.

But it was his look of utter frustration with his own failed attempt to care for himself that speared Jane's heart. He had been proved wrong. He had been made aware of just how necessary she was to his survival, and it obviously distressed him terribly.

Jane stood and took immediate command of the situation. "You're right, Maisie. I should have never allowed him to talk me into hurrying down here to greet you when he needed my help."

"Good gracious," Maisie said with alarm. "You mean to tell me his disheveled appearance is my fault?"

"Not at all," Jane corrected and walked in front of Alex, her hands reaching out slowly, her eyes silently seeking his approval of her help.

His look softened and he gave her a slight nod.

Jane fussed with his shirt buttons, righting them in proper sequence. "I really should have been more diligent in my duties. It doesn't do to allow the patient the upper hand."

Maisie agreed, adding her own bit of wisdom. "You're absolutely right, my dear. After all, you are schooled in such things." She focused her attention on Alex. "You should listen to her, Alex. Jane knows best."

"Thank you for your advice, Maisie. I don't know what I would do without it."

Jane credited Alex's sweet sarcasm with a pleasant grin.

He in turn acknowledged her with a wink.

"Sit," she told him. "I'll see to your breakfast."

He did as she directed, eyeing the flapjacks with a mouthwatering glare. She was glad to see he had allowed the tense situation to pass. This last week had been filled with enough tension to last her forever.

It seemed they were constantly at odds, constantly disagreeing, and yet other times? Other times they actually got along quite well.

Maisie delivered Alex a grand smile and patted his hand. "Now, hasn't this arrangement worked out perfectly?"

Alex looked to Jane when he answered. "Without a doubt."

Jane hurried to fix his plate. His blue eyes were so intent upon her that he made her feel like a bundle of nerves. He would do that from time to time, look at her as though probing beneath the surface, searching more deeply within her. It made her jittery, and she would often find her hands trembling and her stomach quivering.

"I was just, this morning, saying to Minnie that I had no doubt this arrangement would be successful," Maisie said, accepting with a gracious nod another cup of coffee Jane poured for her. "But Minnie being her stubborn self refused to acknowledge my success. Her mulish nature can be so trying on one's nerves."

"Stubbornness is a fault difficult to deal with," Alex added, his eyes fixed on Jane.

Jane picked up a crisp slice of bacon, bit into it, and ignored Alex's deliberately aimed remark altogether.

Maisie released a weighted sigh. "Minnie would never admit to her stubborn nature."

"Stubborn people never do," Alex said, his look still on Jane as he popped a fork full of flapjacks into his mouth.

Maisie concurred. "You're so right. Minnie is always going around bragging to anyone who will listen how her apple jelly is far superior to any in Harmony. When everyone knows *my* apple jelly is superb. Yes, Minnie can—"

"Did I hear my name?" Minnie asked, entering the kitchen, a basket covered with a yellow-and-white checked cloth hooked in her hand.

"We were discussing jelly," Jane explained.

Minnie beamed with pride, her chest expanding as she announced, "I make the best apple jelly in all of Harmony."

Maisie rolled her eyes heavenward.

Alex bit his lower lip to prevent himself from laughing.

Jane politely responded. "So we've heard."

"I also make the best biscuits in Harmony, and I've brought over some fresh-baked ones for you both." Minnie cleared a spot on the table and placed her basket down, removing the cloth.

Maisie peered down into the basket. "Not exactly golden brown; a bit undercooked if you ask me."

"No one asked you, dear," Minnie said politely and turned to Alex. "Try one of these, Alex. It will melt in your mouth, it's so good." Minnie didn't wait for his response. She carefully broke one open, lathered it with butter, and held it in front of his mouth.

Not knowing how to politely refuse the offer, even though he was thoroughly stuffed from the dozen flapjacks he had consumed, not to mention the bacon, he opened his mouth. Minnie popped the biscuit in. He munched and tried for a smile, managing an awkward one as the three women watched him and waited for his verdict. "Delicious," he announced after swallowing the last of it.

Minnie crossed her arms over her waist and snapped a quick nod. "Told you so."

"He's being polite," Maisie said. "The biscuits aren't cooked enough."

Minnie rose to her own defense. "Just because you prefer burnt biscuits doesn't mean everyone does."

Maisie picked up one of the biscuits and shook it at Minnie. "Perhaps not, but at least mine are cooked."

Minnie's eyes narrowed. "Burnt, dear, burnt."

Jane cast Alex a worried look. If something wasn't done soon, biscuits were sure to fly.

Alex handled it surprisingly well. "I'll have that biscuit, Maisie, and when you get a chance I'd love to have some of your tasty apple jelly."

Both women were lost to his compliments, giving Jane a chance to change the subject without difficulty. "Dr. Tanner informs me that Alex is recovering remarkably well."

"Of course, dear, your excellent nursing skills have seen to that," Maisie praised.

Minnie joined them at the table, offering her own opinion. "Jacob tells me your attentive nursing far surpasses any he has ever seen. And that he welcomes the chance to further your medical education."

"Jacob has been wonderful," Jane agreed. "He's thoughtful and so thorough in his lessons."

Jacob? Thorough? Lessons? Alex wondered when she had started calling the doctor by his first name. *Thorough* and *lessons* really had him stumped. He had assumed she spent all her time at his place—she certainly had enough chores to fill her time. But then there were those hours during the day when he talked with Billy or worked on the newspaper articles. He had always assumed she was around somewhere, that he just had to call out to her and she'd answer. But was she?

"And he says you learn so fast," Minnie encouraged with a smile.

Maisie interfered on Alex's behalf. "Jane should concentrate on Alex right now. There's time enough later when Alex is well for her to spend time on her studies."

Jane answered quickly, giving the two sisters no room for disagreements. "I only spend a couple of hours one day a week with Jacob. After Alex is fully recovered, I'll be spending most of my time with Jacob."

Alex swore she sounded delighted over the prospect of spending more time with Dr. Tanner. The idea irritated him. He needed her now. She had agreed on helping him. She had no business spending time with Tanner. "My arm pains me," he said, intending to see that she was kept busy right here at his place with him.

Jane cast him a concerned look. Guilt instantly assaulted her. She had made him see to his own needs this morning and had brought on his discomfort. She should have ignored his ill mood and saw to her duties. Now he would suffer, not her. "I think it's best you go upstairs and rest. You have probably taxed yourself too much."

Maisie stood. "It's time for us to be going, Minnie."

Minnie was about to object when Maisie sweetly added, "Alex needs his rest."

"Of course he does and Jane needs to be off to see Dr. Tanner," Minnie said and also stood.

Jane looked to Alex. His eyes seemed troubled, probably from the discomfit in his arm, and his body appeared tense. He was obviously in distress. "I don't think I'll be seeing Jacob today. I think it best I stay with Alex."

"But Jacob's expecting you," Minnie protested.

"Alex needs her," Maisie said.

Jane settled the matter. "I'll send a note to Jacob with Billy Taylor explaining why I can't join him today. I'm sure he won't mind if we postpone our lesson until tomorrow."

Not likely. Alex had no intentions of feeling better for a few days, maybe even a week or more. He gave a disgruntled moan, sounding more like a man in debilitating pain.

"Up to bed," Jane ordered and ignored the two women as they hurried out the door with a quick goodbye trailing them.

Alex didn't argue. He took the stairs slow and shuffled down the hall to his bedroom with Jane on his heels.

"You're to stay in bed today," she instructed. "And no writing, lifting, or doing anything that puts pressure on either arm." She fixed his bed, drawing his quilt back to the foot of the bed and stacking his pillows against the brass frame.

She gently nudged him to the bed and he sat. She saw to removing his boots and then carefully saw to easing him back on the bed and making sure he was comfortably settled against the stack of pillows.

Jane was covering his stockingfeet with the counterpane when he spoke. "Your biscuits are better."

Jane stopped, quilt in hand, and looked at him. "What was that?"

"Your biscuits. They're better. Much better."

"You mean *I* make the best biscuits in all of Harmony?"

Alex laughed, tilting his head back and enjoying their mutual humor.

Jane joined in, sitting on the edge of the bed. When her laughter subsided she spoke. "They are a pair of characters."

"That they are," Alex agreed and winced when he attempted to sit up a bit more. The pain was real this time, no act, and he silently cursed his own stupidity.

Jane immediately chastised him and moved to fuss over him. "I told you no unnecessary pressure." She checked his sling and the wrapping on his arm. Satisfied all was well, she leaned over him to arrange his pillows comfortably behind his back.

Alex felt his breath catch. Her chest was planted right in front of his face. The blue-and-white gingham check brushed dangerously close to his mouth. Her nearness was too tempting, much too tempting.

Jane stepped back. "There now, you're—" Abruptly she fell silent and reached her hand out to feel his head and cheek. "You're flushed and feverish."

"I feel hot . . . and uncomfortable."

The guilt fell over Jane like a wet blanket, burdensome in its weight. His condition was all her fault. "I'll fix you some chamomile tea. It will help relax you."

"I don't feel like tea."

"Then what can I do to make you more comfortable?"

"You could have been more diligent in your duties," he snapped, more irritated with himself than with her. He was acting foolish, and his heightened emotions wouldn't allow otherwise.

Jane opened her mouth to defend herself but found any excuse senseless. He was right. She shook her head slowly. "You're right and I'm sorry."

Alex stared up at her, feeling worse than ever, which

caused his emotions to flare even more. "When you're hired to do a job, you do it correctly. You don't let your stubborn nature stand in the way."

Her stubborn nature certainly had interfered. She hadn't handled herself professionally. And worse was that she didn't know what to do to correct her misjudgment.

"Rest, you need it," she said, her voice hushed, as she walked to the door.

Alex closed his eyes against Jane's retreating back.

Why had he berated her? She had done nothing but tend to him since taking on his nursing care, and she had done an excellent job.

His ill behavior was inexcusable. He found it difficult finding a reasonable justification for his actions. He certainly couldn't blame his foul temperament on his arm. His injury had far from pained him to the point of severe discomfit.

Actually Jane's skills and attentiveness had abundantly paid off. He had suffered far less than he had anticipated. The scope of her medical knowledge amazed him. He had not expected it to be so extensive.

His eyes drifted open as Jane's name spilled softly from his lips. "Jane, you are a rare woman."

He recalled with clarity his wife and her constant complaints. She detested tending to the house, cooking meals, and even caring for their daughter. She felt herself above everyday tasks. Not so Jane. Seeing to his care and that of the house consumed her day. But then, he thought a bit melancholy, it was her job to do just that.

He hated to admit to himself, and never would he to anyone, how much pleasure he derived from her care. Sure he balked about some things, but it was more from pride than anything. What man would want to be dependent on a woman? Especially an independent woman who spoke up and spoke her mind as she saw fit. An attribute Alex admired—at times. Other times she could be downright pigheaded and immovable in her decisions. Plain stubborn aptly described her.

His mouth crinkled into a half smile, recalling Jane's usual, mule-headed stance. Hands on hips. Nice hips at that, round and curvy, not too wide, but not too narrow, either. The kind of hips a man could grab hold of and—

Alex shook the intimate thought from his mind. He had to stop these mental wanderings about Jane. Why, most of the time they were snapping at each other. They didn't get along. Probably never would. They were too opposite, or perhaps too much alike to be compatible.

He'd keep himself busy, he thought. Articles needed writing for the newspaper. Some of the townsfolk had approached him about advertisements. He had much to keep his hands and mind occupied for some time. He'd focus his thoughts on more productive matters. Jane's duties and her lessons with Dr. Tanner would limit her free time.

The remaining weeks would pass quickly, and finally, Alex thought, his life would return to its usual routine.

He closed his eyes and mind against a little voice that whispered, "Will you really want it to?"

Six

"GOOD. Good. Your arm is healing nicely," Jacob Tanner said with a smile and a nod after a thorough assessment of Alex's arm. "I'm pleased with your progress these last two weeks."

Alex acknowledged him with an abrupt nod.

"Any pain? Discomfort? Questions?" Jacob asked, rinsing his hands in the bowl of tepid water next to him on the table.

"When will the splints come off?" He expected the familiar answer, having asked it often enough, but he needed to hear is again.

"At least four weeks, no time sooner." Jacob dried his hands on the clean towel beside the bowl. "Getting itchy, are you?"

Alex grinned. He couldn't help but like Tanner. He was the likable sort. Congenial and pleasant to be around. "Itching to be getting back to doing for myself."

Jacob's laugh echoed like a deep rumble in his throat. "Don't like Jane's pampering?"

"Pampering?" Alex's question sounded more like a shout. "She issues orders like an old army general dictating to his troops and expecting immediate compliance."

"A general usually reaches that distinguished rank

due to skill and knowledge." Jacob delivered his response with a smile and a hint of pride.

Alex shifted around in his chair, resting both his arms on the kitchen table. "I don't doubt either. She's one heck of an intelligent woman."

Jacob pulled a chair out and joined him at the table. "She's quick to learn. I show her a procedure once, and she absorbs the knowledge like a sponge. I give her books to read, and she comes to me with a list of questions. Some of her questions even stump me."

Alex heard the admiration in Jacob's voice and caught the way his eyes rounded when he spoke of Jane. "I often wonder where she finds the time to do all she does."

Jacob shook his head. "I can't believe she finds the time to help me at my office."

Alex almost demanded to know just how much time she was spending with Tanner, but he stopped himself. Instead he voiced his concern for Jane. "She works too hard."

"A doctor's lot," Jacob informed him with an accepted shrug.

Alex's brow went up and this time he didn't stop himself from speaking his mind. "Do you think Jane will ever really succeed in becoming a doctor?"

"You doubt her capable?" Jacob's tone was defensive.

It was Alex's turn to shake his head. "You misunderstand me. I feel Jane is more than capable, and with your help I see her refining her skills but . . ." Alex paused, almost reluctant to voice his misgivings. "She's a woman."

"This is true, and sadly women are not openly accepted into the field of medicine. I have heard many of my own colleagues joke about their lack of intelligence or pass suggestive remarks as to why a woman would even venture to become a doctor. They give absolutely

PLAYING CUPID 57

no thought to the fact that women instinctively nurture and heal."

"Then Jane is fighting a losing battle." Alex felt a twinge of regret for her.

"Not so," Jacob argued. "Here in Harmony she has established friends and a reputation for healing people before I came along. Those same people still trust her, perhaps even more so since they have seen her working side by side with me. And the women of Harmony?" Jacob laughed and gave a dismissive wave of his hand. "The women will have no other person birth their babies except Jane Carson."

"She's well liked and respected here, but if she ventures to practice elsewhere, would she so easily be accepted?"

Jacob gave thought to Alex's question, rubbing his chin slowly. "I don't suppose so. It will take time for women to be accepted in many fields and with much fight on their part. I'm afraid many—men and women—are too set in their ways to accept change, even when it is so obviously for the better."

Alex laughed lightheartedly. "I'm afraid I fall right into that category. I'm set in my ways, and having Jane around is difficult—sometimes impossible."

"Keep it in the right perspective," Jacob advised. "She's here to help you. Nurse you back to health."

"Nurse me or order me?"

"Jane does have a distinct way about her when tending her patients."

"Tyrannical!"

"Caring," Jacob corrected, his voice softened with obvious respect. "Jane cares about each and every patient she treats. She feels their hurt, their pain, and she does all in her power to help heal and comfort them."

Alex wondered if Jacob's feelings for Jane went beyond that of a teacher and friend. He spoke with such obvious emotion. The notion irritated Alex, but he set it aside, warning himself it was none of his concern.

"Where is Jane anyway?" Jacob asked, standing and slipping into his brown jacket he had removed before examining Alex's arm.

"Errands," Alex explained. "The pantry needed replenishing."

"Cooking up a storm, is she?"

"A mighty tasty one," Alex offered and realized the truth to his own words. Jane was an excellent cook. Every meal she had prepared for him so far had been more than just tasty. They had been downright delicious.

"I wholeheartly concur," Jacob added. "She favored me with some of her biscuits, and my mouth still waters when I think of them."

She made her biscuits for him! The thought pierced his chest and set his mind to wandering. What was she up to? Was she trying to win the doctor over? Not that she had to. The man was obviously besotted by her. Not wanting Jacob to think Jane went to any special bother just for him, he said, "She's always baking biscuits."

Jacob snapped his black bag shut and sent Alex a lively grin. "I'll eat Jane's cooking anytime. Being a bachelor makes home cooking hard to come by."

Alex didn't need reminding of Jacob's marital availability.

"I need to be off. I've other patients to see. Tell Jane I'll see her tomorrow. Follow her instructions and I'll check on you some time next week."

Alex offered a brief thanks and walked Jacob to the door.

Home cooking. His thoughts wandered lazily as he returned to the table and attempted to clean up. Occasionally he had considered how comforting the scents were that hovered in the house since Jane had moved in. They tempted and teased with one sniff of the tantalizing aromas that frequently filled the air.

Mornings he often woke to eggs and bacon frying, and then there were Jane's flapjacks. Simply mouthwatering. Though mouthwatering didn't do them justice. Jane would add special ingredients to make them more appealing. Bits of apple, cinnamon, raisins . . . He shook his head.

"Getting close to supper," he reminded himself.

"Hungry?" Jane asked, pulling the screen door open and maneuvering herself around it, her arms too laden with packages to do otherwise.

Alex moved forward to help her, but she shook her head. "Your arm . . ."

"Is better," he finished and reached out to take a package with his good hand.

She turned her back to him before he could grab it. "Better, but not one hundred percent healed," she reminded him.

Alex grumbled beneath his breath and sat down in the chair, feeling helpless as usual.

Jane busied herself with unpacking and returned to her first question. "Hungry?"

"Yes."

"I'll have supper together in no time." She grabbed her white apron she kept on the peg by the door and tied it around her waist. "So Jacob said you were better?"

"Yes."

Jane grabbed the chopping board from the cabinet. She took a sharp knife from the crockery tub on the counter that held frequently used utensils and then pulled four fat potatoes from one of the packages. She began peeling the potatoes and ignoring his curt response she continued on. "So did Jacob leave any instructions?"

"No."

"I suppose then that I'm doing an excellent job."

Alex grunted his reply.

"The other day," she said, cutting the peeled potato in four pieces, "when I was in his office helping him, he remarked on what a fine job I was doing in tending you."

Alex remained silent, staring at her, though she didn't notice. His eyes were set on her form. He liked when she wore the red calico dress she had on now. The plain white collar and cuffs added to its appeal, not to mention they way the material hugged her in all the right places. He liked, too, the way her brown hair fell in soft disarray on her forehead. Then of course there was that white apron that wrapped so snugly around her waist. She looked like the kind of wife that made a husband anxious to get home and—

"Alex, are you listening?"

Alex moved his glance from her waist up to meet her eyes. His expression clearly told her he hadn't heard a word.

Jane patiently repeated her question. "I wondered if you finished writing your newspaper articles?"

He smiled. It pleased him that Jane appeared honestly interested in his work. He could talk to her about his writing, and she would ask questions, sincere questions, not just conversational ones. They actually shared thought-provoking topics, and he had found himself looking forward to their talks. He relaxed back in the chair, his tension and irritability fading away.

He eased into a conversation with Jane, discussing the issues he had chosen to write about. She questioned. He answered. And all the while Alex watched her. He watched her bend from the waist to stack the logs in the stove and light them, her hips swaying suggestively as she worked. When she finished she stood straight and wiped her hands on her apron, then without delay pulled a cast-iron pot from the cupboard.

Alex continued talking, though his glance sought her every movement. She was at home here in *his* home. She worked the kitchen as if it were hers, knowing exactly where things were. And still she paid attention to him, her eyes lighting, her smile widening when certain comments of his caused her to remark.

Jane dumped the chunks of meat, potatoes, and carrots into the water-filled pot on the stove. While it cooked she turned her attention to mixing her biscuit dough.

The scene cried out of domestic bliss. *If* she were his wife, he'd reach up and kiss her this very moment . . . and supper would wait.

"You're not tiring yourself, are you?" she asked. "Doing things you shouldn't."

Alex looked at her. Concern was evident in her questioning expression, and Jacob's words rushed back to him. *She cares.* About her patients, she cares. The sudden thought disturbed Alex, but he kept his irritation from reaching his voice. "Hardly, I haven't needed to lift a finger—which you well know."

"Good. That means I'm doing my job—though . . ." Jane sent him a chastising glance. "I heard you were checking on the printing press the other day."

"I have a spy in my midst," Alex joked with a laugh and a shake of his head.

"A concerned spy," Jane corrected.

"Billy?"

"He worries you may hurt yourself again."

Alex liked Billy, for a young'un of fourteen he was responsible and dependable. If it hadn't been for his help the last couple of weeks, the newspaper would have never gotten out. "Billy's doing an excellent job."

"Then let him do it," Jane said, stirring the bubbling stew.

For a moment Alex felt himself struggle with his annoyance over her commanding remark. Then he relaxed, a wide grin spreading across his face. "I can't."

Stunned over his honest admission, she turned to stare wide-eyed at him, his smile that of a mischievous boy. Her stomach fluttered strangely and her heart thumped wildly. His forthright response and innocent expression stole her heart, and a reply escaped her.

He continued, an explanation necessary for himself as well as Jane. "The *Sentinel* is my baby, and babies need constant attention. My baby can be more demanding than most, protesting with a clank and a rattle when she isn't attended to properly."

Jane laughed softly, moving back to the table where she proceeded to dust the top with flour. "I empathize with you. I have a patient who makes the same demands."

"Really," Alex said and watched her knead the biscuit dough on the floured surface before she picked up the rolling pin to roll it out. "Tell me about this patient. Perhaps I can offer some advice."

Jane laughed once again, liking his playful mood. She picked up the tin cup, its edge smeared with flour, and began cutting biscuits out of the inch-thick dough. "He's obstinate and set in his ways."

"Traits that could be termed amiable."

Jane cast an incredulous look at him. "Amiable?"

"Think about it," he suggested seriously. "A person who is obstinate—though I prefer resolute—and set in his ways can also be called dependable."

"Dependable?" Her astonished response caused her tone to rise a few levels.

"Of course," Alex insisted. "He could always be counted on to act accordingly, no surprises, always there for someone, dependable."

Jane found her laughter returning. "I don't believe you actually made those traits sound appealing."

"Tell me more about this patient," he said. "He sounds interesting."

Jane placed the biscuits in a round pan and set them in the oven to bake before answering. "He works himself too hard when he should rest and heal."

Alex caught and held her tender expression. "A man is often set in his ways. It comes from years of routine, of depending on no one but himself. A man such as that would find it difficult, near impossible, to accept help."

"Perhaps this man is more complex than I realize."

"A thought," Alex said. He liked the way she held his gaze, not afraid or nervous but with confidence.

"I'll think on the advice you've offered me."

"I'm glad," Alex said.

Their gazes held, suspended in time for a few seconds before Jane hurried to clean the table off to set it for supper. They continued a congenial conversation, choosing safer topics to discuss. They laughed over childhood remembrances and discussed the trials of adolescence. They talked of favorite family members and not-so favorite ones. They continued talking through the meal, Alex remarking over and over on Jane's cooking talent.

By the time Jane cleaned up and placed the last dish away in the cupboard, they both knew much about each other.

Jane yawned, turning around to face Alex.

"Would it do any good for me to tell you you do too much and wear yourself out?"

"Nope," she said while another yawn sneaked up on her and almost robbed the word from her.

Alex knew better than to argue the point, and he knew how to make certain she got herself off to sleep as soon as possible. "I'm feeling rather tired myself."

"Off to bed with you, then," Jane said and ushered him out of the chair and up the steps like the little commanding general she had become.

Jane saw to pulling down his quilt and fluffing his pillows before helping him rid himself of his boots. Alex had become proficient in unbuttoning his shirt by himself, and he had even managed to handle his belt buckle. There was little for Jane to do except to see to his comfort.

She kept her eyes averted from him once he had shed his shirt. For some reason his naked chest set her stomach into the nervous quivers. She had given thought to her strange reaction and concluded that perhaps it was due to his chest being so hard with muscle and not an ounce of fat. Most men she had seen without their shirts had little in the way of muscle and much in the way of fat. Alex was trim and lean and definitely appealing to the eye.

Her thoughts drifting, Jane turned quickly without looking and almost collided with Alex's bare chest if it hadn't been for his quick thinking. His good arm reached out and grabbed her about the waist, bringing her to rest easily up against him.

She tossed her head back to look up at him and offer an apology for her clumsiness. Her words locked in her throat when her eyes caught his.

Desire ignited in the depths of his eyes like a flame to dry kindling. So blatant and heated was it that Jane almost felt her flesh singe. His hold on her had tightened as though demonstrating his refusal to let her go.

She moved to respond, finding speech difficult though necessary. Her lips parted, her words slipped out, and Alex lowered his mouth to hers.

Seven

JANE woke with a start. Her dream had been more real than reality itself, so like a protective mother hen her inner emotions had startled her awake in warning or prediction of future events, which she wasn't certain.

She stretched lazily, easing her muscles awake before settling once again in a comfortable cuddle beneath the colorful patchwork quilt. Her room was just beginning to fill with the first faint light of morning. She was in no hurry to begin the day. She had too much on her mind and needed time to think.

A yawn sneaked from her mouth followed by a secretive smile. Her fingers edged up from beneath the quilt, and as lightly as though she might discover a forbidden secret, she traced her lips with her fingertips.

No hint of last night's kiss remained, but memories did. Jane recalled the soft feel of Alex's lips against hers, and the feel of his arm circling her waist and drawing her up against him. Her heartbeat had quickened. Her limbs had weakened.

Jane shivered remembering that moment. Instinctively her hands had reached up to catch hold of Alex's bare arms in hope of steadying herself. His flesh had felt warm as though heated by the sun and his muscles ... her body tingled at the vivid memory.

She hadn't expected such an intense reaction last

night or now. It had felt foreign and unsettling yet in a pleasurable sort of way and only made her want to explore more.

At that precise moment her senses had returned, registering a warning to tread lightly and take care. She had hesitated a brief moment, his kiss turning more complex and sensuous, robbing her of sensible thought. Before her emotions completely surrendered she shoved at his chest.

He had released her immediately, his words uttered so softly Jane had barely heard them, "It's been so long."

Jane had quit the room with haste, not trusting her own jumbled emotions. Hearing those words in her thoughts now gave her reason to wonder over his meaning. Had it been long since he had kissed a woman? Somehow she doubted that. Then what had he meant? How long since what?

She, herself, had shared a kiss or two with a man, though thinking back and taking last night into consideration, they were nothing more than pecks.

Jane sighed thinking of her once youthful dreams and the promises they had held. The man of her dreams had always been large and strong. She had imagined he would love and care for her forever. As she matured so did her fantasies. Now when she thought of that *someone special*, he was a man who understood her aspirations and encouraged and supported them. A man who accepted her with pride for who she was, not what *he* expected her to be.

A soft noise from down the hall caught her attention. Alex sounded as though he was rustling about.

She hastily jumped from the bed and then abruptly stilled her movements, the edge of the quilt held steadfast in her hand. Would he remark on their kiss last night? Should she?

Jane shook the disturbing questions from her thoughts and hurried out of bed. She would face him as

PLAYING CUPID 67

she did every morning and see to her tasks. What was meant to happen would happen. There was no point worrying over a simple kiss. She and Alex would probably never share another one. It had been late. They had been tired. She was making more of this than she should.

Rationalizing last night's kiss away and not admitting the disappointment her own thoughts brought her, Jane hurried to dress.

In no time her face was scrubbed to shining, her fair complexion highlighted by two blushed cheeks, and her brown hair falling in its own usual disorder close to her face. She slipped into her dark blue skirt and white cotton blouse; simple, plain, and perfect for helping out at Jacob's office. Which she was scheduled to do this afternoon.

She made her bed, placed her light cotton nightdress beneath the pillow, and hurried along to Alex's room.

A rapid knock warned of her immediate entrance before she walked in with a flourish. "Good"—she caught her hesitation and followed it with a quick—"morning."

Alex stared at her, water beading on his naked chest and a wet washcloth hanging from his good hand. "Morning." His greeting sounded little more than a grunt.

Jane had walked in on his morning wash. He was dressed, except for his shirt, and memories of him holding her tightly against his bare chest flooded over her rushing color to stain her already blushed cheeks.

She turned away and busied herself in making his bed as she spoke, avoiding direct eye contact with him. "Are you sure you are feeling up to washing?"

"I'm sure," he answered with an air of finality.

Jane didn't argue and turned back around now that she felt more in control of herself. "Shall I shave you?"

Alex sent her a long, hard glare. "I was thinking of growing a beard."

Jane placed a finger to her lips and gave the suggestion serious thought. She shook her head. "A beard wouldn't suit you." She walked over to him and positioned the lone wooden chair in front of the washbowl. "Sit," she commanded.

Alex raised a brow.

"Sit," she repeated her order with a sweep of her hand to the chair. "I don't have all day. I have breakfast to see to, ham, eggs, and fresh apple biscuits, and then there's the wash. The rugs need a good beating, and this afternoon I'm off to help Jacob."

Alex took the seat, folding his arms across his chest and trying not to make note of his annoyance. With all she had to do, where in heaven's name was she going to find time to spend helping Jacob?

Jane patted dry the remaining beads of water across Alex's neck with the towel before she draped it around his neck and over his shoulders. She ignored the way her stomach fluttered and her heart's tempo increased a step or two upon standing so close to him. She had a job to do, and by goodness she was going to see to her job.

She poured hot water from the pitcher in the empty bowl. The last few days Alex had risen before her and had set the pot to heat, so by the time she woke, hot water was ready for her. At first she had argued against such a strenuous chore for him. But he had insisted, determined not to remain completely dependent on Jane.

She soaked and rinsed a towel and wrapped it gently around the lower portion of Alex's face.

He moaned in satisfaction, tilting his head back and closing his eyes.

She smiled. Truth be told she enjoyed shaving him each morning. She liked that moan of his so deep and satisfying in his throat. She liked the way he trusted her so completely that his muscles relaxed as she glided the razor along his jaw. And then there was the feel of his face when she was finished. His smooth, warm skin felt downright sinful.

Jane's eyes widened against her own wandering thoughts. Whatever was the matter with her? She removed the towel and set about her chore determined to be done with it and get on with other things.

She lathered up his face, her fingers working the soap shavings into a thick lather. Round and round her hands worked, kneading his stubbled skin until she had a rich foam. She opened the razor, noting the edge was sharp and ready, having seen to its care the last time she had used it. With a tilt of Alex's head up and over, Jane began to shave him.

Alex's breath caught in his throat. His face was so near her chest, his mouth a bare half inch from her breasts. He closed his eyes and concentrated on her strokes. Even and tempered she glided the razor across his skin. He had doubted her skill with a man's blade the first time she had wielded it, but she had assured him she had the experience necessary to perform the task more than adequately, and he now believed her. He had never had such a close or more pleasurable shave than when Jane shaved him.

But . . . his thoughts turned reflective. After last night and their shared kiss, his usual morning shave had suddenly taken on an air of sensuality. He peeked from beneath his almost closed eyelids, focusing on her lips. Rose petal soft and faintly pink, they looked just as they had last night when he had found them too disturbingly appealing to ignore.

Her taste still lingered on him, sweet and fresh; it beckoned him to savor her again and satisfy his thirst, which had been tempted but not quenched.

"Almost finished," Jane said, gently patting the remaining residue of lather from his face with the wet towel.

Not quite, was Alex's silent response. At that moment his instincts all but shouted to kiss her.

Take her in your arms, his emotions urged. *You want to.*

But does she want me to? his sensible side challenged.

How do you know if you don't try? Look at her. Your thoughts mirror her own. You can see it plainly. Look.

Alex studied Jane. She licked unconsciously at her lips, then tugged at her bottom lip with her teeth as if in doubt or question. Had their forced closeness charged her emotions as well? Was she warring with the same doubts?

Jane caught the steady stare of his glance then and their eyes locked, each strong and curious in the silent message they sent.

It was all Alex needed. He stood, grabbed her by the wrist and pulled her to him. Her name rushed hungrily from his lips before his mouth descended over hers.

Jane went willingly, the urge to kiss him again far too potent to resist.

He claimed her with a sensual intensity that sent the shivers straight through her. His passion for her was as hungry as her passion for him. Neither could deny the strong attraction.

"Good morning!" Maisie sang up from the bottom of the stairs.

Jane, feeling like a child caught red-handed in a wrongful act, tore away from Alex.

His possessive hold prohibited their entire parting. Their bodies remained close, so close Alex's warm, fresh breath fanned her face when he spoke.

"No," he protested gently.

"But—" she whispered, and he kissed her remaining protest away.

"Good morning!" Maisie repeated more strongly in her singsong tone.

This time Alex interrupted their kiss to answer. "Just stirring, Maisie. What can I do for you?"

Jane parted her lips in protest. Quickly Alex pinned his lips to hers.

"Brought some of my apple jelly for you and Jane.

I'll leave it on the table. Tell Jane I'll see her at Dr. Tanner's later today. Toodle—oodle!"

Alex released her reluctantly, but not before Jane took note of the way his fingers had possessively tightened at her waist at the mention of Jacob's name.

She took a step back and stared at him, not certain how to respond.

Alex felt the same unnerving reaction. What did he do now?

Jane, feeling an overwhelming sense of self-consciousness, stammered a hasty response. "Patients often find themselves attracted to the woman caregiver in their time of illness."

Alex smiled and held back his laugh. "Is that why you think I kissed you?"

Jane tilted her chin up. "Of course. Why else?"

"Could the reason possibly be that you have lusciously inviting lips?"

Jane's immediate response pleased the devil out of Alex. She blushed like a red rose in full bloom.

She fought to hide her embarrassment, turning away to snatch his dirty shirts off the nearby chest. "You are obviously in a humorous mood. I shall ignore your remark *and* the kiss. When you come to your senses and reflect on your actions ... then you may apologize." With her command issued, Jane marched out of the room without looking back at him.

Alex's smile grew into a laugh. A broken arm did have its benefits.

Jane hurried along the boardwalk, her steps steady and full of purpose while her thoughts wandered from last night's kiss, to this morning's kiss, to the breakfast she had shared with Alex and how they had conversed on safe subjects, avoiding any mention of kisses.

She had attempted to convince herself that it was gratitude he felt for her, not passion. And in a few short weeks his arm would be healed and they would part company, returning to their former status—that of a friendly acknowledgment when they passed each other on the street. To win her own debate with herself she recalled his grumbling and complaints over the duties she performed for him.

Why, just last night he had complained vehemently that she had misplaced his most recently written articles for his newspaper when she had cleaned his parlor. She had simply moved them to his desk, where she had stacked them neatly. He had grumbled further when she had easily located them and handed them to him.

"Jane."

Jane stopped in her tracks and returned the friendly smile Minnie greeted her with.

The older woman looked fresh and radiant as usual. Her gray hair was neatly styled and her blue-and-white striped, high-collar dress was pressed to perfection. Jane often wondered how Minnie, or Maisie for that matter, managed never to have a wrinkle in any clothing they wore.

Minnie hooked arms with Jane, retracing her steps in the direction she had come. "I was just asking Jacob how you were doing."

Jane smiled. Minnie was so obvious in her matchmaking that it was almost comical, and at times frustrating, but Jane played along. "I do hope he gave me a glowing report."

"Oh, my dear," Minnie said seriously. "He is simply raving about your skills. And he tells me that the townspeople often ask for you to treat them."

Jane had found that statement to be true. Several of the women patients, not men—understandably so since they were more thickheaded in their ways—had requested that she treat them. It had pleased her immensely to know that they thought so highly of her.

"Jacob also told me how quickly you learn. He claims you are a natural healer."

Jane couldn't help the pride that swelled in her chest.

Jacob had been patient with her, extremely patient. She couldn't have asked for a better or more generous teacher. He answered all her questions, was never curt in his responses, and genuinely sought to explain all procedures as precisely as he could.

Minnie continued to sing Jacob's praises. "He says you will probably put him out of business one day."

"I seriously doubt that," Jane said, stopping in front of Jacob's office.

Minnie gave Jane's arm a squeeze. "He truly thinks the world of you."

"And I of him."

Minnie's eyes widened in interest. "Do you really?"

"I certainly do. He has been kind and generous to me, and he has a delightful manner about him. He is pleasant and so very interesting to converse with."

"And you share so many common interests," Minnie encouraged.

"I have many years of study to come even close to Jacob's knowledge."

"But think, dear, think of how gratifying it would be to share so much common ground with a man. You would never lack for stimulating conversation."

"Bored, that's what she'd be," came the curt and unexpected response.

Jane turned around, hiding her smile, to face Maisie. "Thank you for the apple jelly, Maisie. Alex and I both enjoyed it this morning."

"And how is dear Alex?" Maisie asked, directing the conversation away from the doctor.

Jane recalled the strength of his arm around her waist and the tug of his fingers at her side. "He's feeling *much* stronger."

"Good," Minnie announced. "Then you will be able to spend more time with Jacob and your lessons."

"Alex isn't recovered that much," Maisie insisted. "He still requires Jane's attention."

"Not as much as he did before," Minnie argued back.

"Just as much," Maisie returned with a dangerous squint to her eyes as though she was prepared to battle to the end.

"He's not an invalid," Minnie stated.

"But he does require help and that's Jane's job."

"She can do it and still see to her lessons with Jacob."

"Her patient comes first."

"Her lessons are necessary."

"Ladies!" Jane remarked loudly, afraid the two sisters would come to blows since with each response they had taken a step closer and closer to each other until they were almost nose to nose.

Both women focused their intent looks on Jane.

"I see the validity to both your opinions, and I am certain I can handle my patient and my lessons without any difficulty. But I do thank you both for your concern."

"Always there to help you, Jane," Maisie offered pleasantly.

"Naturally," Minnie agreed.

Jane smiled. "Why, thank you both for that vote of confidence."

The two sisters sent each other an alarming look. They had agreed on something, a rarity to be sure.

"Good day, ladies," Jane called to them and disappeared into Jacob's office, leaving the two women to wonder over the oddity of their mutual agreement.

The outer office was empty when Jane entered, and she stopped to straighten the two spindle-back chairs that sat in front of the wide window. Two benches sat flush against opposite walls, and a small desk and chair occupied the corner space near the door to Jacob's examination room.

Jane surveyed the room with a pleased smile. At home—that was how she felt here. Each time she entered, whether patients were waiting or not, a sense of coming home would rush over her and fill her with contentment.

She supposed in a way the office stirred memories. Lately she thought often of her grandfather and the days she had spent in his office watching him work. Or the days she had peeked in the room, after having been issued orders to stay away, and watched her grandfather work to save someone's life.

Her decision to help heal people had come early in life; only her grandfather's stubbornness and love had interfered. Now she had a chance to follow her dream, and she intended to do just that.

"That you, Jane?" Jacob called from the examination room.

"Yes, it's me." Jane hurried through the door to find Billy Taylor sitting on the table scrunching his face as Jacob worked over his hand.

Jane tensed a moment, fearing the printing press had gobbled Billy's hand as well.

"Splinter, and it's deep," Billy said through gritted teeth.

"I've had my share of those," Jane sympathized and walked over to take a peek at Jacob's progress. She scrunched her own face and suggested, "Why don't I see to the splinter for Billy while you get some of your paperwork done?"

Jacob looked up prepared to inform her it wasn't necessary when he caught the hopeful look on Billy's face. "Good idea."

Jacob contained his laughter when he heard Billy sigh in relief.

Jane slipped on a white bib apron, washed her hands, and filled a white porcelain bowl with lukewarm water.

She had Billy soak his hand while she collected gauze and a jar of finely crushed powder from the medicine cabinet.

"You sure are taking good care of Mr. Evans," Billy complimented. "He's been telling me about you."

"Has he now?"

Billy nodded his head vigorously. "He says you make the best biscuits in Harmony."

Jacob laughed out loud. "So that's the secret to your doctoring."

Billy rushed on. "Says your flapjacks are great, too."

"Perhaps you'd like to try my flapjacks some morning, Billy?"

"Gee—" Billy grew silent, cast a quick look around the room, and spoke softly so only Jane and Jacob could hear. "I'd really like to do that, but I don't want Miss Minnie to hear about this because she kind of thinks her flapjacks are the best and she's always inviting me over for some. But Mr. Evans says your flapjacks leaves his mouth watering for more."

Jane couldn't hide the pleasure his compliment had brought her. She glowed. "I'm glad he enjoys my cooking so much."

Jacob coughed and cleared his throat. "Maybe we should have you cook away all the patient's illnesses."

Jane heard the teasing note in his voice and turned a smile on him. "Perhaps a few oatmeal cookies for the waiting patients would help."

"Boy, would they!" Billy offered his opinion with a quick lick of his lips.

"Hold still now," Jane said after patting dry Billy's hand. She probed the area lightly and in seconds plucked the offending splinter from his palm.

"Wow, I didn't even feel it. You're a lot better than Doc—" Billy caught himself, but too late.

Jacob swung around in his swivel chair. "That's all right, Billy. I admit I don't have a gentle hand. I'm glad Jane was here to see to you."

"Me, too," Billy said, his cheeks heating in embarrassment. In no time Jane had Billy's had bandaged. He left in a flourish with thoughts of fresh-baked oatmeal cookies filling his head.

"Sounds as if your patient is recovering nicely," Jacob said, looking up at her.

Jane furrowed her brow. "It was only a splinter."

"I wasn't talking about Billy."

A pinkish glow tinged Jane's cheeks. She had been blushing all too frequently lately, and it was beginning to annoy her. She was no young schoolgirl dreaming of her beau. She was a grown woman studying medicine.

"Alex is doing just fine. I wouldn't be surprised if in another week or so he won't require my services at all."

"Don't rush his recovery. His arm needs to set properly to heal correctly. I've seen too many men with simple or severe breaks who thought they could resume work before a reasonable healing time. Some were left partially disabled, so make certain he takes the full six weeks to recover."

Jane nodded, feeling a bit guilty she had even thought of deserting Alex, but then he didn't make her job easy. Her thoughts rushed out of her mouth before she could retract them. "He's so stubborn."

Jacob laughed. "Most patients are. There's a reason a patient is referred to as a *patient,* though the meaning is lost to most."

Jane smiled in understanding. "A *patient* needs *patience* to recover."

"Exactly, though few, if any, have the necessary patience to see their recovery through to the end. That's why it's important to keep control of your own patience when dealing with ill people. It isn't an easy profession, Jane, for anyone."

Jane understood he was once again warning her of the pitfalls in becoming a doctor, especially since she was a woman. But it didn't matter—medicine was in her blood. It always had been since as long as she could remember.

Her time with Jacob passed swiftly, and the few hours she spent there were rewarding. It didn't matter that she and Jacob had more patients than usual to see to or that the medicine cabinet needing restocking and the examination room needed cleaning. She enjoyed every minute of her work, leaving her in high spirits when she returned to Alex's home.

Jane had supper on the table in no time. Crispy fried chicken, hot mashed potatoes, fresh-baked corn bread, and cherry pie greeted Alex when he joined her at the table.

He spied the delicious fare with confusion. He couldn't understand where she found the time to do as much as she did.

"I'm starving," she announced and proceeded to fix a plate for Alex and a plate for herself. "It was a busier day than usual at Jacob's office."

She placed a generously filled plate in front of Alex. He had to admit he was hungry himself and the food smelled great. So great that he found his mouth watering for the first bite.

Jane poured them each a glass of lemonade from the glass pitcher on the table. "Did you know about Billy's splinter?"

Alex nodded, having placed a spoonful of potatoes in his mouth.

"It's nothing serious," she informed him, picking up a chicken leg from her plate.

Alex swallowed and took a drink of the lemonade before responding. "He told me you took real good care of him."

Jane smiled. "I'm glad he thinks so."

"I've been hearing a lot about your talent in tending people. Most I've spoken with say you have a gentle hand and a caring nature."

Jane looked perplexed. "Who have you been talking to?"

Alex fussed in his chair and purposely slipped a good-size helping of potatoes into his mouth.

It was obvious he was hiding something from her, and she was about to find out what it was. "Have some more lemonade." She refilled his glass and handed it to him, giving him no choice but to drink. "Who have you been talking to?" she repeated the question as he moved the glass away from his mouth.

"To the folks who have stopped by the *Sentinel*."

Jane's eyes grew wide. "You've been working in the *Sentinel*'s office?"

Alex felt like a kid about to be chastised by his schoolteacher. But being he was an adult and feeling guilty, his defenses automatically went up. "Yes, I've been working in the office."

"I've warned you about returning to work too soon, and you still don't listen."

"I'm a grown man responsible for my own actions."

"Wrong! When you agreed that I was to care for you, I became responsible." Jane couldn't help but hear Jacob's earlier warning. She couldn't bear the thought of Alex being left with any disability in his arm. He was too strong, stubborn, and vibrant to be anything but whole.

Alex groaned in defeat, realizing the argument was senseless. They had debated the point often enough, and he had gotten nowhere. Jane, he had discovered, had an exasperatingly stubborn nature. "How long do I have left to my sentence?"

Jane sent him a victorious smile. "Three, possibly four more weeks."

Alex returned to their previous conversation, feeling the topic was safer. "Folks in Harmony are impressed with your doctoring."

"Really?" Jane asked, hesitant to believe him.

"Really," he confirmed and sliced each of them a piece of cherry pie.

"It isn't easy," she confided, both her tone and expression serious.

Alex looked at her. She wasn't exactly a young girl, being twenty-eight, but at that moment she reminded him of one. All her doubts and fears were registered plainly on her face. Her brown eyes were open wide with concern, and her mouth wore a uncertain smile. His heart went out to her, and all he wanted to do was wrap her in his arms and protect her. But he had come to know and understand Jane in the short time they had spent together, and he realized that at the moment she needed his support and encouragement.

"I can only imagine the challenges you must face."

His empathy was like a soothing tonic instantly bringing her relief. Jane relaxed. Her whole body lost its rigidness. Her smile became more confident. "Some people just can't accept the fact that a woman is intelligent enough to study medicine."

Alex nodded his response while he sampled the cherry pie. He felt it was best to let her talk. She needed to, and he, to his surprise, needed to listen to her.

"Sometimes the women are worse than the men. They think the only illness I can tend to is birthing babies. Of course, the men help fuel the doubts. They fill their wives' heads with crazy thoughts like 'Why does she want to be a doctor? It don't seem right. She's got no business tending to men.' "

Alex felt the need to offer his support, and without hesitation he said, "You need to educate them."

"Educate them?" Jane asked curiously.

"Let them know that a woman not only has the intelligence, but the ability to learn about medicine. It seems to me you've already begun educating them."

"I have?"

"Sure," Alex said with a nod. "As I told you before, the townsfolk are talking about you and the great work you're doing with Jacob. So word is already spreading."

"You've helped in that."

Alex looked at her, puzzled. "Me?"

"You," she reaffirmed, pointing her finger at him. "Billy told me how you talked to him about my cooking, and to a lot of folks that's a surefire way of taking care of someone. Feed them mighty good and you're taking good care of them."

Alex laughed. "Then you sure are taking mighty good care of me, Jane Carson." Without thinking he reached his hand across the table to cover hers. His simple gesture caused them both to tense.

Memories of the kisses they shared flooded both their minds and sent their emotions soaring. His touch was soft, her skin smooth, and their hands . . . heated.

Alex looked at her, removed his hand from hers, and slowly reached up to stroke her heated cheek with his fingers.

"Your skin feels so soft, like a young petal that just blossomed."

Jane thought his compliment relevant since she likened herself to an unfurling flower each time Alex kissed her. And in her secret thoughts, she wondered about the passion he would blossom in her if he brought her to full bloom.

He teased her lips with a faint brush of his finger. "I love the taste of you."

Her stomach fluttered. His words were as suggestive as his touch.

"I could get addicted to you, Jane Carson."

Jane chose to remain silent, though her thoughts registered similar feelings.

"I want to kiss you, Jane," Alex said softly. "I need to kiss you."

She fought back her response: *I need you to kiss me, too, Alex.*

"I won't stop with one kiss. I can't," he warned.

Jane didn't hesitate. "I—"

The door burst open, and Billy rushed in like the devil himself was on his tail.

Eight

He stopped abruptly, grabbing the back of a chair for support. He struggled to catch his breath, but found his news too urgent to wait. "You're—needed—other—end—of town."

Jane jumped up. "Calm down and breathe slowly," she ordered. She pulled a chair out from the table, forced Billy to sit, and hastily poured him a glass of water.

Billy obeyed and greedily took the glass of water Jane handed him.

"Now calmly tell me what this is all about."

Billy took one last deep breath and spoke. "A couple of wagons pulled in and made camp at the edge of town this afternoon. They needed to restock and rest. One of the women is with child, and she's about to have the baby any minute." Billy's voice grew high with excitement as he rushed on. "Doc Tanner is at the Last Resort tending to two patrons that got into a fight. So I came straight for you."

"There's no one to help her?" Jane asked, a bit surprised. Women traveling by wagon usually tended to help each other.

"This is the woman's first baby and the other woman there has no children and she's never helped birth a baby."

PLAYING CUPID 83

"Let's go," Jane said, reaching for her knit corn-blue shawl hanging on the peg near the door. "I'll need to stop by Dr. Tanner's office for a few items. Billy, you'd better go ahead and tell them I'll be right along."

Billy rushed out the door as quickly as he had entered it.

Alex stood. "I'm going with you."

Jane shook her head adamantly. "You are not."

"The issue isn't up for debate."

"You're right about that. You're staying here."

Alex grabbed his coat off the back of the chair. "I'm going."

Jane attempted to argue, but Alex didn't give her a chance. He walked to the door and held it open. "The woman needs you. Why waste time arguing with me?"

"Right again," she said, hurrying over to him and stopping to plant a gentle poke to his chest. "You're not going."

Alex grabbed her finger and gave it a gentle squeeze. "Unless you're strong enough to rope and tie me, I'm going."

"Stubborn," she muttered and stormed out past him.

"A trait we have in common," Alex said, following her.

Jane made a quick stop at Jacob's office, then was off with Alex.

The crackling campfire and a soft murmur of voices greeted Jane and Alex when they reached the campsite. Two men sat opposite the fire talking softly. Both men appeared no more than twenty. One was tall and lanky, where the other one was of average height and weight. The taller of the two stood and rushed over to greet them.

"I'm Ben Campbell," he said, and with a quick turn of his head toward the other man by the fire he added, "and he's Ray Winston. I'm glad you could come, Miss Carson." He removed his worn hat in a gesture of respect. "Billy says that you've birthed a lot of babies and haven't lost a mother or babe."

Jane had no doubt Billy had embellished her skills as a midwife, but at the moment his praise of her work served a purpose. She hoped it help to calm the father-in-waiting. "I've delivered my share without much fuss or fanfare."

Ben relaxed a bit, but tensed instantly when he heard his wife's wretched moan from inside the wagon. "Nora's in pain," he announced the obvious to everyone.

"Most women are when they're in labor." Jane sent an anxious glance toward the wagon. "I'd best see to your wife." Jane gave a quick introduction of Alex to the two men. "Alex will keep you company. He's been through this before." She left the three men to fend for themselves and hurried over to climb into the back of the wagon.

Alex watched her swaying backside disappear beneath the canvas cover and shook his head. The woman amazed him. She waited for no one's help, and she didn't ask for assistance. She possessed an independent nature, and he realized he not only respected her, but admired her courage.

"We'd better make ourselves comfortable, Ben," Alex said, turning his attention to the restless man beside him. "This may be a long night."

The night wore on and proved more difficult with each passing hour. Nora Campbell's moans had grown stronger and had caused her husband's apprehension to escalate. Ben had paced around the campfire so often that he had left an embedded circle in the dirt surrounding the flames.

Obviously Ben's nervous tension needed an avenue of escape, so Alex didn't comment on Ben's repetitive actions. Alex sat in front of the fire drinking his fifth cup of coffee and recalling old memories.

His wife Liza had detested being pregnant and hated

her delivery time even more. The almost twenty-four hours of labor she had suffered through hadn't helped. When Samantha was finally born, Liza couldn't have cared less about the squalling baby. She wanted nothing more than to be left alone to recover from her *ordeal.* Of course she had allowed him a brief visit and had, in that short time, informed him that she had no intentions of *ever* having another child.

A scream from inside the wagon drew the men's attention. All movement stopped as they focused their intent looks on the wagon.

Alex, feeling older and more responsible, commented, "Shouldn't be long now."

Ben gulped loudly. "You sure?"

"Can't be sure about any birth, but it seems as if her pains are increasing in strength and intervals—that usually means delivery is close at hand." Alex tried to sound confident and encouraging.

Ben nodded, accepting his explanation, and resumed his pacing.

Ray poured himself another cup of coffee from the pot on the iron grate over the fire, then offered Alex a refill.

Alex gladly accepted it. He cupped the hot mug in his hands and cast a concerned glance toward the wagon. He hoped Jane was all right and that his comment would prove positive. He didn't care to hear the woman's suffering, but then he didn't care to think that Jane was possibly having a difficult time with the delivery. She had looked tired enough this evening from taking care of him, his house, running to help Jacob, and then returning to make him supper. She needed some time for herself and to rest.

Another scream pierced the late-night air and caused Alex's hair to stand on end and brought a woeful moan from Ben. It had been too long, Alex thought. Too long since he had worried and cared so much about a woman birthing babies.

* * *

Jane wiped Nora's sweat-soaked brow with a damp cloth. "You're doing fine."

Nora rubbed her painfully protruding belly. "I don't feel fine."

Jane gave her hand a reassuring pat. "Giving birth to a baby isn't easy, but believe me when I tell you you're doing fine."

"I believe you," Nora said, bracing for another pain that was beginning to spread over her belly. "I have no choice."

"Don't hold your breath and don't fight the pain—try to go along with it," Jane instructed, studying Nora as she released her held breath and attempted to follow Jane's suggestion. Jane saw no problem with the woman's delivery, though she was still cautious. Birthing babies was too unpredictable, and one always took precautions against emergencies.

Nora was strong and healthy. She didn't complain or carry on like some women did during labor. She had stamina and courage. Her size, at least five six, her solid form, and her fresh complexion all added to her picture of health.

"Is it always this painful?" Sara Winston asked, sitting on a small crate at the back of the wagon.

"Every woman's degree of pain is different," Jane informed her. The poor girl looked as though *she* were going through the labor, so pale was her complexion.

Jane surmised on first meeting Sara that she wasn't prepared to help birth a baby. She appeared the type that had been pampered. Not an ideal trait for survival in the West.

"It's worth it in the end," Nora said after the pain subsided.

A pleasurable smile blossomed on Jane's face. "You've been looking forward to holding your baby, haven't you?"

Nora sent Jane an anxious grin and a quick nod. "It's all I've dreamed of the last month or two."

"I don't know if I want children," Sara commented.

Nora grew wide-eyed, although Jane couldn't be certain which caused her startled expression, Sara's announcement or the labor pain that gripped her.

"Why?" Nora managed to ask before the pain took her speech away.

Nervously twisting her hands, Sara answered, "The pain. Good Lord, you're suffering so much. I feel awful for you."

Jane cast a surprised glance at Sara. She had not thought of her as considerate, but apparently she was, and it would be the one saving grace for her if she settled in Kansas. Jane also realized that for a young girl who had never been present at a birthing, this could be a harrowing experience.

Nora dismissed Sara's concern with a rough hand wave. "That's nonsense. So you suffer a little pain—the baby makes up for it. Right, Jane?"

It was Jane's turn to look startled. "I don't have any children."

"You don't!" both women cried out in unison.

For the first time in her life she felt *different*. Heaven knows her childhood days had been anything but normal. Even now with her medical studies, her daily life didn't run along the common. It had been years since she had given thought to having a husband and children. Yet now, hearing these women talk about children, gave her a sudden sense of not belonging, of being *different*.

Nora reached out and squeezed Jane's hand. "You may still have children someday."

Jane realized the two women assumed her married and childless. She purposely avoided clarifying their misassumption. If she hadn't she would have had to suffer their pitiful looks of sympathy upon their discovering her an *old maid*.

Jane was grateful when Sara spoke.

"I still don't think I want children."

Nora chuckled. "I don't think you'll have a choice. Ray looks like the virile type to me."

Sara blushed unmercifully.

Jane laughed, though if they knew she was unmarried, she wondered if the remark would have been made. Some married women didn't think intimate conversation was appropriate in front of unmarried ladies.

Another pain attacked Nora, and Jane returned to her duties, certain the young woman's time was near.

Ben had stopped pacing and had returned to his seat beside the fire. He cast a worried glance to the wagon every now and then and one to Alex. He was looking for reassurance.

Alex wasn't certain how to handle the young man. He was concerned himself, but his concern was for Jane. The hour had grown late, and she was sure to be exhausted. He wished this whole ordeal were over.

As though his thoughts were heard and his wish granted, the men heard a baby's strong cry from the wagon.

Ben jumped up and Ray and Alex followed. The three men stood there looking at the wagon and waiting.

Ray began to pace before the fire once again when no news was forthcoming, and Alex attempted to explain that the new babe had to be taken care of and the mother seen to before the news could be delivered to the father.

Sure enough a short time later Jane emerged from the wagon, a small bundle cradled in her arms. She approached the men with a warm smile.

Jane stopped in front of Ben, who had stepped forward past Alex and Ray. "Ben, meet your new son." Jane drew back the blanket that wrapped around the small body like a cocoon. Red and wrinkled, the baby made a face at his warm nest being disturbed, but Jane soothed him with a few soft words and a gentle rock.

"He's tiny," Ben said.

"He's sturdy enough," Jane responded and tested the baby's weight with a slight bounce of him in her arms. "I'd say he weighs six or seven pounds. He could even be pushing eight."

"Big guy you got there," Ray offered and caused Ben's chest to puff with pride.

Ben cautiously touched his son's cheek with his finger. The baby sighed contentedly and won his father over completely.

"Nora?" Ben asked anxiously.

"Fine and dandy, but mighty tired," Jane assured him. "You might want to go see her before she falls asleep."

Ben turned to hurry off and stopped suddenly, turning back around. "Ma'am, I don't know how to thank you for your help."

"No need," Jane answered, her smile spreading wide. "He," she said, glancing down at the sleeping baby, "made it all worth it."

Ben hurried off and Ray followed him, noticing that his wife Sara was climbing down from the back of the wagon.

Alex moved to Jane's side and peeked down at the baby. "Is he all right?"

"He's a good baby."

"How do you know?" Alex asked, and itching to touch the wrinkled red face, he reached out and stroked the baby's cheek.

"He didn't give his mother a hard time during delivery. He made his entrance into this world fast and easy. He drew his first breath without trouble and hardly fussed at all. I'd say Ben and Nora have a little darling on their hands."

Alex had to agree; the baby captured your heart at first glance. It didn't matter that he resembled a red prune and had brown peach fuzz covering his head. "I had forgotten how tiny they are," he said, gently lifting one of the baby's small curled fingers.

"They grow fast," Jane said. "Most mothers complain they grow too fast."

"Much too fast."

His melancholy tone caused Jane to glance up at him. The baby's birth must have rekindled memories of his daughter's birth. She hadn't considered his role as a father—and a single father at that. It couldn't have been easy for him, raising Samantha on his own. She understood well the difficulty of a single parent, since it was her grandfather who had reared her. It took a special man to raise his little girl without the benefit of a mother, Jane thought.

Alex caught her studious stare. She looked tired. Her eyes didn't hold their usual brightness. Her mouth appeared too weary to smile, and her shoulders drooped just enough to hint at her fatigue.

"You're tired," he said and without thought reached out to stroke her cheek as gently as he had the baby's cheek.

Jane would have gladly surrendered herself to his arms, if she hadn't been holding the baby. She *was* tired. Tired of always being on her own. Tired of no one being there when she needed a caring shoulder to lean on. Tired that there was no one who showed concern for her. She nodded her head in response, not trusting her voice. The night had been emotional enough; she didn't need to shed tears and make a complete fool of herself.

"You need rest." His solicitous tone lulled her.

Careful, a silent voice in her head warned. *You're exhausted and vulnerable.* She sighed in an attempt to release some of her apprehension. "It's been a long day."

"Too long." His comment sounded stern to her ears. "Are you needed here much longer?"

Jane shook her head. "I only need to tuck this little

fella and Nora in for a good night's sleep. They're both plumb tuckered out."

"I know the feeling," Alex said with a dramatic sigh. He had come to understand Jane well over the last couple weeks. He realized she would respond to his need for rest before her own.

Her apprehension vanished in a flash, and concern registered instantly on her face. "I knew I should have insisted more strongly that you stay home."

"I wouldn't have listened," Alex said with a challenging smile.

"I could have forced the issue."

"As I said before, you would have had to rope and tie me."

"An easier solution could have been found."

Alex disagreed. "Nothing would have stopped me."

Her eyes brightened and she picked up the proverbial gauntlet of challenge he had issued with confidence. "It would have been simple to keep you there if only I had given it rational thought."

Alex anxiously awaited her explanation. "How simple?"

Her smile widened. "As simple as a walk next door to fetch Maisie and Minnie."

Alex winced at the thought of the two elderly women descending on him. "That's playing dirty, Jane Carson."

"I'd do anything that was necessary to see to my patient's full recovery."

"Anything?" Alex asked.

His tenderly sensuous tone caused goose bumps to run up Jane's arms. Nervous tremors attacked her stomach whenever he spoke to her in suggestive riddles. She was in no condition to verbally fence with him. Being as tired as she was made her mind sluggish and her responses not what they should be.

"I'd do what was necessary," she said, drawing her attention back to the sleeping baby in her arms. "I best see to this little fella and his mom."

"I'll wait right here for you." Alex watched her walk away. He wondered over the word *necessary*. He doubted his meaning matched hers. He shook the suggestive thoughts from his head. What was *necessary* now was getting Jane home and to bed . . . to rest.

She returned in minutes. Her gait lacked its usual bounce and vitality. She hugged her shawl around her, fending off the late-night chill of early June. She yawned, her hand going to cover her mouth as she approached him.

"You're going directly to bed when we get home. You need rest."

Jane laughed, only to have it interrupted by another yawn. "Are you offering me medical advice?"

"Common sense," Alex corrected.

"Of which you think I have none?"

Alex slipped his good arm around her shoulders and drew her near to walk alongside him. "You have tons of common sense. You just misplace it at times, especially when you concern yourself with other people's welfare."

"That's my job," she said, snuggling against him as they walked. His arm felt good around her, protective and strong. She liked the feeling.

"Working yourself into exhaustion is not part of your job."

Another yawn sneaked up on her, and it took her a second before she could respond. "Sometimes it is."

"What good would you do a patient if you're too tired to tend him adequately?"

"A point well taken," she agreed, almost tripping on the uneven boardwalk that ran in front of the buildings.

Alex's arm tightened around her. "See what I mean? You've walked along here day after day never paying any mind to this crooked boardwalk. But tonight you're tired and not your usual self."

Jane argued the point. "But I delivered Nora's baby without any problem. I didn't let my fatigue interfere.

Now that I know I'm not responsible to care for anyone, I can relax."

"What about me?"

Jane stopped dead, forcing Alex to do the same since he refused to let go of her. "Oh, Alex, I'm so sorry. I never meant that I wasn't responsible for you. I—"

"Shhh," he ordered, silencing her apology with his finger pressed gently to her lips. "I know what you meant. And I know you're exhausted and need rest. Now let's get you home."

He led her down the boardwalk to the *Sentinel*. This time he followed behind her up the steps to his living quarters. He trailed her down the hall to her room and entered behind her, turning her around to take her shawl from around her shoulders.

"I can—"

"Allow me to tend to you just one night," he finished and didn't wait for her response. "Do you want some hot water to wash up?"

Jane sighed at the pleasurable thought. "I'd love some."

"I'll be right back."

Jane watched him hurry out the door. She wondered over his concern for her. Was he returning the favor and caring for her out of guilt, or did her fatigue actually worry him?

She moved to the bed and sat down, her legs unable to support her any longer. It had been a long and busy day and unusual. It had started with a memorable kiss and escalated emotionally and physically. She didn't recall being this tired or confused in a long time.

She dropped back upon the pillow to rest until Alex returned. Her eyes closed of their own accord, and in an instant she was sound asleep.

Alex returned only moments later. He placed the pitcher of hot water in the blue ceramic washbowl on the dresser. He walked over to Jane and bent down beside the bed.

"Stubborn," he whispered. He reached out, brushing back the stray curls that ran along her forehead. He couldn't deny his attraction for her. Right now he wanted to kiss her luscious lips, caress her slim neck, and lie down beside her and gather her in his arms.

Damn, but he had a problem. A big problem. He had to spend four more weeks with Jane Carson living in his home and sleeping just down the hall from him. *How the hell was he going to keep his hands off her?*

He brushed a kiss across her lips, stood, turned the lamp flame down and walked to the door. He glanced back at her and shook his head. Four weeks never seemed so long.

Nine

THE mouthwatering scent of fresh-baked oatmeal cookies cooling on the table permeated the kitchen as Jane spooned another batch of oatmeal dough onto the baking pan.

She impatiently pushed her hair off her forehead with the back of her hand, making certain the batter-covered spoon she held didn't touch her straying locks. She sighed in satisfaction, turning her face to feel the refreshing breeze that drifted in through the window over the pump sink. She sniffed lightly at the rich scent of mint that floated in from the potted mint plant she had rested to sun on the windowsill.

Be careful, her inner voice whispered. She was beginning to dislike that little warning voice that made itself present from time to time. She disliked even more the fact that she paid attention to it.

She had cautioned herself recently against feeling comfortable and at home in Alex's living quarters around the *Sentinel*. The kitchen had slowly become her domain. Potted herbs took up spots on the windowsill, besides being lined on sunny shelves and grouped in a basket on the table. Dried herbs tied in batches hung from wooden pegs near the door while sun-yellow curtains, stitched by her own talented hands brightly framed the lone window. Little by little her skill with a needle and her feminine touch brought his bland quarters to life. And to her dismay she was growing more and more accustomed to residing there.

She liked rising early and seeing to his shave, and though she had managed to avoid further kisses from him, she valued the closeness the time afforded them. She had to admit she also enjoyed cooking for him, mending his clothes, tending his quarters, and most of all sharing the evening meal with him. He would always ask about her day and especially question her about her work with Jacob. His interest and concern appeared genuine, and she looked forward to their conversations.

Jane felt, of late, as though they were husband and wife, except of course that they didn't share the same bed. A thought she had pondered all too often recently.

The voice cautioned her once again against such dangerous musings. Thoughts of a husband and home would only manage to interfere with her medical studies. No man would tolerate a wife who chose to devote her time and energy to becoming a physician.

Not even Alex?

The notion caused her to stop spooning dough onto the pan and consider the idea. Alex took great pride in his work. The *Sentinel* meant a great deal to him. He labored daily over articles for the newspaper, producing fact-filled and informative news.

Could he understand her need to give the same energy and fervor to her work? Or would he prefer his wife home tending to him and his needs and following the dictates of society?

"Yoo-hoo!" Maisie called out before opening the screen door and entering the kitchen. Minnie trailed in behind her.

"Hello." Jane issued her greeting with a welcoming smile. She had felt a momentary pang of annoyance at their intrusion, but all things considered, their interruption of her wandering thoughts was for the best. She was dwelling too much on her daydreams. Concrete thoughts were more productive. So were her plans for the future—that of becoming a doctor.

Minnie, without invitation, sampled a warm oatmeal cookie. "A bit underdone."

Maisie wasted no time in doing the same. She munched a moment and announced, "The cookies are perfect."

"Doughy," Minnie contested.

"They're cooked just right," Maisie argued and proceeded to demonstrate. "See, the cookie doesn't snap apart like a dried twig; it separates with just the right amount of moisture."

"Nonsense." Minnie grabbed another cookie. "It's too moist. It should separate with a gentle snap."

Jane, seeing her cookies being torn apart, hastily offered a solution. "I'd be grateful for any advice offered, but a demonstration would prove more beneficial."

She held out a spoon to Minnie and then to Maisie.

The two women, weapons in hand, looked armed for battle. And battle they did—each burst into action, spooning the batter onto baking pans.

Jane shook her head, her eyes alight with humor as she watched them. The sisters' actions were so similar you would think you were seeing double, especially since each wore a rose-colored dress almost identical in style. They were a mirror image of each other, yet they disagreed and bickered about everything.

"How are your lessons with Jacob going?" Minnie asked, removing a portion of cookie dough from the spoonful she had just dropped onto the pan.

Maisie on the other hand had decided her recently dropped spoonful was too thin and added more oatmeal batter.

Jane shook her head once again.

"The lessons aren't going well?" Minnie asked with concern.

The shake of her head having given the wrong impression, Jane corrected the misunderstanding. "The lessons are wonderful. I've learned so much and look forward to learning more."

Maisie wagged her empty spoon at Jane. "You're not neglecting Alex, are you?"

Jane reached for both finished trays to put in the oven. "Not at all. He's recovering nicely."

"Wonderful," Minnie said, her smile wide. "Now you can expand your lessons."

"It hasn't been six weeks yet," Maisie corrected. "Jacob insisted on at least a six-week recovery period."

Minnie's smile grew so wide she looked like a cat about to swallow an unsuspecting bird. "The Fourth of July picnic is around that time."

"Alex may still need looking after," Maisie insisted.

"Nonsense," Minnie said. "Alex will be fit as a fiddle and will probably be escorting a lady to the picnic."

The idea of Alex with another woman caused a sudden rush of panic to run through Jane. She pictured Alex cleanly shaven and dressed in freshly washed and pressed clothes escorting one of Harmony's finest ladies to the gala Fourth of July picnic. And of course to make it worse Jane could clearly see the woman's arm snugly wrapped around Alex's now mended one. The one she had patiently cared and tended back to health.

"You're taking them out too soon," Minnie warned as Maisie pulled her tray of cookies from the oven.

Jane ignored the squabbling women. The picture her mind's eye had painted lingered too vividly. She didn't care for the scene at all. Why? she asked herself. Why did the thought disturb her so?

"Oatmeal cookies, my favorite."

Jane glanced up at Alex as he entered the kitchen. He winked at her and smiled. He was so handsome, especially when he smiled that way. She had convinced herself it was a special smile, one he saved only for her. One that whispered of secrets and understandings that no one else had knowledge of but the two of them.

She understood instantly that he was aware that Minnie and Maisie were driving her crazy, and he, like a knight in shining armor, had come to her rescue.

"Try one of mine, Alex," Maisie offered. "It's fresh from the oven."

Alex sent the woman into giggles when he gave her a generous smile and reached for the cookie. He finished it in only a few bites and licked his fingers appreciatively. "I think I've died and gone to heaven."

Maisie blushed like a young schoolgirl in love.

Minnie quickly whipped her cookie tray from the oven and practically shoved a hot cookie in Alex's hand.

Alex obliged, popping the cookie in his mouth.

Jane reached for the pitcher of lemonade on the table and poured a large glass. By the way Alex was hastily chewing the hot morsel, she had a feeling he would need a cool drink. She held the glass out to him.

He sent her a grateful look of relief as he downed near the whole glass. "I think I hear angels singing," he said, turning his praise and charm on Minnie.

Minnie followed her sister's blush with one of her own.

"You know, ladies, if you ever find yourself in a baking mood, I love sugar cookies."

"I make the best sugar cookies," Maisie said. "Golden brown and delicious."

"Burnt," Minnie corrected.

"I do not burn my sugar cookies."

"You always burn your sugar cookies."

"The one time I did was because you had stoked the oven fire too high."

Minnie wagged her finger at her sister. "I didn't know your cookies were in the oven."

Maisie rolled her eyes heavenward. "Then why do you suppose the baking bowl, flour, eggs, sugar, and all the other baking materials were on the table?"

"I thought you had just started."

Maisie dusted her hands off, then wiped them with the towel draped over the back of the nearby chair. "Well, I'm going to bake some sugar cookies right now for Alex. So keep your hands off the stove fire."

Minnie wiped her hands as well and followed behind her sister. "I'll bake some, too, since you'll probably burn your batch anyway."

Jane sighed when the screen door slammed shut behind the two bickering women. "Thank you, Alex," she said with a sincere smile of gratitude.

"It was purely a selfish act on my part," he admitted.

"Selfish?"

Alex cast a tentative look about the room as though checking to see that they were alone before he whispered, "I like your oatmeal cookies the best."

Jane laughed, moved in closer to him, and whispered back, "Then I'll finish making the rest for you."

Alex felt her warm breath sweet with the fragrance of lemons caress his cheek. He liked her unusual scent of lemonade and oatmeal cookies, a strange combination but oddly enticing. He also liked her domestic appearance, rosy cheeks, apron tugged snug around her slim waist, and a spot of flour resting below her bottom lip.

He reacted without thought. He reached up and gently wiped the flour spot off with his thumb. His thumb grazed her lower lip, and he tensed when he felt her shiver.

He wanted to kiss her, ached to kiss her, and ignoring all his staunch warnings about not getting involved because she was his nurse here to care for him, he lowered his lips to hers.

"Oatmeal cookies!" Billy yelled before throwing open the screen door.

Alex and Jane jumped apart.

Jane returned to spooning oatmeal batter onto the baking pan, but not before she raised and pressed the back of her hand to her heated cheek.

Alex caught her motion. He remained standing on the opposite side of the table watching her. She was as heated with passion as he was. He could almost feel the strength of her desire for him. This was no good. It bordered on dangerous sharing his living quarters with her and being in such close proximity. He didn't know how long it could last before their situation turned intimate.

"These cookies are delicious," Billy said, though not coherently. His mouth was too full to understand him.

"I'll give you some to take with you," Jane offered, turning to open a nearby cabinet drawer and taking out a blue check cotton napkin.

"I saw to the delivery of all the papers, and some of the merchants gave me the advertisements they wrote up for next week's paper." Billy reached for another cookie and continued talking. "I told them that since you're so good with words that you'd probably change what they've written some."

Jane wrapped half a dozen cookies for Billy in the napkin and handed it to him. "You want some lemonade?"

Billy, still munching on the cookie, nodded his head.

Jane poured him a glass, handed it to him, and returned to work on her cookies.

Alex noticed that she completely avoided eye contact with him. Their near kiss had obviously affected her more than she cared for him to know.

Alex picked up the papers on the table where Billy had set them down and gave them a quick glance. "Good job, Billy. I don't know what I would do without your help."

"I like the work. It's interesting and fun to gather up news and stuff for the paper." He paused a moment as though debating with himself on whether to address an issue he was obviously concerned with.

"Something you wanted to ask me?" Alex offered, hoping it would ease the young boy's concern.

Billy hesitated a second, then shrugged his shoulders

as if deciding it was now or never. "I was wondering if maybe, that is if it's all right with you, if I tried writing an article for the newspaper?"

Alex answered immediately. "You already write one."

Billy made a face. " 'Under the Shell' is a gossip column. Gossip can get you into trouble. I want to write a real article for the *Sentinel*."

"I think you should write a *real* article. You've a talent with words."

"I do?" Billy couldn't contain the excitement in his voice.

Jane couldn't help but smile.

"You do. If you have a topic in mind, we could discuss it. Then, if I find it newsworthy, you could write it up, and we could go over it and get it ready for print," Alex explained.

Billy jumped at the chance. "I was thinking about doing a story on the history of Harmony. You know, how the town got started. What families have been here the longest and the changes they've seen take place."

Alex nodded with a thoughtful smile. "That sounds mighty interesting. I think the folks in Harmony would like to hear about that. But I think it may be too long for just one piece. What about a series of articles to run once a month?"

Billy's eyes almost popped from his head. "You mean it?"

"I do mean it. I think you have a good idea, and I'd like to see it run in the *Sentinel*. But you have a lot of work to do before you start writing it. You must research all your information and get your facts correct."

Billy grabbed for the napkin with the warm cookies tucked inside. "I'll get started right away. I'll talk to my ma first since she knows everyone and everything that goes on in Harmony."

"Just remember to double-check your information.

We want this series on Harmony's history to be a dandy."

"I'll check with everyone in town," Billy said. "I'll talk to my older brother Joseph. He hears a lot of stories and knows a lot of people, being he's the stationmaster."

"I look forward to reading it," Alex encouraged.

Billy made a beeline for the screen door, but halted in his tracks and swerved around. "Thanks for the cookies, Jane, and thanks for giving me this chance, Alex."

"I have a feeling you're going to make a good newspaperman," Alex said with a smile.

Billy grinned. "The best. I'm going to be the best."

The screen door slammed behind him and left the couple alone in silence.

Jane broke the awkward stillness quickly, her heart beating much too rapidly and her stomach fluttering much too nervously to allow the tension to continue. "Why don't you go rest? I'm going to clean this up and then get supper started."

"I can help," he offered, though he knew she would refuse him.

"That's all right, I can manage on my own. I'll call you when it's ready."

He didn't want to leave. He wanted to stay and watch her work around the kitchen. Watch her cheeks deepen with heat, watch her hips sway gently when she moved about, watch her tongue sweep over her lips when she concentrated on her task. He had discovered so many of her little nuances. Intimate nuances that usually a husband was only privileged to learn.

Husband.

The thought struck him profoundly. "I'll be upstairs working," he said and hurried out of the room.

He took the steps quickly and walked with vigor down the hall to his bedroom. He dumped himself on the bed with a bounce and leaned back against the pillows.

Husband.

He had thought at one time or another throughout the years of marrying again. But he never met a woman that interested him enough to consider marriage. He had also been too busy establishing his business, watching it grow and prosper, watching his daughter grow and blossom.

He didn't regret remaining single, though at times he had found himself lonely. He supposed that was why he had buried himself in his work. If he kept his mind active and busy, he didn't think of climbing into an empty bed at night, or waking in the morning alone with no one to wrap himself around.

He hadn't even considered the little things a wife did to make a home a home. Jane had reminded him of those extra touches. He liked waking to the smell of bacon and flapjacks cooking. He liked the fresh scent of his daily laundered clothes and the way his quarters were kept so neat and clean. He liked the cool pitcher of lemonade that was ready every afternoon for him and the added treats of fresh-baked cookies or cakes. He especially like sharing the evening meal with Jane and the easy conversation they always drifted into. She listened and appeared honestly interested in his work, and he honestly enjoyed hearing about her medical studies.

He closed his eyes against his thoughts, but they haunted him. He grew annoyed with himself for his fanciful musings. He had remained a bachelor for more than enough years. He didn't need to entertain any notions of changing that status. He had done just fine on his own. He had raised a fine daughter and had established a thriving newspaper. His life was full, and he was finally free of any burdens. He didn't need a wife and didn't want one.

He could wash his own clothes, clean his own quarters and cook his own meals. He didn't need anyone doing those chores for him.

"Alex, supper is ready," Jane called upstairs.

He stood, stretched what limbs he could, and gave his face a quick wash and his hair a quick combing before heading out the door.

He stopped dead in his tracks at the top of the stairs and sniffed. "Roasted chicken and mashed potatoes," he whispered and appreciatively sniffed the air again.

He thought of Jane downstairs, her cheeks rosy, her apron tugged snug around her waist, the gentle sway of her hips, and her lips pink and wet and ready to be kissed.

"Damn," he muttered and headed down the steps disappointed that only one of his appetites would be satisfied tonight.

Ten

JANE poured herself and Alex a cup of coffee before slicing two pieces of butter cake. She gave Alex his slice and relaxed back in her chair to enjoy her own.

Alex dug his fork into the moist cake. "I can't figure out why you never married."

Jane sent him a quizzical look and shrugged her shoulders. "I could say the same of you."

"Oh, no, I asked you first," he challenged with a smile.

Jane laughed before popping a piece of cake into her mouth, preventing an answer.

"It's obvious you'd make an excellent wife. You keep a spotless home and you're a fantastic cook."

Jane put her fork down. "Are those the only two requirements necessary for becoming an excellent wife?"

"I suppose neither are absolutely necessary, though I'd find it difficult to imagine a home without either spouse capable of performing everyday tasks."

"That could prove difficult, and it was one of the reasons that I learned to take care of a home."

With his coffee cup cupped in his one hand, he leaned forward and rested his injured arm on the table. "Tell me about it." He enjoyed listening to her tales of her childhood. She had grown up so differently from him, so independent and free. He almost envied her her earlier life experience.

Jane poured herself more coffee and settled herself comfortably in her seat. She smiled when she spoke, recalling happier days. "I felt sorry for, yet proud of my grandfather. I was dumped in his lap when I was young. He was accustomed to taking care of himself and busy with his medical practice. How in heaven's name could he possibly tend to a little girl?"

"I'd say the little girl had a knack of tending to herself."

Jane laughed with a shake of her head. "I had no choice. You wouldn't believe some of the meals he tried to cook for me. It was either learn to cook and take care of us both or starve to death."

Alex pointed to the butter cake. "He couldn't have been that bad. You did become a mighty good cook."

"I didn't learn from him. One of the women in the mining town where my grandfather was the doctor had a sick husband that needed weekly medical care. They were poor and didn't know how to pay my grandfather. I suggested that in turn for my grandfather's medical services the woman, a far better cook than I could ever hope to be, give me cooking lessons. Needless to say my grandfather hastily agreed."

"I'm surprised you didn't find a husband in that mining town."

Jane shook her head, her smile turning sad. "My grandfather held much higher aspirations for me. He didn't want me doomed to that kind of life. And he didn't feel my interest in doctoring would set well with a husband. That's why he moved me here to Harmony and set me up in the sewing shop."

"And still no husband? There are plenty of eligible men in Harmony." Alex felt his throat constrict. He thought he'd choke on his own words and wondered over his reaction.

"I've had a simple date from time to time, but as soon as I begin to discuss my interest in medicine, the men lose interest in me."

"So your interest in medicine surpasses your interest in men?"

Jane sighed and nodded. "There are times I wish I could blend the two, but unfortunately all men are of the same thought—a woman's place is in the home."

"And yours isn't?"

"At times it is. I get pleasure from tending to my home and cooking. Actually, cooking relaxes me. It allows me time with my own thoughts. Time to collect my wanderings and make some sense of them. Time to plan and set my course of action. I suppose it's more of a hobby than a chore."

"Then medicine comes first with you."

A smile wide with pleasure and pride filled Jane's face. "Medicine challenges me. It proposes questions and makes me search for answers and then tests my knowledge. It teaches me something new day after day. It gives me a sense of fulfillment."

"Mighty huge competition for a man to go up against."

"An ordinary man, yes. But I'm looking for an extraordinary man."

"He may be difficult to find."

"But not impossible," she said with such confidence that goose bumps ran up Alex's arm. Could she have possibly found that man? *Tanner.* Tanner was a kindred spirit to Jane. He would certainly understand her love of medicine and encourage it. The thought irritated him.

"How about you?" Jane asked, pouring another cup of coffee for Alex and herself.

"Why haven't I remarried?"

Jane nodded and sipped at her coffee.

Alex shrugged. "I suppose I'm married to the *Sentinel.* When I moved here with Samantha, I wanted desperately to make a success of the newspaper. I worked day and night in producing the paper and raising Sam."

"You did a great job on both. You should be proud of your accomplishments."

PLAYING CUPID

"Thank you." Alex sincerely appreciated her praise. The years hadn't been easy, but he had succeeded.

"You never thought of marrying again?"

"At times the idea entered my mind, but somehow a marriage never materialized. I suppose I didn't give the notion much consideration. The newspaper always demanded my time and I always gave it. Freely, mind you, I'm not complaining. I truly enjoy my job."

"That's obvious," Jane said. "I watch you sometimes when you're writing an article. You sink deep in thought. You write and rewrite until you produce pieces that to me are not only informative but relevant to the town. You wake up people to issues and get them thinking."

"I try," Alex said. "It doesn't always work."

"But most of the time it does, and if you just get people to thinking, I feel the article served its purpose."

"You see what I mean?" Alex said. "What woman would allow her husband to give most of his time to his work? What woman would understand when I wake in the middle of the night and begin to write a piece for the newspaper?"

I would. Jane's silent response haunted her. She could easily adapt to Alex's ways. Too easily.

A knock on the back door interrupted the odd look the couple exchanged. It seemed almost as if each could read the other's thoughts.

"Come in," Alex called out.

Jacob Tanner peeked his head around the door as he opened it. "Not disturbing your meal, am I?"

"Not at all," Jane said. "You're just in time to have some dessert—butter cake and hot coffee."

Jacob shut the door behind him and with a lick of his lips took the seat opposite Jane and next to Alex.

Jane cut him a generous slice and poured him a cup of coffee.

Jacob didn't waste any time in tasting the cake. "Delicious," he said between mouthfuls.

"Is this an official visit or neighborly?" Alex asked with a hint of sarcasm.

Jane caught his tone and sent him an odd glance.

Jacob either ignored it or did not bother to acknowledge it. "A bit of both. I wanted to see how you were doing, and I had hoped Jane had been busy baking and I could sneak a taste."

"Taste to your heart's content," Jane said and cast Alex a look that warned him to behave.

Alex fussed in his chair in response, then settled down and politely acknowledged Jacob's concern. "I'm doing fine. I haven't experienced any pain in a couple of weeks, and I find myself itching to get this splint off me."

"Then you're healing just fine," Jacob said. "When you start getting annoyed with the splint that means it's getting close to the time for it to come off."

Panic hit Alex. When the splint came off, Jane returned home. No more suppers and shared conversations. No more tasty smells filling his home. No more Jane sleeping down the hall from him. No more shaves from her, so close his lips could brush her soft flesh. He'd be alone again.

"A week or two should do it," Jacob said, "and then I can take that irritating splint off. You should be good as new, though I wouldn't exert the arm too much at first. Maybe Jane could stay one extra week with you to make certain everything has healed properly."

Alex looked at Jane.

Jane's eyes were concentrated on Jacob. "If you feel it necessary I can stay an extra week."

Jacob nodded. "It may be a thought to consider."

"The extra week won't interfere with your studies?" Alex asked, forcing Jane to turn her attention to him.

Surprised and pleased that he thought first of her medical studies than of her sewing shop, she answered him with a pleasant smile. "I've managed so far. I don't think an extra week will interfere. If it's necessary."

"If you say so," Alex said, relieved that she would remain with him for a bit longer. Somehow he would face the inevitable, but for now he intended to enjoy Jane's company.

Jacob held his plate out to Jane. "Mind if I have another piece? It's mighty good."

Jane sliced him another generous slice. "You can have as many as you like."

"No, he can't," Alex objected with a laugh. "There won't be any left for me."

"I don't blame you a bit," Jacob said, cutting into his cake with his fork. "I wouldn't let anyone have more than say, three slices?" He looked to Alex and waited.

Alex thought a moment with a studious eye on the remaining half of the cake. "Three sounds about right to me."

Jane scolded both men. "Shame on the both of you, squabbling over a cake. I can always bake another one."

"But this one is here right now, and that makes a difference," Jacob said and popped a piece into his mouth.

"A big difference," Alex agreed and held his plate out to Jane for another slice.

She obliged him, cutting a bigger piece for him than she had for Jacob.

A pleased smile spread across Alex's face when he took the plate back.

"I hear you've had several visits from Minnie and Maisie," Jacob said.

"I think each of them possesses a built-in divining rod that draws them to any incident that even hints at competition," Alex said.

Jacob laughed. "They are a pair. Zeke at the barbershop is kind of pleased that you've diverted their attention away from him for a while. Though he did say he missed the treats they plied him with day after day."

Alex shook his head in amusement. "All of Harmony

knows Minnie and Maisie have their sights set on Zeke Gallagher."

Jane disagreed. "I don't think either is really interested in him. They just seem to enjoy being in competition with each other."

"I'd say it's more like a war," Alex said.

"The ladies do get highly agitated at times," Jacob added.

"It adds spark to their lives," Jane said.

"And sparkling gossip for Harmony," Alex finished.

Jane glanced from one man to the other. "They're really a lovable pair and really concerned with everyone's welfare."

"That they are," Jacob agreed. "Although at times they interfere a bit too much."

"Like when it comes to their matchmaking," Alex interjected.

"Exactly," Jacob nodded.

Jane felt the need to defend the two elderly women, though she doubted they needed her help. If they were here, they would do just fine on their own. "They mean well."

"Actually," Jacob said after taking a sip of coffee, "I've heard tell that their matchmaking often turns out quite well."

Jane's and Alex's glances met instantaneously, and for a second both felt the heat rise in their bodies. They tore apart just as rapidly.

"I'd best be off," Jacob announced, standing. "Thank you both for sharing your dessert with me. The cake and the conversation were both appreciated."

The door closed quietly behind Jacob, and the kitchen remained silent for several minutes. Neither Jane nor Alex looked at each other. The heat still lingered in each one, and neither dared to glance up and betray his emotions.

"I'd better clean up," Jane finally announced.

"I'll help," Alex offered.

"It isn't necessary. Go rest."

"I rested before. I want to help this time."

"You only have one good hand," she reminded him.

Alex held up his uninjured hand. "I may have only one workable one, but I can clear the table, stack dishes, and put them away."

She shrugged. "Suit yourself."

They worked in silence and with compatibility. It was almost as though each anticipated the other's next move and was prepared for it.

With the table finally cleared and the dishes dried and ready to put away, Jane turned around from the cupboard to dismiss Alex from the remainder of the chores. His nearness affected her far more than she expected, and she wanted him gone from the room.

She moved swiftly, too swiftly, and collided with his chest. His good arm instantly went around her, clasping her up against him to steady her.

She found her face nuzzled in his chest, his white cotton shirt open several inches down from his throat. The hair on his chest tickled her nose and beckoned her to bury herself further against him. She turned her cheek to the curly hairs and without thinking gently rubbed against him. He felt good. He smelled good, too. His familiar scent of lemon and spice tickled her nostrils and her passion.

"Jane," he whispered almost breathlessly.

She ignored him and turned her face, rubbing her other cheek against his furry chest.

"Jane," he said, his voice full of desperation.

"You smell good," she murmured and lifted her face up to look at him.

He lost all control when his eyes met hers. Her brown eyes shone bright with sensual passion. She wanted him as much as he wanted her.

"Jane," he whispered harshly one more time before he lowered his head and claimed her lips.

She drew her arms up and around his neck, needing and wanting to taste all he had to offer.

His tongue delved deep, and hers answered willingly. They mated in a dance that excited them both and their bodies responded by pressing urgently against each other, demanding that their needs be met as well.

He tore free of her mouth, and she protested with a whimper, but he satisfied her when he gently kissed her lips, then moved to each cheek. He trailed down to her neck, and she threw her head back, offering him her tender flesh.

He tasted her and marveled at her sweetness. He couldn't get enough of her, couldn't satisfy his need, it was so intense.

His arm released her slowly, but she remained up against him. His hand drifted up to beneath her breast, and he looked into her eyes for a brief moment. She made no move away from him, and as he once again brought his lips to hers, his hand slipped up and over her breast.

She whimpered again, and he captured the sound in his mouth, his tongue delighting her and turning her whine to a soft pleasurable groan.

His hand cupped her breast and tenderly caressed it. His desire soared along with his need to feel her flesh. He worked at the buttons on her blue blouse and slipped his hand inside, meeting her cotton chemise. Determined to feel her warmth, he slipped beneath the barrier and found her full breast fell into his hand.

He groaned this time and deepened his kiss, searching for far more than this little intimate interlude could bring him.

His thumb grazed her nipple again and again, and he reveled in her hardening response.

His lips reluctantly left hers, and breathlessly he whispered her name. "Jane?"

She heard the query in his voice. He was asking, seeking permission to go further. Reality hit her like a cold splash of water in her face. She was standing in the kitchen while her patient touched her intimately. Touched her where no man had ever dared to tread. But she had allowed Alex access to that intimate part of her body, and she had enjoyed it. *She had allowed and enjoyed.* What in heaven's name was she doing?

She tore away from him, clasping her blouse closed with her two hands. She looked at him, her anguish and confusion plainly written on her face. She opened her mouth to speak, shook her head, and ran from the room.

Alex ran his hand over his face and shook his head as well. He wanted her. God, how he wanted her. He looked at the steps, where she had run up, and took a step toward them. Then he stopped himself, swerved around, and headed out the door, slamming it behind him.

Eleven

JANE hurried across the street to her You Sew and Sew shop. She had only a few matters to attend to there. The two women she had hired to fill her sewing orders were working out perfectly, leaving her time to tend to Alex and pursue her interest in medicine. In a way her grandfather had been right. A little seamstress shop was just what she needed to secure her future.

After attending to business, she intended to enjoy her hour of free time. She had rushed through her chores this morning purposely ignoring Alex, not that he hadn't ignored her. They had barely spoken two words to each other since they had risen.

Last night had placed a severe strain on their relationship. They had crossed the line from nurse and patient to just plain man and woman. Intimate man and woman, she reminded herself.

They had avoided any close contact all morning. Alex had gone off to Zeke's barbershop for his shave, having informed her that starting today he'd take his shave there every morning. She had intentionally given him a wide berth when he entered the kitchen, placing his morning cup of coffee on the table instead of handing it to him as she usually did. They were walking a tightrope, and she wondered when the rope would snap.

"Good morning, Jane. How's my father?"

Jane stopped abruptly and looked up to greet Samantha. "He's doing fine."

Samantha smiled. "I know him too well to believe that hogwash."

Jane thought her a beautiful girl, taking her father's most striking features and having improved on them. Not to mention her gorgeous long blond hair and blue eyes, which would make any man's head turn her way. "Good, then you know how stubborn your father can be."

"Do I ever. Why do you think I don't stop by as often as a dutiful daughter should?"

"Because you know what a pigheaded man he is."

"Precisely," Samantha agreed. "That newspaper is his life. Day and night that's all he thinks about. I've warned him over and over not to give so much of himself to his work. But does he listen? No."

Jane felt the sudden need to defend Alex. "The newspaper is important to him."

"Too important."

"He's worked hard to establish it and make the success of it that he has."

Samantha raised a brow. "But he should relax and enjoy life some."

Jane continued to defend him, not realizing the zeal with which she spoke. "But he's relaxed when he writes his articles. He works on them, reads me what he's written, and then rewrites them again to improve on them even more. He's very talented, and his talent shows in his newspaper."

Samantha smiled knowingly and nodded her head. "So all this work isn't harming his recovery?"

"Not at all. You couldn't expect a vibrant man like your father just to sit around while he recovers."

"If you say so," Samantha said sweetly. "You're the nurse."

"Who you shouldn't be bothering with a million

questions," Cord Spencer said, coming up behind his wife and wrapping his arms around her waist.

"I'm just checking on my father and making certain he's behaving."

Cord laughed and gave her slim waist a squeeze. "Your father's behavior is just fine. It's yours that needs watching."

Jane smiled at their playful banter. They were obviously made for each other, the perfect couple, happy and in love. Her smile faded, though she stopped it from completely disappearing. Love had eluded her these many years. Besides, her interest in medicine had been a strong deterrent to any relationship she had attempted.

"I hear you're doing a mighty fine job of taking care of Alex, not to mention your fine work with Dr. Tanner," Cord said, catching her attention.

"Thank you, I've always enjoyed the challenge medicine presented."

"Dr. Tanner says you have a real talent for it," Samantha added. "That's why I'm pleased that you're caring for my father."

"Thanks for the confidence, but your father's almost healed and won't be needing my services much longer." Her heart ached as she heard herself admit her time with Alex was near an end.

Samantha instantly became concerned. "You can't leave him on his own too soon. You know how stubborn he is! He could break his arm all over again because he insists on doing something he shouldn't."

Cord looked at his wife strangely. "Your father's a big boy. I'm sure he'll know what he can do and can't do until his arm has healed completely."

Samantha shook her head adamantly. "He's too stubborn."

"Like his daughter," Cord said with a grin.

Samantha pulled away from her husband and placed

PLAYING CUPID

her hands on her hips. "Cord Spencer, I'm concerned about my father's health."

Cord reached out, grabbed her arm, and pulled her toward him. "Too concerned. Leave the doctoring to Jane—she knows what she's doing." He sent Jane a wink. "Have a nice day and don't mind my wife." With that he took Samantha's arm and whisked her down the boardwalk.

Jane stared at the couple, shaking her head. Suddenly Samantha forced her husband to stop. He leaned down, listening to her, then looked back at Jane and shook his head before he started laughing and walking off with his wife, who was poking him in his ribs.

"Strange," Jane mumbled and hurried off to her shop.

She immediately saw to business, making certain all orders were up to date and material was plentiful. Though Jane's talent with a needle showed in her shop's attractive displays and pleasant atmosphere, she didn't find contentment there. She found herself more at peace when she worked in Dr. Tanner's office.

Jane made a list of supplies she needed from the store and a few items she needed for baking. She locked the shop's door behind her and headed next door to the mercantile.

"Jane. Jane Carson!" An excited voice called out.

Jane stopped in her tracks and turned. "Hello, Zeke," she said, his twinkling blue eyes bringing a pleasant smile to her face.

"Need to talk to you," Zeke said, halting in front of her. His smile was generous, as was his disposition.

"Talk away." She was certain he was about to ask her for a favor.

"Thought you'd be the perfect person to organize a few activities—games, races, and such—for the Fourth of July picnic."

"Me?" she asked, curious as to how he came to that conclusion.

"Who better than you? You would know what games would be less likely to get people hurt, and even if someone did get hurt you'd be right there to fix him."

Jane held her smile in check or it would have spread from ear to ear. Zeke was a sly one, filling her head with compliments to get her to agree to help him.

"You gotta do it for me, Jane," Zeke pleaded with a sorrowful look that demanded sympathy.

Jane shook her head at his playful dramatics. He definitely was a sly one. "You don't need to plead—I don't mind helping."

Zeke laughed. "Had to make sure I hooked you for those games. Couldn't let you get away."

Jane's laughter joined his. "Well, you hooked me good and solid. You'll have the best games ever for this Fourth of July."

"I have no doubt about that." He rubbed at his white whiskers and grinned. "I see another good citizen of Harmony who is about to volunteer his services for the picnic. Don't forget, the fourth is only a short time away."

Zeke left with a quick wave goodbye, chasing after another unsuspecting volunteer.

Jane watched his retreating back, though she wasn't interested in his actions. Her thoughts were on the Fourth of July picnic. Would Alex take one of the lovely ladies of Harmony? Or would he attend alone?

She shook her head, chasing her disturbing thoughts away. Her actions mirrored a love-struck young girl, not a grown woman. She had more important matters to worry about than whom Alex would be escorting to the picnic. She had to worry what games would be played, and determining the entertainment and fun for the day was more important than guessing whom Alexander Evans would be taking to the event.

She stomped her foot. "Damn," she mumbled, annoyed that once again she sounded like a girl in the throes of puppy love.

Locking her bothersome thoughts in the back of her mind, she swung open the door to the mercantile and marched in. She walked straight to the material counter and examined the bolts of cloth and looked at various color threads, then debated on a new thimble for herself.

"How's the patient?" Lillie Taylor asked, coming up beside her.

Jane smiled sweetly, aware that Lillie loved to gossip and was just dying for a small morsel of news to spread around Harmony. "Which patient?"

Lillie's bubbling laughter caused a few heads to turn. "The one whose house you're residing in, dear."

"Alex is doing just fine, thank you."

"So does that mean you'll be moving back to your home above your shop?"

"Shortly," Jane answered, fitting the thimble to her middle finger to see how comfortably it fit.

"I hear Alex has Zeke see to his shave every morning," Lillie said. "How ever did he manage before that?"

Jane recalled the mornings she had shaved him. She had enjoyed the closeness they had shared, the feel of his smooth face, the fresh scent of his skin. *I miss shaving him.* The thought shocked and irritated her all at once.

"He couldn't have shaved himself," Lillie said, still probing for an answer.

Jane turned on her. "I shaved him. I washed him. I helped dress him."

Lillie Taylor turned three shades of red.

Jane continued her assault. "That's what a nurse does. She takes care of her patient. She sees to his care. *Whatever* it may be. Now I'd like to buy this thimble." She handed the small item to Lillie and waited, her arms crossed.

Lillie produced a weak smile, nodded, and stepped

around to the other side of the counter. "Will that be all?"

Jane wasn't prepared for what came out of her mouth next. She hadn't intended to say it; it just sort of slipped out. "Shaving soap. I need shaving soap so Alex doesn't have to go to Zeke's every morning."

Lillie blushed a deeper shade of red and hurried to collect the soap. Most of the patrons in the store were staring at her. She realized that by this evening the gossiping tongues of Harmony would have the news of her ill-behaved conduct in the mercantile spread all over town.

Lillie handed Jane the small wrapped package.

"Thank you," she said and walked out of the store with her head held high. Once out of the store her bravado deflated. She released a sigh and her shoulders sagged. What in heaven's name had gotten into her?

She walked slowly across the street to the *Sentinel*. What would happen when Alex heard about her remarks? She all but announced that it wouldn't be necessary for him to go to Zeke's for his shave any longer and that he had only done so because she hadn't gotten around to buying more shaving soap. She had really put her foot in her mouth this time.

The light screen door weighed heavily in her hand as she pulled it open. She plopped down on a chair and rested her elbows on the table, cupping her face in her hands.

Her free time, which she had so looked forward to, had turned out disastrously. She had caused the heated situation between Alex and herself to turn volatile. How was she ever going to explain her unusual behavior to him? And how was she going to rectify the matter?

No solution came to her as she remained at the table brooding. She wondered when and who Alex would hear the gossip from, since most of his time after breakfast and before supper was spent in the *Sentinel* office, where people came and went with much frequency.

Her face brightened for a moment, and she lifted her head. What if he didn't hear the gossip? Her smile faded quickly. She'd have no choice but to tell him herself. He'd find out eventually if she didn't.

Her sigh grew heavy. She stood and looked about the kitchen. She'd start supper. Idle hands only caused more worry. If she kept herself busy, her mind would challenge her problem and perhaps find a solution.

She grabbed for her blue apron from the peg near the door and slipped it on, tying the strings extra tight. She took the bowl of freshly washed string beans from the counter and sat back down in the chair by the table.

She'd settle this matter in no time. She snapped a bean with determination. In no time, she told herself once again and snapped another bean.

Twelve

JANE pushed at the green beans on her plate. The helping she had served herself thirty minutes ago was minus only one bean. Her slice of ham remained untouched, and her mashed potatoes sat cooling in a mound. She wasn't in the least bit hungry.

Alex on the other hand was joyfully finishing his second helping of everything, not to mention polishing off his fifth biscuit.

He had spoken of everything from the weather to his printing press. She had no idea if he had an inkling of what had transpired at the mercantile this morning.

"Zeke made an odd comment to me this afternoon when he dropped by the *Sentinel*," Alex said, placing his fork and knife on his plate.

Jane continued to annoy her green beans with her fork and chose not to glance up at him.

Alex rested his arms on the table. "Zeke wanted to know that since I replenished my supply of shaving soap did that mean I wouldn't be coming to him any longer for my morning shave?"

Jane rested her fork on the edge of her plate and looked up at him. *He knew.*

"Want to tell me about it?" His voice was gentle, his tone full of concern.

Jane didn't hesitate; her hand rushed out to grab at his.

Alex wrapped his long fingers around her slender ones protectively. "Tell me about it."

Jane sighed and shook her head. "I don't know what got into me. One minute I was standing at the counter looking at material and a thimble, and the next thing I knew I was announcing how—" She shook her head again, recalling her own words.

"I heard it all," he said, sparing her the embarrassment of repeating it.

Jane squeezed her eyes shut as though her words would cause her pain. "What exactly did you hear?"

"Do you really want me to repeat it?"

Jane nodded vigorously.

Alex obliged her recounting Zeke's words. "I was told how you cared for me from washing me to dressing me, and of course Zeke questioned your thoroughness in performing those tasks."

Jane groaned.

"Then he explained how many good citizens had dropped by his barbershop to let him know that you would be shaving me from now on and his services weren't necessary."

Jane's groan turned pitiful.

"Who put the bee in your bonnet?"

Jane looked at him and smiled. "Thank you," she said, grateful he understood her enough to know she normally wouldn't act as she did this morning.

"You're too intelligent a woman to respond as you did unless someone put a bee in your bonnet," he said with a grin.

Jane laughed this time, and a little groan followed it. "Lillie Taylor and her probing questions got the better of me." Though if her mind hadn't been on Alex all morning, she thought, Lillie's remark wouldn't have disturbed her half as much.

"You should have confided in me about this immediately," Alex said, threading his fingers with hers.

Jane shrugged her shoulders. "I didn't have the courage."

"You mean you didn't trust my reaction."

"I thought you might get mad at me," she admitted.

"At first I found it amusing, and then the more I thought about it the more it disturbed me."

"Disturbed you?"

He nodded and squeezed her fingers gently. "It isn't necessary for you to defend your profession to anyone. If your job requires that you wash and dress a man, it should be accepted just as that. Not viewed as something to gossip and speculate about. You're good, actually excellent, at what you do—doctoring people—and you and the residents of Harmony should be proud of what you do."

He's my champion, she thought and smiled. "Thank you, Alex."

"You're very welcome," he said and winked playfully at her. "But we have another problem."

She perked up ready to solve anything now that she had her champion beside her. "What is it?"

"When Zeke asked me about my morning shave, I told him that since you finally got around to picking up the shaving soap that I wouldn't be needing his services any longer."

"You did?" He had defended her actions instantly without thought to the consequences. His reaction amazed her.

"I did, but—" he paused again.

Jane jumped right in. "I'll shave you, that's if you don't mind. I really don't mind shaving you. I did so often for my grandfather that I'm used to it, so if you want I can—"

Alex interrupted her rambling. "I'd appreciate it if you would give me my morning shave. You do a better job than Zeke does anyway."

"Do I?" she questioned curiously, thinking that perhaps he was only trying to make her feel better.

"Believe me you do," Alex insisted strenuously. "Your strokes with a razor are gentle and accurate. Zeke shaves me fast and furious, and I'm left with more than one nick in my flesh."

"It's a woman's touch that does it. A woman has a tendency to take care as she wields a razor. A man doesn't."

A pregnant pause forced their glances to meet and hold steady until Alex spoke. "I surrender to your care." Passion laced his words, and he slowly brought her hand up to his mouth and brushed his lips across her fingers.

Jane felt a shiver run down to the tips of her toes. Her stomach flip-flopped and her heart skipped a beat or two. His words of surrender concerned more than a shave.

"Dessert?" Her voice quivered as she attempted to change the subject.

He released her hand with some reluctance, holding on a brief moment as if he questioned letting her out of his grasp. "Something sweet sounds tempting."

Tempting. The word drifted overhead. She had a strong feeling he wasn't referring to dessert. She stood and cleared away a few of the dishes. "Bread pudding sweet enough?"

He nodded, his heated stare setting her nerves on edge.

"Zeke also said he put you in charge of the games for the Fourth of July picnic."

Jane looked at him with relief, glad that the subject had turned to a lighter topic. "Is there anything you don't hear about that happens in Harmony?"

"Nothing. The residents of Harmony feel right at home sharing their news with me, especially since I run the newspaper. So what have you got planned?"

Jane placed the white ceramic bowl on the table and sat down. "I haven't even given it thought yet. Zeke only asked me this morning. I haven't—"

Minnie swung open the screen door and burst in. She was flushed and appeared upset. "Jacob sent me for you. A cowhand out at the Double B Farm was injured badly, and he asked that you come over to the office and help him."

Jane jumped out of her chair.

"I'll tend to Alex," Minnie offered.

"Not necessary—I'm going with her."

Jane turned around, ready to protest. Alex sent her a look that told her not to bother. Then he walked over to the peg by the door, grabbed her shawl, and held it out to her.

She was accustomed to his stubborn demeanor by now and knew any protest from her would be senseless. She hurried over to him, took her shawl, and walked out the door.

"Coming, Minnie?" he asked, holding the screen door open.

Minnie shook herself out of her dazed state and rushed out the door past Alex.

A few recently hired cowhands from the Double B stood outside Jacob Tanner's office. Jane gave them a quick nod and strode past them and into the office.

Alex stopped and extended his concern. "I'm sure with the combined efforts of Dr. Tanner and Miss Carson everything will be fine."

One cowhand shook his head, his face full of sorrow. "It was a bad accident. Joey's leg is badly wounded."

"It don't look good," another cowhand added.

"I've seen many a leg in a lot less worse shape taken off," a nearby cowhand said.

"Joey ain't gonna like the idea of losing his leg," another said.

They all nodded in agreement.

Alex gave the one cowhand a sympathetic pat on the back before heading inside to check on Jane.

Minnie and Maisie both were bustling around the office, preparing strips of cotton bandage and fussing to try to make the young cowhand comfortable.

Alex glanced over at the wooden examination table. The cowhand couldn't have been more than seventeen. His complexion was deathly pale, and he tossed his head from side to side and moaned. His leg was a mess. Alex couldn't even tell what was left of the limb, there was so much blood. It was going to take a mighty lot of luck and some good doctoring to save the leg and the boy.

He turned to look for Jane and saw her scrubbing her hands at the washstand. He went to her.

"Are you going to be all right?"

"I'm fine. It's him I'm worried about," she said and nodded toward the boy.

Alex should have known her first concern would rest with her patient. But he was worried about her. He wondered how far her medical studies had taken her and if she was prepared for the difficult task ahead of her.

He frowned, thinking of the night that lay ahead for Jane.

Her hand instantly went out to him. She carefully touched his arm cradled in the sling. "Is something wrong? Are you in pain?"

Again her concern was for someone else instead of herself. "No," he said softly and reached up to brush a tiny water spot off her cheek. "I'll wait outside. If you should need me . . ."

A pleased smile crossed her face but vanished instantly when Jacob anxiously summoned her.

"Jane, hurry!"

She rushed past Alex to Jacob's side. They huddled in whispered conversation like two trusted comrades mapping out a plan. Alex experienced a momentary pang of jealousy and hastened out of the room, not looking back.

Alex sat in relative silence in one of the chairs

Minnie and Maisie had supplied for the cowhands. Most of the men were too anxious about their friend's condition to sit. Some paced while others exchanged brief episodes of conversation.

Fred appeared lost in his thoughts, leaning forward in his chair and staring blankly at his boots.

Alex was lost to his own thoughts as well. His musings centered on Jane and the relationship she had formed with Jacob. It was more than mere friendship. Admiration and respect were clearly involved and perhaps more ... much more.

The idea irritated him. He had grown accustomed to Jane in his home. It felt as though she should always be there. That she belonged there and should remain. But she only *belonged* there as long as he required her services.

Services. At first he had thought of her presence in his home as her providing a necessary service besides her being a nuisance. But living in such close quarters and sharing certain intimate moments had forced a strange relationship to form between them. He had learned much about her, and he had grown to respect her determination to achieve credibility in the medical field.

Help and support in her endeavor were essential to her now. She required someone who could strengthen her confidence and encourage her when she became despondent. Someone who cared enough to love her no matter the circumstances.

Love? The implications of the unexpected word struck him hard, stealing his breath away. He took an anxious breath, drawing in the cool night air, and leaned back in his chair.

When had love entered the picture? It had been too many years since he had last experienced or even thought of that emotion. And the memories he recalled were not pleasant ones. He had loved Liza deeply, or he'd thought he had. Unfortunately, Liza was not the woman he thought she was, and he had learned that truth too late.

No hidden secrets lurked in Jane's personality. She was stubborn, intelligent, caring, outspoken, and determined. She possessed a mixed bag of attributes, and he found each one interesting.

Love.

Again the word crept into his mind. Was this a warning or a promise of things to come? Was he releasing an emotional side of himself he had locked away for so many years ago?

Do you want to love again?

The strange query haunted him. He remembered the hurt he had suffered when Liza had left him and their little girl. He had thought the pain would never go away, and he had thought his emotional loneliness would consume him. He supposed that was why he had packed up and left, leaving behind his hurtful memories and locking away his emotions.

Somehow over these last few weeks that tightly sealed lock had managed to come undone, laying his emotions bare once again. He had found himself looking forward to seeing Jane in the morning and sharing breakfast with her. He enjoyed the way she fussed over him. He delighted in sharing his work with her and hearing of her work. And he ached—Lord, how he ached—to touch her intimately.

He shut his eyes against his own admission. His ache, need, desire—whatever he suffered from—had grown considerably in the last few days. He not only worried over her completing her duties and leaving him, but he worried over the urgency of their passion. He wanted her. He wanted her badly.

Over the years when his desire had flared, he'd seek out relief from a willing woman and be done with it. But this time was different. His passion was directed toward one woman in particular. Not just anyone would do. He wanted Jane.

He was aware that she experienced the same urgency as him, but they had both tempered and controlled their emotions. How long could that last? How long did they want it to last?

"Alex," Jacob said and gave Alex's shoulder a shake.

He opened his eyes and stretched as he stood to his full height. "Jane's all right?"

Fatigue tainted Jacob's brief smile. "Jane is fine, but exhausted. I want you to take her home, though she refuses to go. I thought you might have more luck persuading her than I did."

"She'll go if I have to drag her."

Jacob rubbed at his chin and shook his head. "She's upset. We did all we could for the young man. The outcome is in God's hands now."

"His leg?"

Jacob didn't look happy. "He insisted we do all we could to save it, claimed a cowhand couldn't work with one leg. He told Jane he'd rather die."

Alex immediately understood Jane's predictable response. She would do everything she could to save the young cowhand's leg.

"Actually," Jacob continued, rubbing the back of his neck, "Jane's skill with a needle and thread is what helped the boy. She stood over him and meticulously stitched every piece of torn muscle and flesh. I don't know how her fingers didn't cramp."

"Will the young man be all right?"

"Time will tell. Jane's given him something for the fever and pain. She wants to stay by him, but he'll be out for hours and she's not only physically exhausted, she's emotionally exhausted."

"Excuse me, gentlemen," Fred Winchester said, interrupting their conversation. "I just wanted to let Jacob know we'll be on our way. I've convinced the cowhands there's nothing more they can do for their friend except pray. If there's any change in Joey's condition, please send a message to the Double B."

"I won't hesitate," Jacob assured him and shook his hand.

Alex followed Jacob into his office. Minnie and Maisie worked silently, cleaning up. Both women looked tired themselves, but their pace reflected no sign of their weariness. Jane sat in a chair next to the examination table where the cowhand rested in a deep slumber.

"We didn't want to move him yet since the wound is so vulnerable at this point. In the morning some of the cowhands will return, and we'll settle him more comfortably in one of the rooms in the back."

Alex nodded his understanding. "Are you sure she's not needed here?"

"Positive." Jacob spoke softly in deference to the patient's condition. "I'll probably need her help tomorrow, and I'll need her fresh and well rested."

Alex nodded again and walked over to Jane. He gently placed his hand on her shoulder. "Time to go," he announced firmly as she looked up at him.

Her disturbed frown warned him of her imminent objection. He placed a finger to her lips and with his eyes directed her to move away from the patient to the other side of the room.

"I can't leave yet," Jane insisted as they stopped by the medicine cabinet.

"You need some rest." Alex delivered his response softly yet sternly.

"I'm needed here." Her voice sounded determined and ready for battle.

"Jacob disagrees. He feels you've done all you can for now. Tomorrow is another day, and you need rest to face that day."

Jane thought to argue, but it was impossible to protest the truth. She'd do her patient no good if weary on her feet. The cowhand would sleep the remainder of the night. He would need her to care for him tomorrow.

A yawn escaped her, followed by a tired smile. "You're right."

Alex grabbed at his chest dramatically. "What did you say? I'm right!"

Her smile grew stronger. "Don't push your luck. I'm not often given to admitting other people are right. It must be my weakened condition."

"And one I intend to take advantage of," he said and took her arm, directing her straight for the door.

"I need—"

He cut off her protest. "To rest." He issued a softly spoken good-night to all in the room and propelled her out the door and right to the *Sentinel*.

Jane brought a halt to their progress a few steps into the kitchen. "Alex, you're being—"

"Sensible." He released her arm.

Jane felt the impact of the night's difficult work cover her like a heavy wool blanket. Her body sagged and her legs weakened. She reached out for the back of the nearest chair for support.

Instead she found Alex's arm wrap supportively around her waist, and he eased her back to rest against him. His large frame sustained her weight easily, and she relaxed in the comfort of knowing he was there for her.

"You work yourself too hard, woman."

"Sometimes it's necessary." She raised her hand to cover an escaping yawn.

"Sometimes," he emphasized, "one should look after one's own health."

Jane tilted her head back against his chest to look up into his eyes. She had a teasing retort prepared, but it died on her lips as soon as her eyes met his.

In the depths of his blue eyes lay bare his emotions. Need soared, concern lingered, and passion ruled.

"Jane." Her whispered name drifted around them while his hand moved slowly up to stroke the smooth column of her neck and his mouth reached down to descend over hers.

His kiss was thoughtful, tasting her desire to submit. When she eagerly responded, reaching out for more from him, he graciously complied with her wishes.

Their kiss grew strong, full of passion and intent. His hand searched her body, caressing a path from her neck to below her breast, then moving up to cup her breast gently.

She made no move to protest. His intimate touch felt too good, too right to deny.

He reluctantly parted his lips from hers, his teeth tugging playfully at her lower lip before he planted kisses along her cheek up to her ear.

She opened her mouth, intending a dramatic sigh of pleasure, when a yawn shoved past and escaped.

Alex laughed softly and low. "It's a bed you need." His whispered words tickled her ear and sent shivers down her arm.

Another yawn quickly followed. "You're right about that." Though a sudden thought didn't have her entering her bed alone.

She looked up wide-eyed at him and he looked down. They both knew at that precise moment that intimacy between them was inevitable. Shivers ran through them both, and Jane hurriedly stepped away from him.

"I'm not that easy to discard," Alex said seriously. Too seriously to Jane's way of thinking.

"I don't need any further assistance tonight." She heard her own voice quiver, and she silently scolded herself for lack of emotional control.

Alex stepped toward her, his gait like that of a predator bearing down on his prey. "I could return your favor and help you undress."

Jane stood her ground, intending not to display her nervousness. "I can undress myself."

Alex stopped in front of her. His fingers reached up,

toying with the buttons on her blouse. "Sometimes we aren't aware of our own weaknesses."

Jane chased his hand away with a brush of her own hand. "I have two good hands that work just fine." She couldn't help but think how deft he was with only one operable hand. What would he be like with two?

"You're tired," he reminded her, as though it made a difference.

"Not that tired."

Alex slipped his hand around her neck and massaged the stiff muscles firmly. "Are you sure?"

Jane felt her tense muscles ease. She involuntarily melted to his touch. "That feels good."

"Turn around," he ordered.

She did so without question, his touch too soothing to deny.

"I can make you feel good, Jane. Relax for me, just relax," he whispered near her ear. He dug his fingers expertly into the tense muscles of her neck, stroking and massaging the soreness away.

"Mmmmm, so good," she murmured, eagerly awaiting each stroke.

"Don't think about anything," Alex cajoled. "Don't think."

Jane listened, freeing her mind of everything, concentrating on nothing but the play of his fingers and the strength of his touch.

Her body relaxed. Her thoughts rested. Her eyes drifted closed. And she yawned. A deep, satisfying yawn that warned her of her body's limitations.

Alex understood her response completely. "You need rest."

"I agree with your advice, Dr. Evans," Jane said, attempting humor, but sounding bone-tired.

"Are you sure I can't help you?" He spoke sincerely and with concern for her.

Yes, climb into bed with me and hold me. Her

thoughts remained silent, and instead she shook her head. "You've done more than enough."

Alex tilted her chin up. "If there's anything you need, just ask."

I need you.

As though hearing her silent declaration, he kissed her gently. "I'll help you to your room."

Jane stepped away from him, her heart hammering like a beat of a blacksmith's hammer gone crazy. "Thank you, but it's not necessary."

"If you should need anything—"

"I'll call out for you," she finished and turned in a flourish and headed for the steps.

"Jane."

His strong summons stopped her in her tracks, and she turned.

"Good night."

It took her a minute to catch her breath and speak. "Good night, Alex."

She hurried up the steps and down the hall, closing the door behind her and collapsing against it. Lord, that man stirred her passion. Ignited, fired, and blazed it all at once. And with a devious smile she wondered when the devil he'd put out her fire.

Thirteen

"My raspberry preserves are going to take first place this year at the Fourth of July picnic jelly contest. I'm sure of it," Maisie said. She finished her declaration with a proud smile and a bright twinkle in her eyes.

Jane nodded in response, only half paying attention to her. She had risen early and had hurried over to Jacob's office to check on the young cowhand. He had been restless and feverish. She had eased his condition with some swallow bark tea.

She was now in the process of making a comfrey salve for his wound, the first step being to chop the rootstock and add it to hot water to form a thick mash.

Maisie interrupted her thoughts and actions. "Make certain you make that salve thick enough if you want it to work properly."

Jane had made comfrey salve time and time again. She had used it often on her grandfather's patients with satisfying results. You could say she was an old pro at it. But instead of explaining the extent of her skill to Maisie, she decided a simple "thank you for the advice" was enough.

"That's what I'm here for, dear, to help," Maisie said and returned to folding the freshly laundered linen bandages spread out over the lye-scrubbed examination table.

Jane focused once again on preparing the salve while

Maisie continued talking about her preserves. It wasn't that she wasn't interested in raspberry preserves. It was just that her mind was cluttered with more important matters at the moment. Another time Jane would have paid close attention since she enjoyed putting up her own preserves, but lately she didn't seem to have time for simple pleasures. Not even her gardening, particularly her herb garden, which she loved tending to and which brought her immense pleasure.

Her medical studies consumed a good portion of her time, and last night she was grateful she had paid such close attention to her studies. Sewing up the cowhand's leg hadn't been easy. She had actually doubted her own ability after having seen the extent of the damage his leg had suffered. But one look at the young man's face told her she had no choice. She had to help him.

Now this morning she was grateful she had stayed up so many nights reading the medical journals Jacob had provided her with and for having listened all the times Jacob had so thoroughly explained a procedure.

"Minnie thinks her blueberry preserves will win the contest, but I know the judges prefer raspberry over blueberry," Maisie said, stacking the folded bandages neatly in the cabinet.

Jane remained silent, still lost in her own thoughts. Maisie happily rambled on detailing the ingredients that made her raspberry preserves a surefire, first-prize-winning jelly.

Jane concentrated on spreading the linen cloth Maisie had left beside her, with the comfrey salve, acknowledging Maisie every now and then with a nod.

She had to remind herself that her medical studies were important and that she could allow nothing or no one to stand in her way of accomplishing her dream.

Last night after she had retired and had thought more on the intimate exchange that she and Alex had shared, the more upset she had become. Sleep had eluded her until well into the night. Finally she had dozed off just before dawn and was up shortly thereafter.

She had berated herself for allowing her feminine emotions to rule. She had a golden opportunity to achieve acknowledgment in the medical field. Yet last night she had succumbed to emotions that would only interfere with her plans.

Her independence had been hard won. First with her grandfather, who had postponed but not completely eliminated the possibility of her becoming a doctor, and then with the town of Harmony, when she had arrived a woman on her own.

How many times had she been questioned about her marital status and had been cast a sympathetic glance for having not secured a husband for herself and at her *advanced* age? There wasn't a woman, and certainly not a man, who could understand her desire to pursue her interest. She had been dependent on herself for so long that she feared she could never be dependent on anyone ever and certainly not a husband who would expect an obedient wife.

"Sugar, Jane, it's the amount of sugar that most women make the mistake with when preserving," Maisie said, her voice rising in excitement.

Jane sent Maisie a nod and thought about the sweetness of sugar. Most women were sweet and thoughtful, doing as their husbands dictated. Some even attempted to speak their own minds, but not around their husbands. She recalled how freely the women spoke when they gathered for their quilting meetings. But when it came to certain matters, their husbands' word was law and they would not go against it.

Jane on the other hand lived her life as she chose. She had no one to dictate her actions, no one to answer to.

Independence and freedom created her biggest problem at the moment. The problem being that she wasn't willing to give them up for a man. She had the distinct feeling that if she became involved with Alexander Evans, her life would change completely and not for the better.

"You have to learn what a man likes in his preserves and make sure the batch turns out just the way he likes them. Yes, sir, you've got to please a man," Maisie said, still talking about her preserves.

Jane didn't mind pleasing a man, but she wondered if a man thought about pleasing a woman. Could she even hope to find a man that cared enough to attempt to understand how she felt about medicine? Or was she doomed to spinsterhood because she chose a field unacceptable for women?

The idea rankled her, and she slipped her hands under the bandage to pick it up. Pain shot through her hands, forcing them to cramp instantly, and she cried out.

Maisie rushed to her side. "What is it?"

"My hands," Jane answered, biting down on her lower lip.

Maisie slipped the bandage off her hands and winced when she saw Jane's fingers gnarled from the cramps that had attacked her. "I'll get Jacob."

Jane shook her head adamantly. "No, don't bother him. He's getting some well-deserved sleep which he'll need when he relieves me later tonight."

"But what shall I do?" Maisie seemed baffled for one so sure of herself all the time.

"First put this comfrey bandage on Joey's leg, then get me a bowl of warm water for my hands."

Maisie complied quickly with her instructions, arriving back by her side in minutes. She placed the bowl of water on the table beside Jane. "I can look after Joey while you rest. You have been here since early this morning, and it's already late afternoon."

"I'll wait until Jacob wakes," Jane said between deep breaths as she eased the cramps from her fingers while they were emerged in the warm water.

"I'm capable of looking after the young man," Maisie said.

Jane glanced up at her. "I'm not questioning your capability. I need to inform Jacob of when the bandages need changing and the quantity of swallow bark to use."

"No problem, I can see to that," Maisie said confidently.

"I can wait."

Maisie shook her head. "No, you can't. You look boned-tired. Why, I bet you didn't sleep a wink last night. You need a good night's sleep. So take yourself off right now."

Jane attempted to protest. It did no good. Maisie insisted she could handle everything, and Jane realized the woman was more than competent to handle the matter until Jacob woke.

With a promise from Maisie that she would fetch Jane immediately if necessary, Jane left Jacob's office, her fingers feeling better from their short soak.

Jane set to work to prepare a quick supper as soon as she entered Alex's kitchen. In minutes she had a vegetable stew simmering and the dough for her biscuits ready to knead. Her hands folded the dough over and over, kneading it skillfully. Another few folds and she'd be done and ready to sit and rest with a hot cup of tea to add to her pleasure.

She kneaded the dough one last time. Painful cramps instantly locked her fingers. She cried out.

No one heard her. A tear stung her eye. She told herself the pain had nothing to do with her highly emotional reaction, that she was overly tired and therefore more sensitive than usual. She would just see to taking care of herself and—

She cried out again when she attempted to extricate her fingers from the dough. Another tear slipped free, followed closely by a third one.

This was stupid, she thought, and without considering her actions she called out, "Alex!"

Her cry was pitiful and so were her tears, but she cried out again to him. "Alex!"

Alex rushed down the stairs and into the room. "What the devil is the matter?" He took one look at her tears and at her gnarled fingers in the bowl and hurried over to her.

"Cramps!" she cried and the tears ran down her cheeks.

"It's all right," he said softly and attempted to brush her tears away. They wouldn't stop flowing, so he left them to fall and saw to her hands.

He produced a tepid bowl of water and after sitting Jane on a chair at the table he took one hand at a time and submerged each into the bowl.

"Your arm?" she questioned between sobs, worried he was taxing his broken arm.

"My arm is fine and I've managed perfectly fine with just one for several weeks now. Thanks to your help," he added. He shook his head when she cried harder.

He pulled a chair up beside her and sat down. With his good hand he massaged the fingers of her one hand, easing the cramps from it. "You work yourself too hard."

"I—I—kn-know," she said between sobs.

Alex couldn't help but smile, keeping his lips to a slight tilt, not a wide grin. She looked like a lost child. Her brown eyes sparkled from her tears, her long lashes curled gracefully, her cheeks were flushed pink, her lips were plump and red, and her brown hair framed her attractive features, setting each one off to perfection.

"You didn't sleep last night, did you?" He asked because he hadn't slept himself. His thoughts had been on Jane down the hall from him, so close yet so far out of his reach.

She shook her head and sobbed.

His expression turned serious and stern. "You're going to eat and then go straight to bed afterward, and I'm warning you now, I'll have it no other way."

Jane stared at him for a solid minute, and just when Alex was about to ask her if she understood, she burst into a flood of tears.

Alex shook his head and slipped his good arm around her shoulder, drawing her near. "You're overly tired."

Jane nodded against his chest.

"A good night's sleep will set you right again."

Jane responded with another nod.

"I'll take care of you, don't worry."

Jane pulled away from him, stared at him again with her wide wet eyes, and cried harder.

He reached for the towel on the table and patted her teary eyes. "No need to cry. You won't be eating my cooking."

Jane smiled, laughed, and cried all at once.

He wiped at her eyes more gently, catching the tears as they ran down her cheeks. "I can guarantee you would cry even harder if you had to eat my biscuits."

Jane sobbed and attempted to control her tears.

Alex continued to soothe her. "After supper I'll massage your hands with some of that lotion you use all the time. I don't know what it is, but it sure smells good and I bet it would make your hands feel better."

"Witch hazel," Jane said, sighing heavily from her crying.

"The lotion has witch hazel in it?" he asked doubtfully and turned the towel on her hands to dry them.

"It's better"—she paused to take a breath—"to use witch hazel on my hands."

"If you say so, Doc," he said with a wink.

Jane stared at him, and she fought the tears that struggled to break lose. She lost her fight, and tears fell from her eyes.

Alex caught one lone tear on his finger. "No need to cry, Doc. I'll take care of you."

His words were so tender, so sincere that Jane

couldn't stop the tears that followed. For a moment, a brief moment, she allowed herself to believe that Alex was different from all men. That he could care for her, maybe even love her for who she was and understand, especially understand, her dream.

"No more tears," he ordered sternly, but in a whisper, and leaned closer toward her to gently kiss her tear-stained cheeks and then her eyes. "Shhh," he murmured. "Don't cry anymore. Don't cry. I'll take care of you."

She wanted nothing more at that precise moment than for him to do just that. Take care of her.

He kissed her lips, a featherlight kiss. "I'm going to take you upstairs and settle you in your bed. Then I'll fix you a cup of tea while you wait for supper."

"Settle me?" she queried so softly she was afraid he couldn't hear her, not that she wanted him to. She recalled the many nights she had settled him and the reaction their actions had caused the two of them.

"Settle," he repeated firmly and eased up from the chair. "Come on."

He walked behind her up the steps, his hand in the crook of her back just below her waistline.

His hand remained there, warm and comforting as he walked her down the hall to her room. Once inside he asked, "Do you need help undressing?"

She shook her head, her verbal response caught in her throat.

"But your fingers?" He stepped toward her.

She backed away. "They work," she said and wiggled them as she held them up.

"All right, but I'll still massage them later with the witch hazel for you, just like the doc ordered." He smiled and reached out so fast that he caught Jane off guard.

Her protest as he unfastened the buttons of her blouse died on her lips. The look he had sent her warned her he'd tolerate no objections to his actions. "I'll see to your blouse for you. You can handle the rest."

"Thank you," she said, her head bent as she watched

his fingers slip her buttons undone and run his hand along the edges of her blouse to spread it apart.

He lifted her chin to look into her eyes. "That wasn't so bad, was it?"

She shook her head. "Not bad" did not describe the way her heart raced and her blood rushed.

"I'll get your tea unless . . ." He paused and smiled. "Unless you want me to help you undress the rest of the way and tuck you in bed."

"I'd like the tea," she said, her cheeks blushing.

He laughed, leaned down, and kissed her lips. "You wound my pride, woman."

"The tea," she repeated, frightened that if he didn't leave the room soon, she'd accept his teasing taunts and then they would be lost.

"Tea it is," he agreed and left the room, stopping to peek back in and instruct, "Have yourself settled in that bed when I get back, or I'll see that you're settled myself when I return."

He didn't wait for her answer; he vanished out the door.

Jane hurried out of her clothes and into her nightdress. She felt the long day and sleepless night invade every bone of her body and wanted nothing more than to climb into her bed and sleep. Sleep soundly.

She arranged the pillows to sit up against and pulled back the covers and climbed in, folding the counterpane neatly over her waist. She was all settled when Alex returned.

"You take orders nicely," he commented, resting the small tray with her teacup on it on the nightstand beside the bed.

"I know when I've pushed the limits," she said.

He turned his head and looked at her. "Did you push the limits that far, Jane?"

"Much too far," she answered and held her hand out for the cup. Her fingers once again fell victim to torturous cramps, and she cried out as they knotted painfully on her.

"Damn," Alex said and reached out for her hand, sitting down on the bed beside her.

"Ouch," she protested as he massaged the tightened muscles and joints.

"Jacob said he didn't know how your fingers hadn't cramped from the sewing job you did on the cowhand. Guess the cramps waited for a more convenient time for you."

Jane dropped her head back against the pillows and closed her eyes. Alex was making her fingers feel so good, she didn't want to move or speak.

He massaged each finger, carefully and skillfully, easing the painful cramps away. He worked his way up her arm some to ease the muscles that had tightened there. His fingers beneath the sleeve of her nightdress felt cool and welcoming, and she drifted into a peaceful rest.

Alex studied her fingers as he worked. They were long and slim and racked with pain, and he felt every bit as much of her pain as she did. He didn't care to see her suffer, though he knew any objections from him wouldn't matter. And rightly so. She had worked to save a young man's life, and her response to him would be "a few cramps won't kill me." Still, her suffering disturbed him and he had to say something. "I don't want you working so hard. It's not good for you."

When no protest came from her, he looked up. Her eyes were closed and so heavy with sleep that Alex smiled. He slipped her hand beneath the covers and added her other one to it. Then he gently, so as not to wake her, eased her down with her pillows to lay comfortably in the bed.

He leaned over her and pressed a tender kiss to her lips.

"I don't want you working so hard, Jane," he repeated softly. "I care too much about you. Much too much."

Fourteen

"Feeling better?" Alex asked when Jane entered the kitchen the next morning.

"Much," she said and in a glance noted that the table was set and coffee was made.

"My arm still won't allow me certain privileges, or else I would have had breakfast ready for you."

Jane smiled appreciatively. Mostly because he looked so darn handsome in his black trousers and white cotton shirt that he had left unbuttoned at his throat. Even his morning growth of beard, just a mere shade, added to his potent appeal. "I'm supposed to be taking care of you—not you me."

"You needed me last night."

His statement sent the shivers through her. He was right about that. She needed him and in more ways than one. She averted her glance from his, afraid that the depths of her emotions shined in her eyes and would easily betray her. "I'll fix us some breakfast."

"I was hoping you would."

"Eggs and bacon?"

"Biscuits, too?"

"Anxious, are we?" Jane teased, hearing the hopefulness in his voice.

"Starving is more like it," Alex admitted.

"Then this breakfast calls for buttermilk biscuits."

148

"I've died and gone to heaven," Alex joked and grabbed his chest.

"Before you take off to heaven, how about pouring me a cup of that great-smelling coffee?"

Alex obliged, pouring one for her and one for himself. He sat her mug down beside her on the counter where she worked at scrambling eggs in a yellow ceramic bowl. "I make terrific coffee."

She picked up the mug and sipped. "I agree."

Alex put his mug down on the counter, then caught her chin between his fingers, tugging her face up to look at him. "Are you sure you've rested enough?"

His worry was apparent in his cautious voice and in his thoughtful expression. His blatant concern touched her deeply. "More than enough. Why, I probably snored all night and kept you awake."

"You didn't snore."

His look was alarmingly sensual, so much so that Jane pulled free of his hold and bent her head to concentrate on her task. She couldn't prevent the rapidly rising blush that stained her cheeks, but she could prevent him from noticing her embarrassing reaction.

Jane beat the eggs in the bowl a bit harder than necessary. He wouldn't have known she hadn't snored unless he hadn't slept. And if he hadn't slept, why? Had he been thinking of her?

Alex sat himself at the table, his coffee mug held snug in his hand. "So have you given thought to the Fourth of July festivities?"

Jane appreciated the turn to neutral conversation. "I'm open to any ideas you have to offer me?" She cut thick slices of bacon and dropped them into the heated pan while Alex took a moment to think.

"Egg races are mighty popular," he suggested.

Jane agreed with a nod. "I was thinking apple dunking, too."

Alex grinned broadly. "I loved to dunk for apples as a kid."

"I wasn't bad myself," she admitted, arranging the platter with piping hot bacon and eggs and bringing it to the table.

"I bet you didn't dunk your whole face in the pan to get at an apple."

Jane placed the platter in the center and took the seat opposite Alex. "You've got to be joking if you don't think me capable of that."

Alex laughed. "I never met a girl who would dunk her whole head in the water when dunking for apples."

"You just have," Jane said proudly. "And I beat many a young man doing so. And lost many a chance of acquiring a boyfriend."

Alex laughed harder.

"It's not funny, especially to a young girl's ego," Jane insisted, though now she could find humor in the youthful situation. Back then she couldn't. The rejection had hurt her.

"I would have asked you out."

Jane noticed he wasn't laughing. He was dead serious. "You would have?"

"I would have had to."

"Why?" she asked totally baffled by his response.

He leaned forward after having filled his plate. "I would have admired your tenacity and bravery in going after the apples. I would have wanted to get to know you better."

"You wouldn't have been intimidated by my actions?"

He laughed again. "Intimidated? Any man that is intimidated by a woman isn't much of a man."

Jane felt her dander rise. "There isn't any woman that intimidates you?"

Alex threw down his challenge. "Is there any man that intimidates you?"

"No," Jane answered without hesitation.

"That's because we're both alike, you and me, Jane Carson. We don't let people put us in molds. We live our lives the way we want, not the way people expect us to."

"You're right. I like my independence and freedom. I wouldn't want anyone dictating to me." She waited, wondering over his response. Wondering if he could accept that part of her so easily.

"I feel likewise," he said, sending a rush of disappointment through Jane. "I enjoy being on my own, doing as I wish without thought or concern for another person."

Jane hid her disappointment behind her smile. She hadn't considered that he favored his life exactly as it was, no strings attached, no one to answer to. They were alike him and her, in so many more ways than she had imagined.

The attraction between them was just that, an attraction and no more. The close quarters they had shared these last few weeks had fostered a misconception of their emotions. She had to keep that thought in mind. She had to remember that they were both set in their ways. *Settled,* she thought. How ironic.

She changed the subject. "I was considering a sack race for the Fourth of July festivities. What do you think?"

"Sounds like a great idea. Are you going to run the three-legged kind?"

"What other kind is there?" she joked, though not feeling humorous. "I'd better clean up and get over to Jacob's."

"Could you do me a favor first?" he queried softly.
"Of course, what is it?"
"Shave me?"

Alex stood at his upstairs window watching busy Main Street below. Children chased each other playfully while dogs barked and nipped at their heels. Friends stopped to exchange pleasantries or a bit of gossip. Wagons meandered down the dusty dirt street, and horses with lone riders lazily drifted through town. This was the heart of Harmony, this street with its garishly painted buildings. Friends, neighbors, wives, husbands, children . . . they all came together on this Main Street of Harmony. They all shared a common bond. They all cared deeply, for each other and for this town.

He rubbed his hand over his smooth, clean-shaven jaw and shook his head. He had no idea what had gotten into him this morning at breakfast. He had spoken as if his lifestyle were perfect. He had sounded as though he needed no one but himself. And that was a downright lie. One did not exist in Harmony without the solid support of neighbors and friends. He had come to realize that in the last few weeks. And more important he had come to realize just how much he wanted someone to become part of his life. How empty his life had been without someone to share it with all these years.

Not that his life had been entirely empty. His daughter, Samantha, had filled a good portion of it with cherished memories, but his intimate life had been sorely lacking. He understood part of his reason for not seeking a wife had been due to the hurt he had suffered when Liza had left him. He had found it hard to trust again. He had always feared he would find love only to have it slip away from him.

He supposed that was why he was having such a difficult time adjusting to his feelings toward Jane. They puzzled him. On one hand he was intensely attracted to her, and on the other he feared commitment.

He couldn't deny his strong desire for her. It was too blatantly obvious, as was her passion for him. He assumed sooner or later they would face an intimate situation beyond what they had experienced thus far, and a decision would be forced upon them.

Alex moved away from the window to the desk near the corner of the room and sat down in the chair. He pushed a few papers on the desk around as though searching and then stopped. His mind was in turmoil.

He couldn't think about anything without Jane invading his thoughts.

He shook his head again. He had been doing that a lot lately, shaking his head. He wondered if the simple movement helped to clear his mind or troubled it all the more. He shook his head—again.

He recalled clearly this morning when he had asked her to shave him. She agreed with a bit of hesitation and had attempted to keep the task purely platonic. At first she appeared to have succeeded. She remained a safe distance away from him, her arms stretched out as she ran the sharp, straight razor blade down his lathered face.

He had remained a gentleman, keeping his hands folded in his lap and his eyes closed so as not to look at her and be tempted.

Then it happened. She nicked him. She hadn't meant to, naturally, but having never done so before disturbed her and she reacted instantly. She stepped forward, nudging her way between his legs and pressing a warm wet cloth to the bloody spot near his lip.

Her breath was sweet and warm on his face, and her scent was all woman, from the freshness of her morning washing to the soft unobtrusive powder that she had sprinkled over her intimate parts and had mingled so delightfully with her own natural fragrance.

He hadn't give a fiddler's damn about the bloody nick on his face. He only cared that she stood a hairsbreadth away from him. His hand had moved to her waist, slipping around it and drawing her toward him.

He had asked her then, a simple question yet one that had caused her to shiver. "Will you kiss it and make it all better?"

Her hand sprang away from him as though frightened to touch him. She had stared at him oddly.

Then he had added one word sensually soft and sensually pleading. "Please."

Jane stared at him for what he thought was a full

minute or more, and then she lowered her mouth toward his. Her lips descended near his, brushing past his hungry and wanting ones to cover the small abrasion.

He squeezed his eyes shut against the shivers that racked his body when her lips so lovingly soothed his wound. His fingers tightened at her waist and his legs closed her in against him.

He couldn't control his need for her, and he shifted his mouth to capture hers. But he wasn't the only one to capture. Her response was of equal desire.

Jane ended it abruptly, her surprising action causing him to realize she had suddenly come to her senses. She had said nothing. She had stood staring at him, her breathing labored, her chest heaving. Then she had dropped the cloth on the floor, turned, and fled the room.

She had gone off to Jacob's office next door, looking more attractive than ever. Her lips were red and swollen, her color sat high on her cheeks, and she wore a slight wrinkle to her white cotton blouse near her waistband where he had hugged her so possessively.

Now she would share the afternoon with Jacob Tanner. They would confer over the young cowhand's condition and work side by side.

Alex angrily shoved at the papers on his desk and muttered beneath his breath. "Ridiculous." This whole situation was ridiculous. His age prohibited jealousy, or so he thought.

He stood and stalked the room. Back and forth. Back and forth he walked. He stopped abruptly as though hitting an obstacle in his path, and he looked down at his arm cradled in the sling.

It would come off soon. How long did he have left before Jane would be gone?

He swerved around, grabbed his coat from the tree stand by the door, and walked out.

Fifteen

"I'd say another week or two at the most," Jacob said, studying Alex's arm. He shook his head and amended his prediction. "More like a week."

"That's not six weeks," Alex complained.

Jacob laughed and stepped away from the examination table. "I can't help it that you had such good care that your arm healed faster than most."

A week. He only had a week left with Jane, he thought.

"Of course, I suggest you take it easy with the arm for a while, to make certain it's mended properly. Don't overdo it."

Alex grasped at the chance to keep Jane with him for a bit longer. He needed time. Time to straighten out his mixed emotions. And he wanted that time spent with Jane. "Do you think Jane should stay on an extra week with me?" he asked and added quickly, "Just to be sure."

"It wouldn't hurt," Jacob agreed.

"Alex!" Jane's startled cry caught both men's attention, and they turned toward her as she hurried in the room. She rushed over to Alex, who was sitting on the examination table. "When I heard you were at Jacob's, I thought something had happened to you. Are you all right?"

He had been until her cool hand touched his forehead. Her touch extended gentleness and concern, and it completely unmanned him. He liked, liked very much, her caring for him. "I'm fine," he said and took hold of her wrist, moving it away from his face, but not relinquishing his hold on her.

Jacob explained Alex's presence. "He was wondering when the splints would come off."

"Two weeks," Jane answered.

"I think next week is time enough," Jacob said.

"But that isn't two weeks." Jane spoke with a raised voice, sounding anxious and almost regretful.

"It's close enough. Though not the full six weeks, it's about five and a half. And with the excellent care you've provided for Alex, I feel it's safe to remove the splints."

"But Jacob feels I shouldn't overdo it," Alex added, moving his hand from her wrist to hug her fingers.

"He's right. Your arm will be stiff and tender. You won't be able to do all you're accustomed to right away," Jane warned with a cautious tone.

Jacob offered the solution. "Jane, it would be wise for you to stay on an extra week, maybe two to help Alex. I'll be able to better judge his condition when the splints are removed."

"Would you mind?" Alex asked, threading his fingers through hers. "You've already given me so much of your time. I hate to further impose on you."

She smiled and gave his hand a squeeze. "Don't be foolish. I have no intentions of leaving you until Jacob pronounces you one hundred percent fit."

An overwhelming wave of relief washed over Alex. Good Lord, he had grown so accustomed to her being around, he thought. What would life be like without her?

She removed her hand from his and fussed at the sling that supported his injured arm, adjusting it around his shirt collar. "What are your plans for the day?"

He liked the idea of sharing his day with her, of letting her know where he'd be and what he'd be doing. And he liked knowing what she was up to. "I'll be working on an article or two, and then I have a few errands to run."

She smiled. "Could you do me a favor?"

"Anything for you, Jane," he said with a wink.

"We're almost out of flour, and I wanted to make raisin cake for dessert tonight. Could you stop by the mercantile and pick up five pounds?"

Before Alex could answer, Jacob said, "Raisin cake? Did I hear you say raisin cake?"

"Raisin cake?" Minnie repeated, walking into the room with fresh-laundered sheets folded over her arm. "I make the best raisin cake in Harmony."

Maisie rushed in behind her. "You always burn the bottom of your raisin cake, dear."

Minnie huffed and shook her finger at her sister. "I most certainly do not. Once and only once did I burn my raisin cake."

"Jane is making raisin cake tonight for dessert," Jacob informed the two women. "I wonder how her raisin cake is?"

Jacob, Minnie, and Maisie each smiled pleasantly and looked expectantly at Jane.

"You've done it now," Alex whispered in her ear. "They're expecting a dinner invitation to determine the best raisin cake baker in Harmony."

Jane wanted to giggle over the silliness of the situation, but she refrained, keeping a pleasant smile fixed on her face.

"You have no choice," Alex continued in a bare whisper. "You have to invite them."

Jane held firm to his fingers laced with hers and addressed the waiting trio. "Would you all care to join Alex and me for supper this evening?"

Jacob responded first. "How delightful of you to ask. I for one would love to have supper with you both."

Maisie's wide smile declared victory. "I accept with pleasure."

Minnie, needing to protect her vested interest in this matchmaking battle, accepted in a curt tone. "I'll also come."

The young cowhand called out from the other room, and Jane instantly pulled her fingers from Alex's.

He stopped her with a tug to her arm. "Are you rested well enough?"

His sincere concern for her always tempted her heartstrings. "Someone took extremely good care of me, and I'm now full of energy."

He released her. "I'll get your flour."

"And extra raisins," she said, hurrying off to tend to the cowhand.

"Running errands like a husband. How thoughtful," Maisie said with an I-won grin directed toward her sister.

"A favor," Minnie corrected. "Alex is being a gentleman and doing his nurse a favor. After all, she's busy spending her time with Jacob and learing all she can. It's important that she spend as much time with him as possible."

"You're right," Maisie agreed.

Minnie's eyes widened in surprise and then narrowed suspiciously.

Maisie continued. "Jane needs to spend all the time she can with Alex. You never know when he might need her help."

"I wasn't talking about her spending time with Alex. I meant Jacob. She needs to spend time with Jacob and her studies," Minnie argued.

"Alex comes first," Maisie protested.

"Jacob," Minnie countered.

Alex slipped off the table, grabbed his coat from the back of the nearby wooden chair, sent Jacob a wave, and disappeared out the door.

Jacob shook his head and sighed. "Now, ladies . . ." he began.

Alex finished his newspaper articles in no time and made a few notes for tomorrow's edition. The office had been relatively quiet. Billy was off researching his series of articles, and the printing press was all ready for the next print run.

The sunny and warm June day beckoned to him, and he was glad to answer. He closed the door to the *Sentinel* behind him and took himself off across the street to the mercantile to get Jane's flour and a few items of his own.

He anxiously awaited summer every year. He loved the rich hot weather. Sweet and pungent smells were more pronounced. The sky seemed more blue, the clouds a brighter white, and the rain showers more welcome.

His private thoughts brought a smile to his face. This summer held promise, mighty good promise. He swung the door open to the mercantile and walked in.

"Dad!"

Alex looked up as Samantha descended on him.

She gave him a kiss on the cheek and patted his recovering arm gently. "Feeling better?"

He wondered why when children matured they began to speak to their parents like children. "I've never felt better."

"That's good, and how's Jane?"

Alex knew his daughter all too well. She was up to something. "Jane's fine."

Samantha looked alarmed for a moment. "She's still staying with you and looking after you, isn't she?"

"Yes, Sam, she's still with me and will be with me for about two more weeks."

"Two weeks! Only two weeks? Don't you need her services longer than that?"

Alex wondered over Sam's strange remarks.

"Pestering your father again, Sam?" Cord asked, stepping up beside her.

"I don't pester," Samantha corrected.

Both men grinned at each other and shook their heads.

"Men!" Samantha declared and returned to the previous conversation with her father. "I'm going to speak to Jane about staying on longer than two weeks with you."

"No, you're not," both man said simultaneously.

Samantha looked from one to the other.

"She's your wife, you handle her," Alex said and walked away.

"Thanks, *Dad*," Cord called over his shoulder to Alex as he faced his irate wife.

"Children," James Taylor said with a shake of his head when Alex approached him at the counter.

Alex found James's one-word remark humorous. "You should know—you have six of them."

"And you think I would have learned my lesson after the first two or three and stopped."

Alex laughed. "Kind of hard when it's so much fun creating them."

James smiled broadly. "That it is, that it is."

Lillie hurried out from the back room flushed with exertion, and both man brought their conversation to an abrupt halt.

"Alex," Lillian said sweetly and patted her hair, making certain no strands were out of place. "You're looking fit."

Alex dazzled her with a pleasant smile. "I'm feeling fit."

"Jane's taking mighty good care of you."

"Mighty good," Alex said and sent the woman a wink.

Lillian gasped, drawing her own conclusions from Alex's audacious wink.

James patiently set his wife straight. "Jane Carson is a good woman and good at doctoring folks."

"I never said she wasn't," Lillian said snappishly.

"Why, I heard she's doing a fine job doctoring that young cowhand from the Double B farm that had an accident," James said, looking to Alex for confirmation.

Alex proudly informed both Taylors of Jane's skill. "That she is. She stitched his leg up right and proper. Dr. Tanner told me if it wasn't for her skill with a needle, the young man probably would have lost his leg."

"Is that so?" Lillian said. "How wonderful of Jane to attempt such intricate surgery, her being a woman."

Alex was stunned by Lillian's remark. He had thought women would automatically defend Jane's choice to become a doctor, but Lillian even doubted Jane's skill and knowledge. He jumped to her defense. "Jane is one remarkable lady."

"I agree," James said. "Glad she's here in Harmony."

"So am I," Alex said.

Not to be left out, Lillian added, "She's an asset to the community."

"She'll be glad to hear that, Lillian," Alex said. "But I better get what I came for. Jane and I are having guests for supper this evening."

Lillian's interest was piqued. "Oh? Who's coming for supper?"

"Maisie and Minnie and Jacob Tanner. I'll need five pounds of flour."

"Jacob is such a wonderful man," Lillian said while James saw to getting Alex his flour. "He's charming and delightful to talk with. I do enjoy when he stops in."

Alex wasn't in the mood to listen to a list of Jacob's attributes. "He's a good man. I also need ink."

"James, get Alex one of the new inkwells that came in," she called out to her husband and resumed talking with Alex. "He's so intelligent. Jane is lucky to have such an excellent doctor teaching her."

Alex nodded.

"She must spend hours and hours with Jacob. And

when your arm heals, I imagine she'll spend even more time with him."

Alex attempted to control his annoyance. Or was it jealousy he felt? He liked Jacob, he honestly did, but thinking of the amount of time Jane spent with the man and the amount of time she would be spending with him, Alex found himself feeling jealous. A petty, young man's reaction and one that irritated him.

"Pen nibs, almost forgot I needed pen nibs," he said, hoping Lillian would go fetch them and leave him alone.

"Pen nibs!" she shouted to her husband.

Alex groaned beneath his breath.

"Jane is lucky she's not married. A husband wouldn't be understanding about a wife working such long hours and tending to men the way she does. No, a marriage wouldn't work for her."

"It would take a special man," Alex heard himself say.

"In Harmony?" Lillian said and laughed. "The men are all the same. There isn't a man around that would accept her profession without complaint."

Alex considered her remark. Most men would find Jane's profession objectionable. But he wasn't most men.

"Anything else?" James asked, placing Alex's packages on the counter in front of him.

A smile tickled Alex's features. "I have all I need, James."

"It's a bit dry," Minnie declared, helping herself to another piece of raisin cake.

Maisie immediately disagreed after finishing the piece of cake she had popped into her mouth. "It's moist, not dry."

"I said a bit dry," Minnie corrected irritably, slicing off a piece with her fork.

Maisie furrowed her brow and turned to question

Jacob. "What do you think of Jane's raisin cake? Moist or dry?"

Jacob munched hastily on the piece of cake he had in his mouth and washed it down with a sip of coffee before he spoke. "Delicious, absolutely delicious."

Maisie turned a triumphant smile on Minnie.

"A bit, I said a bit," Minnie said in a high, defensive tone.

Jane and Alex remained silent all through the exchange. Alex didn't really care what either woman thought of Jane's raisin cake. He loved it and relished every bite of the two generous pieces he had eaten. It was safe to assume that the way Jacob was going at his third piece, he'd be in total agreement with Alex.

The two sisters continued their debate, and Jacob continued eating his cake. Alex glanced at Jane seated beside him. She seemed lost in her thoughts. Her cake sat untouched on her plate and her tea hadn't been sipped. He wondered what musings occupied her mind so thoroughly.

Minnie's anxious words drew Alex's attention back to the conversation at hand.

"I can't believe the splints come off in one week. Why, it seems like just yesterday you stood at our doorstep, cradling your injured arm. Time does fly."

Maisie jumped right in. "Alex will still require Jane's assistance."

"Perhaps for a week or two, but no more than that," Minnie protested. "It's important she devote her time now to her studies. Right, Jacob?"

Jacob reflected a moment on the question and then nodded his agreement. "You're right, Minnie. Jane is a highly intelligent woman. She can go far in the field of medicine if she applies herself to her studies."

Jane smiled in appreciation of his sincere and thoughtful compliment. "As soon as Alex no longer needs me, I'll be at your disposal day or night."

Minnie giggled like a young schoolgirl, and Maisie

huffed her annoyance over Jane's remark, which implied much more than she had intended it to.

Alex remained silent, his thoughts disturbing. At the moment Jane was at *his* disposal day or night. He didn't care to relinquish that pleasure. And he certainly didn't care for the implication the conversation had suggested. Alex was actually preventing Jane from devoting the time she should to her medical studies. Both notions required consideration and decisions.

"Another piece of cake, Jacob?" Jane offered, slicing a generous piece.

Jacob beamed with pleasure. "Don't mind if I do."

Minnie, not one to miss a trick, smiled with delight. "Just think of all the delicious treats Jane will bake for you when she finishes here with Alex."

Maisie frowned her displeasure.

Alex turned sullen. The idea that Jane would bake for someone other than himself irritated the hell out of him. He had decisions to make. Big decisions and not much time to make them.

Sixteen

JANE worked in relative silence, cleaning off the table after Maisie, Minnie, and Jacob had polished off the entire raisin cake and a second pot of coffee and had finally bid Alex and her good night. Alex had retired upstairs, having complained of being exceptionally tired. She worried that he had exerted his strength today, and she had felt a twinge of guilt for having sent him on an errand.

She stacked the dishes neatly in the cupboard, then glanced out the window at the darkness. A warm breeze tickled her face, and she shut her eyes a moment, enjoying the peacefulness of the night. She didn't mind the solitude; she actually favored it. Time alone gave her a chance to ponder, and she had a whole lot of pondering to do.

Her eyes fluttered open as though unwilling to lose the contentment she had just captured. She cast a quick look toward the steps and sighed.

She didn't care for the emotional seesaw she had been on lately. One moment she wanted nothing more than to tend to Alex as a wife would, and the next she resented her own feelings for standing in the way of her studies. It didn't seem fair, having to choose. Why couldn't she have both?

Because no man would put up with your penchant for tending to the sick.

She hated that sensible voice in her head. Sensible wasn't the way she felt at the moment. Lonely and empty were more like it. She'd be a liar if she said she didn't want to feel a man's arms around her, or to kiss him until her legs grew weak and her heart pounded near to bursting.

She was a woman with all of a woman's feelings, and there was no denying it. And there was no denying she didn't want just any man's arms around her or any man's lips on hers. She wanted Alex. Plain and simple.

Good Lord, she had really gone and made a mess out of this whole situation. Why? Why in heaven's name did she have to fall in love with him?

Love. Lord, she never imagined herself falling so hopelessly in love. Love interfered. Love hurt. Love felt good. Love brought tears. Love was shared.

Alex never mentioned love.

Someday she was going to ignore that annoying voice, but right now she couldn't. Alex had kissed her. He had touched her intimately. But he had never expressed any words of affection for her. She shook her head and once again lamented over the mess she had gotten herself into.

A soft rap on the door startled her, and she wondered who would be calling so late.

"Jane," Jacob called.

Jane hurried to the door, swinging it open.

"Fever," he said, not having to elaborate.

Jane felt a chill run through her. She had managed to keep the young cowhand's fever at bay for the last couple of days, but she'd been afraid her control of it wouldn't last. And she'd been right. It hadn't.

She rushed out the door with Jacob, not bothering to grab her shawl from the wall peg. The door slammed behind them, shattering the silence of the late-night air.

Alex stood at the bottom of the stairs and watched the couple disappear behind the closed door. A wave of jealousy swept through him, leaving him shaken.

He could follow her. He could stay by her side while she worked. He could ... He shook his head over his childish reaction. Jane was a grown woman tending to her profession. She didn't need, probably didn't want him hanging around her when she had work to do. She was more than capable of taking care of herself. She had certainly proved it with her independent lifestyle.

"So is that what's bothering me?" he asked himself softly. "Is it the fact that Jane doesn't really require any man's help? If so, then she certainly doesn't need me."

His own remark irritated him, and he turned, heading back up the stairs and to what he was sure would be another sleepless night.

Dawn was just about breaking on the horizon when Jane left Jacob's office. It had been a long, torturous night. The cowhand's fever had soared, and she had thought without a doubt that she and Jacob would lose him. But the Lord had had other plans in mind, and the young cowhand now slept peacefully, his fever gone.

She rolled her shoulders back a few times, easing out the aches and soreness. She had worked diligently over the fevered patient all night, bathing him and spoon-feeding him an old herbal concoction that her grandfather had sworn by.

Jacob was amazed at the results the brew had produced, and he insisted that she begin to school him in the ancient art of herbal remedies. She promised him the first lesson by the end of the week, pleased that he was so willing to explore old healing methods in addition to the more modern ones.

Jane yawned and made her way to the *Sentinel*. She entered the kitchen, closing the door quietly behind her, and removed her ankle-high shoes. Toting them in her hand, she crept up the stairs with the most delicate of care, in an attempt not to make a sound. She made her way down the hall, avoiding the weathered boards that protested loudly when stepped on. She stopped by

Alex's door and listened a moment, hoping he hadn't needed her assistance at all during the night.

No sound came from within, and she took a step back to move on to her room. Alex's door swung open, causing her to jump in alarm and drop her shoes, just missing her feet. He stood half naked in the doorway, his trousers his only clothing. Another night his appearance would have struck her as sensually appealing, probably downright sexy, especially the way his usually neat hair appeared so temptingly unkempt and his jaw was shadowed with a night's growth of whiskers—but not tonight. Tonight she needed his warmth and understanding. She desperately needed his broad, hard chest to lean against, his arms to hold her, and his concerned words to comfort her.

"Alex." His whispered name sounded desperate on her lips.

He held his hand out to her, and she went to him.

He cradled her against his chest, her arms wrapping around his waist, her face nestling to rest on his naked chest. He was warm, solid, and oh, so comforting.

He stood holding her, his hand gently rubbing along her back while clutching her firmly against him.

She relaxed and sighed heavily in relief of having someone there for her, the only someone she wanted.

"You work yourself too hard, woman," he whispered, worry and reprimand all mixed in his tender tone.

She nodded her head, her cheek rubbing against his hard chest, the friction heating her soft flesh.

"Is the cowhand all right?"

Jane smiled to herself. He understood her absence from his home this evening. It wasn't necessary to explain where she had run off to for most of the night. He understood and accepted, but why not? She wasn't his wife and had no say to her whereabouts. The thought made her sad. "He'll be fine."

His hand ceased rubbing her back. "You don't sound convinced of his condition."

She had allowed her emotions to creep into her tone. "I'm tired." A flimsy excuse but a feasible one, she thought.

"You need an undisturbed night's sleep," he insisted, speaking from experience.

"A whole night of uninterrupted and peaceable sleep. It sounds like heaven."

While Alex agreed with her, he guided her toward his bed. With his arm clamped more firmly around her waist, he lowered them both to the bed together. "You work too hard."

"You've told me that a hundred times before." Her head remained resting on his chest, her arms stayed snug about his waist, and her eyes had drifted closed, too heavy with fatigue to remain open.

"A thousand times is more like it," he corrected and eased them both back onto his pillows, grateful that his arm was almost healed.

Jane didn't protest. He wondered if she even realized she was in his bed. She nestled more closely to him and drew her stocking feet up on the bed. He followed her feet with his own, snuggling his naked ones with hers.

"You won't let me go, will you, Alex?" Her whispered words were barely audible.

"I won't let you go, Jane," he promised her and wished she had meant she wanted him to hold her forever and not only for tonight.

Jane woke with a start, springing up in bed. Not her bed.

"Good Lord!" The words rushed out of her mouth while her hand ran over her flushed face. She had slept in Alex's bed, with Alex. She distinctly remembered him holding her and lying down on the bed with her and—

She abruptly cut off her anxious thoughts. Nothing had happened, she was certain of it. Alex had lent her his support and concern last night, nothing more. This interlude they had shared had been strictly platonic.

"It's about time you woke up. It's noon," Alex said, leaning against the doorframe and smiling.

He looked handsome. Downright gorgeous handsome. Damn him, she thought. His black trousers were neatly pressed, thanks to her, and his blue shirt was freshly laundered and starched just the way he liked it. She on the other hand probably looked a mess. Her clothes were wrinkled from sleeping in them, her hair more than likely stuck out like spikes on a porcupine's back, and her cheeks had to have resembled two bright cherries from her recent blush. Her day had not started off well at all, and here it was noontime.

"Why don't you freshen up? I have plans for the rest of the day for you and me."

Jane swung her legs off the bed, making sure her skirt covered her legs as she did so. "What plans?" she asked, having decided that since he hadn't brought up the matter of her being in his bed, she certainly wouldn't.

"A picnic," he said and walked over to her, extending his hand in assistance.

She took it and he easily pulled her up off the bed. A picnic sounded delightful. It had been so long since she had gone on one, but she didn't have time to spare on such a frivolous activity. "I don't have time—"

He instantly silenced her response with a finger to her protesting lips. "We—that means you and I, Jane Carson—are going on a picnic. I know the perfect spot by the Smoky Hill River. It's shaded this time of day and sweet with the scent of wildflowers."

She smiled at the pleasurable picture his words had painted. "I can't—"

He prevented her protest again, pressing his fingers more firmly to her lips. "You can and you will. I have already spoken with Jacob, and he insists that you go off with me and enjoy the day. He says you've worked hard and are more than entitled to a day of leisure."

She opened her mouth, and he answered her unasked question to her surprise. "Your patient is doing fine. His fever has gone, and Maisie had volunteered to sit with him for the afternoon, freeing Jacob to tend to his patients."

She parted her lips to speak.

He stilled her once again. "Unless you intend to tell me you'll be ready to join me in no time, then don't bother to say a word."

She laughed and nipped playfully at his finger, her action and the taste of him startling them both. "I'll be ready in no time," she said, her breath a bit too rapid.

He nodded and stepped out of her way. She hurried out the door, hearing Alex expel his breath slowly but heavily.

Alex assisted Jane up into the buggy, pleased by her choice of dress. Gone was her usual plain-colored skirt and white blouse, replaced by a pink calico cotton dress that hugged her waist and rounded over her breasts perfectly and temptingly.

He climbed in beside her and directed the buggy off toward Smoky Hill River just past the railroad tracks.

Jane poked at the picnic basket next to her foot. "Who prepared the food?"

"One guess," Alex challenged.

Jane answered quickly. "Maisie."

"Perceptive, Miss Carson, very perceptive."

Jane laughed, already enjoying this short reprieve from her usual hectic workday. "It's a glorious day. Not too hot, just right, like someone ordered it up special."

"I try to please," Alex teased.

"You have good taste, Mr. Evans."

"Thank you, Miss Carson. But if you think the day is grand, wait until you see the feast Maisie prepared for us."

"Just the thought of not having to cook one meal is relaxing in itself."

Alex looked at her, surprised. "I thought you liked to cook."

"I do, but with my work and chores . . ." She shrugged. "I don't always feel like cooking, especially for just myself."

His thoughts raced with memories of too many suppers eaten alone. He'd scramble a few eggs, break off a hunk of day-old bread, and eat, washing it down with cold coffee left on the stove since morning.

He imagined Jane's solitary suppers weren't as tasteless as his, though they were probably just as lonely. He hadn't given thought to the price she paid for her independence. The cost ran high. No partner. No mate. No love.

He at least had had Samantha all these years, and only recently, and for the first time in his life, had he lived alone.

Jane interrupted his wanderings, her voice light and carefree. "I love the summer sky. Its blue color is richer, and it seems to stretch on forever, but in a lazy sort of way."

Alex grinned. "Everything and everybody is more lazy in the summer. The people move at a slower pace. And so do the animals."

"But not the flowers," Jane added. "They grow rapidly, stretching hungrily toward the sun and lifting their faces in glory to the rain. Then they multiply and brighten in their new growth."

He loved the way she smiled. You couldn't help but smile along with her when her mouth broke into that heartwarming grin. Her eyes lit with merriment as well, widening and fluttering with excitement. He wondered if he kissed her at that very moment if he'd taste her pleasure.

"Do you like flowers, Alex?"

"I sure do."

"I love flowers. Their vibrant colors are a sight to behold, and their rich perfume scents can intoxicate. I grow flowers along with my herbs. The plants blend well together."

"The herbs that appear to be overrunning my kitchen are from your garden?"

"Do you mind? I never thought to ask you. I didn't think you would object."

"I don't mind at all." He really didn't mind. The small pots tied around the tops with different colored ribbons were a welcome sight to his once drab kitchen. "So they come from your garden?"

She nodded vigorously. "My garden is my pride and joy, and every plant is my baby. I fuss over every seedling and nurture every one with tender loving care."

"You're good at nurturing. Actually you're natural at it."

"You think so?" Jane asked as he pulled the buggy to a stop near a large maple shade tree.

He shook his head while he secured the reins to the buggy. "No. I know so. You nurtured me."

Jane hurried to respond, but Alex raised his hand.

"If you are going to protest, don't bother. Accept the compliment as just that, a sincere compliment."

Alex climbed down out of the buggy and walked around to Jane's side. He held his hand out to her, and she took it, pausing a moment in her descent. "Thank you for the compliment."

"You're welcome," he answered with a teasing wink.

Jane arranged the plaid blue blanket Alex had brought along for them on the ground beneath the shade of the large tree. He eased himself down on it and handed the basket to Jane. "I'm hungry."

"When aren't you hungry?"

"I'm a healing man. I need my strength."

"You're a healed man," she said and jolted the both of them with the truth of her statement.

Alex needed to express his gratitude for her help, but

the words stuck in his throat. Voicing his appreciation would seem as if he was dismissing her, that their time together was over. And to him their time together was just beginning.

"Not officially," he protested. "Until the bandages and splints come off, I'm still an invalid."

"And still my patient, my duty being to look after you."

"I like you looking after me, Jane Carson." He leaned toward her slowly.

He was going to kiss her, she could feel it. His desire sizzled in the air.

He kept coming, his lips parting, his hunger obvious. A few more inches, and he'd be on top of her, literally on top of her.

She grabbed a fried chicken leg from the basket and stuck it in his face, catching the juicy meat between his teeth. "Chicken leg?" she asked with a laughing grin.

He bit a succulent piece off it and chewed. "Mighty tasty, ma'am. I always liked legs, though I favor breasts."

Heat surged through Jane like a flooding river racing in her veins. His words teased and suggested on purpose. The heat finally reached her cheeks, and she turned away from his while her color settled and left her with two softly tinged pink cheeks.

This attraction between them was growing serious. Much too serious. And their time together was coming rapidly to an end. Would he ask her to stay?

"Your thoughts grow too solemn," Alex said. "This picnic allows only for smiles and laughter."

He was right. This occasion was a memory maker. The kind you stored in your treasure chest of memoirs and saved to recall on rainy days. Jane picked up her glass of lemonade in a salute. "To a gorgeous day, to an abundance of food, and to a charming and delightful companion to share it with."

Alex raised his own glass. "I'm in total agreement

with your toast. And may *I* add a special thank-you to a companion who unselfishly and tirelessly nursed me back to health. Her efforts were sincerely, though not always vocally, appreciated."

Jane sipped her lemonade, trying not to let the nervous tremor in her hand show. He was saying goodbye, letting her know she was no longer necessary to him.

She felt close to tears, but smiled. She mentally calculated the remaining days she had left with him, then it would be over ... all over.

Seventeen

"Bet it seems more like six months instead of almost six weeks," Jacob commented, holding a pair of scissors in his hand.

"It sure has." Alex fussed uncomfortably on the wooden examination table in Jacob's office. He had slept restlessly all night thinking about this moment. Jane stood nearby, though not nearly close enough for his satisfaction. He expected with each snip of the scissors Jane would be cut further and further out of his life. As much as he favored the removal of the confining bandage, he didn't favor losing her.

"All set?" Jacob asked.

Alex immediately looked to Jane. She barely smiled. He sensed her concern and noticed the slight tremble to her body. He wondered if her worries matched his own. "All set," he answered, his gaze remaining steadfast on Jane.

Jacob waved the scissors at Jane, directing her beside him. "You best stand closer in case I need your assistance."

She walked over to Jacob's side, and without prompting, she carefully took Alex's arm and rested it comfortably along her own arm.

"Perfect," Jacob complimented with a smile and proceeded to cut away at the wrappings.

In what seemed like seconds, though several minutes ticked by, the bandages and splints were discarded to reveal his arm, milk white and stiff.

"Don't attempt to move it yet," Jacob cautioned, placing the scissors to the side on a nearby table. "You must remember your arm has been immobile for several weeks. Your joints are stiff and will protest. You must take it slowly."

"Let me help," Jane offered, still holding his arm. She gently worked her fingers soothingly over his pale flesh, massaging and manipulating his stiff muscles to respond.

Alex relaxed under Jane's skilled touch. She successfully forced his resistant limb to respond, moving it little by little until his arm became more pliable to her touch.

"Looks good," Jacob said with a satisfied nod. "But don't overdo it. It might not to be a bad idea for Jane to stay on one more week with you. What do you say, Jane?"

Caught off guard, Jane wasn't prepared to respond. She stared at Alex, unnerved.

"Would you?" Alex asked softly. "Stay on, that is."

"If you would like me to stay on a extra week, I will."

His reply was immediate. "I'd like you to stay."

Jane fought to control the shivers that raced through her. How often had she dreamed of hearing him speak those words? *I'll stay.* And how often had she dreamed of issuing that exact response?

"Good," Jacob concluded. "Now let's see you move that arm on your own."

Though reluctant to break away from Jane's soothing touch, Alex slipped his arm from her grasp. He moved it up and down and back and forth, and with each movement his smile grew wider.

Jacob laughed. "Feels good to have the use of it back again, doesn't it?"

"Does it ever." Alex proudly extended his arm out in front of him. He looked to Jane. "Thanks to your skill, it works as good as new."

Pleasure and pride leaped inside her, forcing her to smile. "I was concerned with your ability to heal quickly, being you're so stubborn."

"Me stubborn?" he questioned. "You're not?"

She tapped her chest. "Persistent. There's a difference when one is tending to a patient."

"Persistently stubborn is more like it," Alex accused good-naturedly.

Jacob joined in the debate. "A preferable trait for a physician."

Alex watched Jane's face register with surprise. Obviously Jacob's remark had pleased her. Her work meant more to her than she would ever admit. Medicine would come first in her life—a man second. He found the thought a blow to his male ego.

But then he had to remember Jane wasn't like other women. She sat apart from them, a breed all her own. She was a woman before her time, pushing the boundaries to succeed in a male-dominated profession.

His pride soared and his ego deflated. Jane was a woman to be proud of and one who deserved respect and admiration. And one who would need a special man . . . like himself.

He found himself singing her praises. "You're mighty lucky you've got Jane working with you."

Jane shot him a look that questioned his sanity.

"That I am," Jacob agreed seriously. "Do you know her knowledge of herbal remedies in phenomenal?"

"Yes, I know. She cultivates her herbs in pots in my kitchen," Alex said with a wink at Jane.

"And she knows the properties of each one," Jacob said in amazement. "When the young cowhand's fever rose dangerously high, she mixed a few herbs . . ." Jacob stopped a minute in thought. His eyes flashed wide in remembrance. "Sallow bark was one part of the mixture. She spooned mouthful doses periodically into that fellow all night."

"And it worked just like my granddad taught me it would," Jane said proudly.

Jacob scratched his head while shaking it. "Wouldn't have believed it if I hadn't seen it myself."

"Herbal medicine's been favored out here in the West for some time," Alex explained. "Though I can't say there's many skilled at it."

"Jane certainly is," Jacob challenged.

Alex didn't care for Jacob's defensive tone. If Jane needed defending, he'd defend her. "That goes without saying."

Jacob continued on, his interest in herbs peaked. "Jane has agreed to teach me about herbs. With you healed and her time caring for you near to an end, we'll be able to apply ourselves to studying the ancient art of herbal medicine." Jacob grinned and looked to Jane. "We'll probably find ourselves burning the midnight oil many a night."

The muscles in Alex's jaw clenched. *Burning the midnight oil?* He didn't care for the sound or implication.

Annoyed with his own musings, Alex grabbed the edge of the examination table with each hand and made ready to shove himself off. His arm, not yet accustomed to such exertion, protested with a sharp pain, causing Alex to lose his balance and fall to his side.

Jane rushed over to him, bracing her weight into his shoulder and preventing him from falling completely over.

"Where is your common sense?" she scolded, her heart pounding in fear of the damage he could have caused himself.

A good question, he thought, since he was certain his common sense had deserted him the day he had agreed to have Jane nurse him. He fixed a teasing smile on her. "I lost my common sense about six weeks ago. Haven't you been able to find it since. I swear it's been kidnapped, but . . ." Alex winked at her. "I have a distinct feeling it will return in about a week's time."

Jane teased him right back. "Are you sure you had any common sense to begin with?"

His fingers drifted up beneath her chin. "I had too much."

"But you don't anymore?"

Alex shook his head slowly. "Completely devoid."

"That could prove dangerous," she suggested in a mere whisper.

"Or fun," he challenged in a soft murmur.

"You all right?" Jacob asked, coming up behind Jane.

Alex nodded, his fingers falling away from Jane's chin. "I just need to remember my arm requires a little coddling for a bit longer."

Jane stepped to the side, allowing Jacob access to Alex's arm.

Jacob gave the arm a quick look. "Be careful. It looks good as new, but it's still tender from its recent and lengthy confinement."

"Will do," Alex said, intending to take no chance in injuring his arm all over again.

Jane stepped back in front of Alex after Jacob turned away and walked over to his desk. She unfolded his rolled-up shirtsleeve, buttoning the cuff and soothing the wrinkles from the white cotton.

I could hold her in both my arms now. The sudden thought jolted him. He had only been able to slip his one arm around her, caress her face with one hand, hold her to him only so tightly. Now he had two working hands and arms. The thought definitely proposed unlimited possibilities.

"Alex?" Jane spoke his name in a soft question.

He focused his eyes on her, his thoughts still bemused by his mental wanderings.

"Is something wrong?"

A tender smile blossomed on his face, and he slipped his healed hand over hers. "Things couldn't be better."

She threaded her fingers with his. "Squeeze," she ordered.

He looked at her oddly.

"Your recovering hand needs exercise. It's been sedentary too long," she explained. "Now squeeze."

He obliged her, realizing she was absolutely correct. He didn't have the strength in his fingers he once did.

Alex's concern showed as the faint wrinkles around his eyes deepened. Jane addressed his worry immediately. "You'll get your full strength back, especially if you keep exercising your joints and muscles."

His expression changed quickly. He cast her a look that was somewhere between sensuous and playful. "Can I use you to exercise with?" He pulled their entwined hands up between their chests.

She sent him a stern and professional look. "We can find you a more appropriate and challenging object."

"You're challenge enough for me."

Jane caught the compelling look in his eyes, his rough yet suggestive tone, and his implied yet not clearly spoken message. Her legs betrayed her and turned to instant mush.

She squeezed his hand more for support than to help him exercise. He squeezed back thinking otherwise.

"Up to the challenge, Jane?"

Her voice was strong, her legs still weak. "Naturally."

He gave a hardy laugh. "Stubborn."

"Persistent," she corrected and unlaced her fingers from his.

He didn't stop her. He let her go. He had time yet. Another week to be exact. A sudden thought struck him, and he hopped off the table.

Jane abruptly took a step back, his size and lithe movement intimidating.

"I'm cooking supper for you tonight."

She cast him a questionable look. "You?"

"Me," he said and thumped his chest.

She called over her shoulder to Jacob. "Get the peppermint leaves."

Jacob pondered her remark a moment, his brow furrowing, and then he broke into a smile and triumphantly announced, "Peppermint eases an upset stomach."

Alex shook his head slowly. "You have so little trust in my abilities."

"It's not you. It's your cooking."

"You haven't tasted my cooking."

"I spoke to your daughter about it."

He folded his arms across his chest and waited.

Jane shrugged. "She told me *caution* was the word to use when you got near the stove."

"She certainly didn't starve while growing up."

Jane covered her mouth to hide her laughter.

"Well, she didn't," Alex insisted.

"You're right, she didn't. She learned, out of necessity, at a young age to cook as I did."

Alex frowned. "I'm not that bad a cook and I'll prove it."

"And I get to be the one you prove it on?"

"Precisely," he said and stomped toward the door. He turned and shook his finger at her. "And don't be late for supper."

The door slammed behind him and Jane laughed even harder as she turned around and faced Jacob.

He shook his head. "I'm glad I wasn't invited. You'd best take extra peppermint leaves with you."

Jane stopped laughing. "He can't be that bad."

Jacob stared at her wide-eyed. "Show me any man that can cook good."

Jane's shoulders drooped and she sighed. "Give me the jar of peppermint leaves."

* * *

Several hours later she stood by the back kitchen door, afraid to open it. She breathed deeply of the fresh summer air and admired the flourishing daisies she had planted in a narrow wooden box next to the door. She hadn't a clue as to what awaited her inside. The kitchen had been spotless when she had left this morning. Now there was no telling how it looked or how it smelled.

She braced herself for the worst, took a deep strengthening breath, turned the handle to the door, and walked in. The sight that assaulted her caused her breath to catch.

The table was set with a white linen tablecloth and matching napkins that were folded neatly beneath the utensils. A bouquet of wildflowers ranging in color from pale yellow to bright purple sat in a blue pitcher in the center of the table. A pitcher of fresh-made lemonade sat to the side of a platter artfully arranged with beef slices, boiled potatoes, and carrots. A small bowl held dark gravy, and a larger bowl was heaped with flaky biscuits.

Jane's mouth quickly watered.

"Good, you're on time."

Jane looked up to see Alex coming down the steps. He was freshly washed and attired. She couldn't help but notice he had recently shaved—very recently, since the scent of spicy lemon balm drifted off his smooth face.

"Any comments?" he asked with a sly smile as he held a chair out for her.

She scooted hastily into the offered seat. "Everything looks delicious."

Alex took the seat opposite her. "I did my best." He fixed her plate for her as she had so often done for him these past weeks.

Jane relaxed, enjoying the attention, and impatiently waited to taste the meal. "The food really does look tasty."

"Then I'm sure you'll enjoy it since it is tasty," he said and planted her plate in front of her.

She picked up her fork ready to dig in.

"Biscuit," he offered, holding the bowl of biscuits out to her.

"Thank you," she said and eagerly took one. "It's light as a feather."

"Of course," he said and helped himself to one.

Jane shook her head, wondering how he or—who—had gotten this delicious meal together. She felt a twinge of guilt for thinking him incapable of preparing such a succulent meal. He could have hidden skills she hadn't known about. While contemplating the thought, she tasted a piece of beef.

It melted in her mouth. The potatoes and carrots tasted just as heavenly. They were perfectly seasoned and cooked, not too mushy and not too hard.

"Another biscuit?" he asked, holding the bowl out to her again.

She eyed him suspiciously this time and accepted another biscuit.

"Aren't you enjoying the meal?"

"This meal is perfect. I'm envious of *the cook*."

"Why, thank you," he said and bowed his head in appreciation of her compliment.

"For a man whose cooking skills fall predominately with eggs, how did you master such a fine meal in such a short time?"

"I learn quickly."

Jane held her tongue. She wanted to ask what it was he learned quickly, conning her or cooking.

"Wait until you taste my dessert."

Curiosity snagged Jane. Most desserts took time to perfect. Her own first pie had been a disaster. And her first cake? She hesitated to recall that memorable moment. Mrs. Benning, the woman who had taught her to cook, had laughed so hard she had brought tears to her eyes—a flood of them.

Jane generously spread her biscuit with butter before

she asked Alex what he so obviously relished to tell her. "What did you make for dessert?"

Alex beamed with pure pride. "A three-layer chocolate cake.

Jane chomped on her biscuit even though the flaky dough melted in her mouth. Absolutely, positively, there was no way his limited cooking skills extended to the complexity of baking a three-layer chocolate cake. There could be only one way for him to prepare a meal like this. He had to have had an accomplice, but who?

"Chocolate cake, especially a three-layer cake, isn't easy to make," she said, looking him directly in the eye.

Alex looked right back. "It's a bit of a chore, but the end results are well worth it."

"You must share your recipe with me."

"Glad to," he said and popped a carrot into his mouth.

Jane picked up the gravy bowl and with the ladle generously dribbled more gravy over her meat. She mentally tabulated a list of suspects. His daughter, Samantha, topped the list. Jane had realized after speaking with the young woman on a few occasions that she loved her father dearly and would do anything for him.

She returned the gravy bowl to the table, then sliced a piece of meat while contemplating the rest of the list. Maisie was another distinct possibility. Maisie intended a match between Alex and Jane. Cooking a meal to help pave the way for success would certainly be in her favor and make her a likely suspect.

"You're quiet tonight. Is something wrong?"

Jane considered her response and decided directness was best, especially since curiosity had gotten the better of her. "Who cooked this meal?"

Alex laughed and leaned back in his chair. "I like your direct manner. No beating around the proverbial bush for you, straightforward all the way."

"You haven't answered my question."

Alex placed his hand to his chest as though wounded. "You don't think I cooked this meal?"

"Never," she insisted. "If it were a simple meal, I might have considered the possibility of you preparing it, but this?" She cast her hand over the table. "This is too involved for a novice. And . . ." She wagged her finger at him. "You took it too far with the three-layer chocolate cake."

"So the cake did me in?"

"Most definitely."

Alex leaned forward, bracing his arms on the table. "I wanted you to have the pleasure of a tasty meal all prepared and waiting for you when you got home."

Jane felt a chill run through her. *Home.* He considered this her home. She responded hastily, afraid to linger on his remark. "Thank you, that was very thoughtful of you. But—"

"I didn't cook the meal."

"Who did?"

"Different folk."

Jane sent him a puzzled look.

Alex threw his hands up in the air in surrender. "I pleaded my plight to whoever I thought would help me."

"What?" Jane asked in surprise.

"Lillian Taylor supplied the buttered carrots, lightly sprinkled with a trace of dill, she informed me."

Jane shook her head in disbelief.

"Minnie, though it took some smooth talking, baked the biscuits. Maisie set straight to work. She roasted the beef, boiled the potatoes—the parsley adds that extra tang of flavor—and she made that smooth—not a single lump, mind you—gravy." Alex rested, out of breath from the detailed rundown of accomplices and their cooking tips.

"You're not finished," Jane reminded him.

Alex stood, walked over to the counter by the cupboard, picked up a glass-covered cake plate, and brought it over to the table. He sat it down between Jane and himself. He looked at her, silently questioning if she was ready for the unveiling, and at her agreeable nod he lifted the glass cover.

Jane almost gasped at the sight of the perfectly formed, eye-catching, and mouthwatering three-layer chocolate cake. The baker had topped off her creation with chocolate shavings over the top and around the sides. Sheer talent, she thought.

"Who?" Jane queried, her eyes still fixed on the confectionery delight.

Alex puffed his chest out and held his head up with pride. "My daughter."

"It looks almost too good to eat," Jane said, then quickly amended, "but I'd die for a piece."

"Samantha will be pleased to hear that."

"Hurry and finish your meal so we can have dessert," Jane ordered impatiently.

Alex leaned back in his chair, folded his arms across his chest, and pouted like a child.

Her tastebuds were all set to experience that rich dark chocolate, so she was in no mood to contend with his childish behavior at the moment. "For heaven's sake, what's bothering you now?"

"You haven't commented on *my* contribution to the meal."

Jane appeared puzzled, hastily surveying the table to take note of what she had missed. She focused on the only item whose preparer had remained unaccounted. She raised her glass and announced, "Alex, you make the best lemonade I've ever tasted."

"You've brightened my day with your compliment," he said with a grin.

Jane turned a serious expression on him and stretched her hand out to cover his. "No, Alex, it's *you* who have brightened my day. Thank you."

He threaded his fingers with hers. "You've done so

much for me, Jane, and you've been so thoughtful. I wanted to return your actions in kind."

"You've returned more than was necessary." She reluctantly slipped her fingers from his. She hadn't wanted to. She would prefer holding on to him forever if she could. His skin felt warm, almost as if it had been drenched by the heat of the sun. And his long fingers entwined perfectly with hers like a long-lost glove that found its match. She feared her action if she continued to hold on to him. She feared she might speak her mind—or more so her emotions—and say something she would regret. So instead she pointed to the cake and licked her lips.

"Can't wait?" he teased.

No, I can't wait, but it's not the cake I hunger for, she thought and hid her silent response behind a wide smile.

"I'll be generous and kind," Alex said, slicing a large piece for her.

Please be generous and kind, her thought murmured in her head. See me as a woman and not a cook, a physician, or an independent female. *Just see me.*

He placed the plate in front of her. "Satisfied?"

Her heart ached and her stomach fluttered. She'd take this moment with him if that was all she could manage, and perhaps one day they would share a more intimate moment together.

"I'm satisfied, Alex," she said and sliced into her cake, dropping her glance to the plate so he wouldn't see the tears in her eyes.

Eighteen

JANE beat the hell out of the round woolen rug hanging over the clothesline in Alex's backyard. She whacked the wire rug beater against the ivory-and-deep-blue floral design repeatedly until she was attacked by a fit of coughing from the dusty dirt that floated and descended in a cloud around her.

Three days, she thought. Three days and her time with Alex would be over. And to make matters worse, the last few days with him had been wonderful. They had talked, they had laughed, and they had teased each other often. He'd hold her hand, touch her face, even kiss her gently on the lips. Anyone watching their actions would surely think them husband and wife and assume them deeply in love. But oddly enough love had not been declared by either of them.

Jane gave the rug another whack, though her energy had abated and it was more of a tap. Her thoughts remained focused on her problem at hand. The problem being that her time with Alex was rapidly running out. And she was rapidly running out of control. She wanted Alex. Plan and simple. She wasn't some young schoolgirl suffering from puppy love. She was a grown woman of twenty-eight, ready and willing to love a man. She wasn't growing any younger, and God only knew when or if she would ever marry.

189

She shook her head, shutting her eyes against her lusty thoughts. Here she was beating a rug and beating herself silly with ideas that would never see reality.

Alexander Evans never once expressed any interest in a relationship with her. A quick roll in the hay maybe, but a permanent, long-lasting and loving relationship?

She opened her eyes and shook her head in answer to her own question. Presumably, he was grateful to her for her services and fancied himself attracted to her out of gratitude. A sorry reason, but a familiar reaction from a person dependent on another for his care.

She beat the rug even harder, annoyed with her own pragmatic conclusion. She didn't desire practical, she desired passion. But that heated emotion eluded her, as did a husband and love. She had paid dearly and highly for her independence and her desire to learn of medicine. She had chosen an uncommon path for a woman, and she couldn't dwell on it or spill tears over her decision now.

Still, she was a woman, with all of a woman's desires. Not that it did her a lick of good. She could count on her one hand how many times she had been kissed.

Twenty-eight. Twenty-eight, the silent voice reminded her. She didn't need reminders. She was all too aware of her old-maid status in Harmony. Had she allowed time to slip past her? Had she expected too much of life and men in general?

Her thoughts irritated her. She carelessly tossed the rug beater to the ground and marched into the kitchen. She was angry with herself, and it showed in her troubled expression and ardent strides.

Once inside she set to work to rid herself of her tormented wanderings. Work not only kept her fingers occupied, but her mind as well. Good, hard work would set her thoughts right and ease her irritation. She grabbed split logs from the large basket by the door, and with her arms stacked full, she marched over to the stove. A hardy swing with one free hand sent the side door of the stove open, and she threw the logs inside one by one. They landed with a heavy clunk, one after the other, reverberating throughout the house.

She shut the door with a loud bang and dusted her hands on her blue apron. She then hefted a big cast-iron pot onto the top of the cookstove from the cupboard and dropped it with a solid clang, sending another disturbing sound echoing noisily through the rooms.

Dishes clattered, pots clanged, and cupboard doors slammed closed. A cacophony of irritating noises resounded steadily throughout the house.

"What the devil is going on?" Alex yelled, entering the kitchen.

The noises ceased insistently, and Jane turned an innocent smile on him. "I'm getting supper ready."

"Getting it or killing it?"

"It's been a long day," she said in way of explanation of her strange actions.

Alex eyed her suspiciously. Even on a long, tiring day he had never known Jane to complain or grow grouchy. "If you're tired, I can fix supper."

Her smile faded. "If you want to cook supper, do so, but cook it for yourself. I'm not hungry." She marched past him, her head held high and her anger running even higher.

Not accustomed to this side of Jane and not one to be dismissed so rudely, Alex's hand shot out and grabbed her arm as she fled past him, abruptly halting her in her tracks. "Wait just a minute."

She glared down at his hand wrapped firmly around her upper arm. If she intended her look to intimidate, she failed. His hold on her remained firm.

"What's wrong?"

She had never heard him use that tone before. She was reminded of a strict parent who spoke with authority. It irritated her all the more. "Nothing." Her voice dripped with sarcasm.

Alex shook his head and smiled. Only it was a half smile, a warning of sorts that sent the shivers through her.

He pulled her toward him, moving forward to meet her. They stood chest to chest, her head tilted, her eyes daringly fixed on his.

"One more time, Jane. What's wrong?"

Jane swallowed the nervous gulp in her throat. How could she lay bare her emotions to him? How could she admit her need, her desire to love?

His stare intimidated, warning her he wouldn't repeat the question.

"Headache," she lied, her courage fading like the daylight.

"Let me make you some chamomile tea."

His suggestion surprised her and gave rise to her guilt. And her guilt grew stronger with each silent moment that passed.

"Sit," he ordered gently when she failed to respond. "Let me get you some tea, and then you can lie down and rest for a while. The rest should help rid you of that headache."

She allowed him to lead her to a chair and sat down in the one he pulled out from the table for her.

"When did this headache come on?" he asked, busily filling the pot with water and setting it to boil on the stove.

Jane held back her moan of frustration and answered him calmly. "While I was beating the rugs."

Alex took a china cup and saucer from the cupboard and placed them in front of Jane on the table. "The combined heat and dust probably didn't help your problem any."

Jane nodded, thinking the heat had more to do with her irritation than the dust, although it wasn't the heat from the late sun that caused her discomfort.

Alex prepared the chamomile leaves for her and

poured the boiling water in her cup. "I can take that upstairs for you if you would like to rest in your room."

Jane shook her head. The last thing she needed was him following her up to her room. "I'll have it here."

"Mind if I join you?" Alex asked, pulling out the chair opposite her.

"Not at all." Her answer was honest. She enjoyed his company immensely, and she enjoyed conversing with him. That would be the hardest part of leaving him. She'd once again return to an empty house. No one would be there to share the evening meal or discuss the day's events. She'd once again be alone.

"Would you like anything with your tea?"

Jane shook her head and sent him a weak smile. "You needn't trouble yourself over me. It's just a headache that is rapidly fading."

Alex raised a finger in objection. "It could return if not attended to."

"You sound like a doctor."

"I've learned from a skilled physician."

A pleasurable grin spread across Jane's face. "I'm not a physician. But thank you for the compliment."

"Not yet you're not, but you will be, and you're more than welcome. Now, do you want to tell me what was really troubling you?"

Jane appeared stunned. Her eyes grew wide and her mouth fell open.

"I've come to know you well, Jane Carson. Heat and dust wouldn't do you in or cause you so much irritation."

Jane wanted to release the heavy sigh resting deep inside her. Frustration quickly replaced her irritation. He obviously was attuned to her emotions, a dangerous advantage. If he read her so easily, could he read her feelings for him as well?

He took a guess when her answer wasn't forthcoming. "Worried about a patient?"

Jane found it easy to nod her head in response. In

truth she *was* concerned with a patient—that patient being Alex.

"Anything I can help you with?"

Jane cast her glance down at her cup, hugged in her hands. She didn't trust herself to keep her eyes focused on him. He looked so handsome, so virile, so utterly male.

He wore tight-fitting jeans today and a white shirt with the sleeves rolled up and the top buttons open. He was dressed casually, intending to work on the printing press. And his casual clothes gave him the appearance of a rugged, down-to-earth male, adding mightily to his sensuous appeal.

"Jane?" he questioned with concern.

She raised her head and looked at him. What could she say? Alex, thoughts of you trouble me. "Nothing I can't handle." *Liar*, her mind tattled.

His hand stole across the table, reaching for hers and capturing it in a gentle squeeze. "I don't mind listening to your concerns."

Her heart pounded violently. Lord, but he could melt her with words alone, especially with such a caring declaration. How many men would be willing to listen to her speak of illness and medicine?

He's returning in kind your thoughtfulness. "No," she said firmly, chastising her silent thought.

Alex looked at her oddly.

"No need," she amended hastily. "I appreciate the offer but I find my headache is returning, and I think an hour of rest would prove beneficial." She stood, slipping her hand from his and ready to sneak away with her warring thoughts to her room.

"Are you sure there—"

An abrupt shake of her head interrupted him. "The tea helped and a nap should do the rest."

She took herself off in a hurry, running like a coward, afraid to face the truth. She loved Alexander Evans, but feared he didn't love her.

* * *

Alex stood looking out the upstairs parlor window, watching the near setting sun. He flexed his healed arm and repeatedly curled his fingers into a fist and released them. The exercise had proved useful, and his hand had regained much of its former strength, as had his arm.

He really hadn't required Jane's help for the last couple of days. He could have easily informed her she was no longer necessary to him, but he had questioned the notion. Had her presence become necessary?

Presence, not service, he reminded himself. He had thought much lately on his life before Jane had entered it. It had been lonely, although he had attempted to convince himself otherwise. Now he had only a few days left to make Jane realize how much she meant to him. But would his feelings matter? Did her interest in medicine take precedence over all else in her life?

He rubbed his eyes with his fingers, the strain of his thoughts disturbing.

Jane was independent, free to do as she wished, pursue interests of her choice. And a man of her choice. He wondered if a husband had ever entered her plans. Had she thought of a home and a family, or did her interest deal strictly with her love of medicine and helping to tend to the sick?

Alex stretched his arm out and folded it back, flexing the once weakened muscle. His biceps tightened and expanded considerably, straining the material of his white shirt.

His stare remained fixed on Main Street below and the hush that began to settle over the town for the evening while his thoughts lingered on Jane and the unsolvable solution their strange relationship presented.

His ears picked up a strange sound from down the hallway. He strained to listen. The pitiful moans alerted him to Jane's distress, and he hurried off to her room.

* * *

Held captive in a tormenting dream, Jane moaned and writhed uncomfortably on the bed. Alex was calling out to her. He needed her, desperately needed her, and she could not get to him. A heavy door barred her way, and behind it she heard his cries.

"Unlock it! Unlock it!" he screamed.

"I can't!" she yelled back. "I can't."

"Only you can unlock it, Jane," he called out, his voice fading away in the distance.

"Alex!" she screamed, frightened by the distance and the door that separated them.

"Only you, Jane. Only you can unlock it."

Jane barely heard his words that drifted off to a faint whisper, and fearful of losing him she screamed. "Alex!"

"I'm here, Jane. I'm here. Wake up."

Her eyes shot open. Seeing him sitting on the bed beside her caused an overwhelming sense of relief to rush over her, and she flung herself up and into his arms.

Alex captured her in a wrenching embrace, holding her trembling body tightly to his. "It's all right. Everything is all right."

Jane squeezed her arms around his middle, drawing herself more solidly against him. She buried her face in his shirt, nuzzling her nose between his open buttons and inhaling the scent of him. A warm manly smell mingled with his lemon-scented shaving balm and favorably stung her nostrils. She breathed deeply of him and faintly touched her lips to his chest.

Alex remained still, her lips sending a shiver of emotion racing through him. "Jane," he whispered, wanting to make certain she was awake and aware of her actions.

Jane responded with a more ardent kiss to his chest.

His body rushed to excitement, his every nerve strung taut, his every emotion on edge. Jane's disturbing dream had set her in a frenzy, and he didn't want her regretting her actions.

"Jane," he said.

She kissed him again, more urgently, pushing his shirt apart with her nose to clear a wider path for herself.

"Jane," he said more strongly.

She didn't respond, she was lost in her intent.

Alex swore beneath his breath and reluctantly grasped the back of her hair and tugged her head away from him, pulling it back and forcing her to look up at him.

Her eyes shone with unshed tears, and her cheeks were flushed with heated passion while her lips sat parted, sleek and hungry.

He whispered softly though firmly, "If you don't stop—"

She didn't allow him to finish. Her response was murmured urgently. "I don't want to stop."

He attempted once again to play the gentleman. "Jane—"

"Don't," she begged softly, innocently wetting her lips with the tip of her tongue.

He shook his head, moaned in surrender, and lowered his mouth to hers as he brought her head forward to meet his aching lips.

Nineteen

JANE tasted of warm chamomile tea and pure passion. He eagerly sought more of the heady combination, deepening their kiss until they both found it difficult to breathe. And still they tasted of each other.

Alex tore his mouth away from hers and trailed kisses over her cheek to her ear. "I want you."

Jane sighed deeply and nodded her head in response, her breath lost to her.

Alex cupped her face in his hands. "Are you sure?"

Jane nodded again, not trusting her voice. If this one night was all she could share with him, then so be it. At least her first time and possibly her last would be with Alex. Besides, she wanted no other man but Alex. Tonight would be her night of love. A night to tuck away in her memories.

She reached up and began to unbutton her blouse.

He stilled her hand with his. "I'll do that."

The sensual softness in his voice sent the shivers through her, enjoyable shivers that raced to ignite her passion even more.

His fingers were deft, and in seconds her blouse was spread open, his hand slipping inside to cup her breast. "You feel so right in the palm of my hand as though you were fashioned precisely for me."

Anxious to experience more of the excitement he

generated in her, Jane reached up and began to unbutton his shirt.

He smiled. "For once I am glad you have such an unconventional nature."

She returned his smile. "And nimble fingers?"

He laughed and lowered her back upon the bed. In minutes they both had each other undressed, and Alex laid stretched out and propped on his elbow beside Jane, admiring her naked body.

His hand ran teasingly over her breast, rolling each nipple in his fingers. "Perfection," he uttered softly. "Sheer perfection."

Jane reached up and traced his jaw with her finger. "Your words, your touch—they stir my soul."

Alex found her words stirred more than his soul; they touched his heart. He leaned down and brushed his lips over hers. "I'm going to kiss every inch of you, Jane."

"Promise?" she whispered, stealing a sudden kiss from him.

He kissed her more soundly. "Promise," he said breathlessly, and his lips scorched a path down her neck to her breast.

Jane didn't think anything could feel so exquisite. In her wildest dreams, or her wildest fantasies, she had never imagined such a sweet, hot passion.

His touch was magic, bringing each fiber of her body to life. Her flesh tingled with his every touch and kiss. His hands would roam and his tongue would follow, and she was soon helplessly lost to his intimate caresses.

Alex couldn't explore enough of her; eagerly he sought to discover every responsive part of her. And she had many. She wasn't a woman afraid to love. She moaned and writhed at his touch, demonstrating her pleasure proudly and passionately. Her boldness excited him and made his desire for her even stronger.

He nudged her legs apart with his knee as his hand dipped down farther to explore the very core of her.

Her moan deepened with his intimate intrusion, and he leaned down and captured her sensual protest in a kiss.

Her hands stretched up and ran over his chest, feeling the hard expanse of his muscles, lingering in spots she found enticing and moving on to explore more.

Alex relished her inquisitive journey and released a moan or two of his own. They continued to explore each other slowly and freely, each reveling in the feel of the other. They ignited dormant emotions, fanning their passion to near exploding only to have them cease, take a breath, and start all over again.

It was a time of learning for them both. Learning each of what the other enjoyed, responded to, received pleasure from, and fulfilling those needs.

Their bodies were sprinkled with a fine sheen of perspiration when Jane finally protested she could wait no longer.

"I want to feel you inside me."

Alex needed no further urging. He slipped over her and eased himself slowly inside her.

She stiffened, but only a moment.

His words encouraged her. "Relax, I won't hurt you."

She did precisely as he requested. She relaxed while he filled her with the strength of him. His full entrance jolted her but only for a moment. And his words helped to soothe her.

"You feel so good, Jane, so very good." He moved slowly at first, allowing her time to grow accustomed to him. Jane began to match his rhythm, and he moved more vigorously, more powerfully, more possessively until she grasped hold of his shoulders and held on tightly as he sent them both spiraling into oblivion.

Alex lay slumped over her, attempting to keep his weight from completely crushing her. His breathing was erratic, his heart beat frantically and his body relaxed in absolute satisfaction.

Jane felt fulfilled. Nothing had prepared her for this

intense and personal feeling of satisfaction, and it moved her to tears she fought to hide.

Alex sensed her cries, silent as they were. Her body alerted him to her distress, and he immediately sought to assuage her. He lifted his head, stared directly into her eyes, and kissed her gently before slipping off her and taking her into his arms.

He positioned her comfortably against him, hugging her to him, stroking her arm, offering comfort. Words failed him. He could think of no appropriate response except "I love you," but he worried that his declaration of love might chase her away instead of draw her closer to him. He still wasn't certain if a relationship was what she sought or if a relationship would interfere with her independent life.

His intimate touch was the only thing he could offer at the moment, and besides he couldn't keep his hands off her. He loved the feel of her petal-soft skin and the way she fit against him. He didn't want to ever let her go.

"Alex." Her voice caught on a sob, and she drew a deep breath for control.

Alex closed his arms more tightly around her and sought to find words that would ease her discomfort. "You took my breath away," he said with a light laughter. "I've never experienced anything quite like it. You're a remarkably sensuous woman, Jane Carson."

Alex felt her body go limp against him, her tension drained away, and she snuggled comfortably in his arms. "May I offer you that same wonderful compliment?"

"By all means, I think we both are well-deserving of it."

Jane's laughter was light and cheerful and her response honest. "Alex, you've made this a most memorable experience."

"I did not accomplish that feat alone, dear heart."

She looked up at him, her smile generous. "We did it together."

"Precisely," he said and gave her playful wink. "Would you like to do it again?"

Jane nodded her head vigorously.

Alex traced her lips with his fingers, and his expression grew serious. "I want to make love to you all night."

Jane looked at him strangely. "Night has only fallen."

Alex grinned wickedly, grasped her arms, and drew her toward him. "I know, dear heart. I know."

The night wore on, but the two lovers hardly noticed. The bark of a dog, laughter from the saloon, and raised voices from Main Street below didn't penetrate their world. They were lost in each other.

"Oatmeal cookies and lemonade," Alex said with a shake of his head. "A combination I would never associate with making love."

Jane brushed the oatmeal crumbs off the sheet that lay draped over her waist and took a drink of her lemonade before she spoke. "Gratifying and satisfying is the combination we sought, and I'd say the cookies and lemonade fit perfectly."

Alex, sitting comfortably propped against the pillows next to her, took a hearty swig of his lemonade and sighed appreciatively. "I agree wholeheartedly. Gratifying and satisfying is the perfect description."

Jane elbowed him in the side. "I meant the lemonade."

Alex snatched her glass from her hand and placed it along with his on the nightstand beside the bed. He turned to her and slipped his arm behind her back, slowly drawing her to him. "I didn't."

Jane threw her arms around him. "You're wickedly sinful, Alex."

"Compliments will get you exactly what you desire," he said and nuzzled at her neck.

"And what do you think I desire?" she queried softly, her flesh quivering from his teasing assault.

He pulled his head up and focused his eyes intently on hers. "Me. You desire me."

He issued a declaration, not a question, though Jane felt he expected an answer, and she gave one freely. "I desire you, Alex." She pulled his head down and stole a kiss.

He stole one back.

They teased. They tormented. They tempted one another as the night wore on, along with their lovemaking.

"It's so silent out there," Jane commented, resting comfortably back against Alex's bare chest while his robe they wore was tucked safely and securely around both their naked bodies.

Alex tightened his arm around her middle, holding her firmly, loving the feel of her cool skin against his warm flesh. "It's well past midnight. Time for Harmony to rest."

Jane sighed in contentment and pillowed her head against his chest, staring out the window at the darkness of the late night. "Sometimes when I can't sleep I sit in my rocking chair by my window and listen to the soothing sounds of the night."

Alex remained silent and strained to listen while his thoughts settled on Jane and her solitary life. Did she prefer living alone? "I don't hear anything," he said, though he wished he'd hear the answer to his silent question.

"Close your eyes and listen," she instructed in a whisper that was meant not to disturb the soft night symphony.

Alex followed her lead, closing her eyes and studying the sounds. His ears picked up toads croaking, insects buzzing, owls hooting, and the nearby river drifting lazily past town. They blended in harmony just like the town itself. "You're right. I can hear the sounds, and they are soothing."

"My grandfather taught me to listen carefully. He told me I would learn much more if I lent my ear willingly to life's lessons."

"You learned well and accomplished much. Your grandfather would have been proud of you."

She laughed and patted his arm that lay across her waist. "You didn't know my grandfather. He never thought medicine a proper profession for a woman. That's why I own the sewing shop. He assumed I'd settle down, find myself a husband, marry, and have children."

"But you didn't."

Jane stroked Alex's arm absentmindedly, her thoughts far from her actions. "Life seemed to interfere. With no doctor in Harmony the townsfolk sought me out when they took ill. Between the seamstress shop and tending to people, my time was limited."

"No socializing for you, I take it."

Jane grasped hold of his arm and hung on as though for support. "A severely limited social life."

Alex needed to probe deeper, find out answers to concerns that plagued him and to discover if she was ready to settle down, at least somewhat. "Won't your social life suffer even more now that you're helping Jacob and studying with him?"

Jane slid around in his arms, hugging his waist. "My social life is of little importance to me. Medicine is of the utmost importance to me."

Her answer stung his heart. Medicine was her first choice. A man was second, or perhaps he was relegated even farther down the line. He'd need to proceed cautiously with her, take one step at a time. He didn't want to frighten her away. He didn't want to lose her.

"It's late, we should get some sleep."

Jane rubbed softly against him. "Are you sure you want to sleep?"

Alex didn't say a word. He released the robe that wrapped around them. It slipped down along their bodies and nestled at their feet. He reached down, scooped her up in his arms, and walked to the bed while his mouth fed hungrily on hers.

Sunrise wasn't far off. It sat just on the horizon in preparation of its brilliant ascent. Jane stared out the window at the fine line of light that preceded the burst of light. She stood alone with her thoughts, her arms hugging her waist.

Tears threatened her eyes. She refused to allow them to fall, holding them back with sheer will and determination. She would not allow herself to cry or feel self-pity.

She turned and stared at Alex sleeping soundly in the bed. He lay tangled in the sheet, exhaustion having captured him only thirty minutes before. They had loved hard and long all night.

I want you, Jane.

Alex had whispered those words to her throughout the evening. She had waited, had hoped that he would say more. But he hadn't, and it was time for her to accept that he never would.

Her heart ached and a tear spilled from the corner of her one eye. "I love you," she whispered so softly she barely heard her own words.

Jane hurried and dressed, then collected her clothes and personal items, hastily shoving them into her satchel. She cast an anxious glance toward Alex before she walked out of the room and closed the door silently behind her.

Twenty

ALEX stirred, disentangling the sheet from around his legs and turning over to reach out beside him. His eyes flew open when his hands connected with an empty space.

He jolted up to a sitting position, the sheet falling completely away from his body as he pushed at it and jumped out of the bed. Ignoring his nakedness, he walked toward the closed door, his nostrils flaring as he tested the early morning air for signs of breakfast cooking downstairs.

No tempting smells drifted in the room, and as he reached for the door handle, his head turned sharply to the side, catching a glimpse of the wardrobe from the corner of his eye.

He rushed over, shoving wide the partially open door. He retreated back as though shocked at what he saw. No clothes lined the wooden pole. It was empty.

Alex stood staring at the blank space. He shook his head and stared more intently. After several minutes he walked over to where his clothes lay and slipped into his trousers and walked out of the room.

He slowly took the steps down to the kitchen and prepared himself a pot of coffee. Then he dumped himself into a seat at the table and rested his face in his hands.

Jane was gone. Her absence spoke loudly of her desire to retain her independence. She had probably not wanted to face him or the issue of her freedom this morning. Leaving before he woke settled it all rather nicely.

He stood and took a cup from the cupboard and poured himself some coffee. He glanced around the room, remembering the smell of frying bacon and biscuits fresh from the oven and pancakes that melted in his mouth. And a vivacious smile and stubborn manner that brightened and challenged his day.

He shut his eyes against the memories. He was going to miss her. Damn, but was he going to miss her.

Alex took his coffee and climbed the stairs, walking down the hall to his room and ignoring the door to Jane's room. He had work to do and decisions to make.

"Jane?" came the anxiously shouted query. "Jane, whatever are you doing here?" Maisie demanded, stepping out the back door of Jane's sewing shop and into her backyard.

"I live here," Jane said, not bothering to stand and greet Maisie. She was too busy on her hands and knees tending to her herb garden. She had neglected it of late, and the weeds had taken command of the patch.

Maisie shook her finger at her as though she were a naughty child. "I know you live here, but you are suppose to be tending to Alex, not your garden."

Jane leaned back on her haunches and brushed the excess dirt from her garden gloves. "Believe me, Maisie, when I tell you that Alex is more than capable of looking after himself. His arm and hand are completely healed. He doesn't need me."

Her words stung her. He certainly needed her the other night and had said so repeatedly. Those very words haunted her dreams night after night. How many times had she woken with a start? She had dreamed of his hands touching her, his lips kissing her, his body . . .

She shook away her thoughts and reached for a young plant beside her, tucking it into the earth a few inches away from its sister plant and shoving the rich dark dirt around it.

Maisie concentrated a moment, collecting her thoughts, and then spoke. "Shouldn't you be certain Alex is well enough to remain on his own?"

Jane had to smile while she patted the mound of earth around the plant. "There isn't a doubt in my mind to Alex's ability to care for himself."

Maisie persisted. "But, dear, you should at least remain the week as you had agreed to."

Jane couldn't have lasted one more day in Alex's home. If he had proclaimed his love for her, she would have gladly and happily stayed, but his silence concerning their relationship spoke clearly that he wasn't ready to establish a serious one.

Jane continued planting. "I agreed to stay if it was necessary. It is no longer necessary and it's time for me to get on with my studies."

Maisie frowned, not at all happy with the situation. "Alex may need you."

Jane looked up at her, shading her eyes from the afternoon sun. "He knows where to find me."

But he hadn't looked, and that had disturbed her, also. If he really cared for her, wouldn't he have come after her, declared his love, and asked her to marry him? He hadn't even acknowledged her absence. He hadn't even sought an explanation as to why she'd left.

"You should plant those closer together, makes for less weeding time," Maisie said, pointing at the young plants standing tall and proud.

Jane tempered her growing annoyance with Maisie's interference. After all, if it hadn't been for Maisie, she wouldn't be in this predicament with Alex. "Mint plants spread rapidly. In no time there'll be no space between them, and if I don't keep them trimmed, they'll take over my entire garden."

Maisie eyed the plants critically, squinting to take a closer look. "Mint plants do have a tendency to hog space."

"I'll save some cuttings for you if you'd like," Jane offered, attempting to change the subject.

Maisie smiled her appreciation. "That would be nice of you. But I still think you should reconsider your decision concerning Alex. Everyone in Harmony has been watching to see how well you nursed him, and it wouldn't look right you running out on him before you should."

Jane sighed wearily and dusted her glove-covered hands once again. "I didn't run out on him. He no longer requires my services."

"Still," Maisie cautioned with a shake of her finger. "You should check on him from time to time, just to be certain."

Agreement with Maisie was the only way to put an end to this chastisement. "A good suggestion. I'll do that."

Maisie smiled with satisfaction or victory, Jane couldn't be certain. Glad that her capitulation had produced her desired results, Maisie left. But not until she had discussed most thoroughly the recipe for apple mint preserves.

Jane rubbed her lower back, the ache making her uncomfortable. She couldn't expect her back not to suffer. Several hours bending over weeding and planting put a strain on the muscles, and she had been at her garden since before noontime.

She slowly unfolded herself, rubbed her back, and stood. She stretched and arched her back to ease the tense muscles. She had gardened to ease her mind, and now her back ached.

Better her back than her thoughts. Physical pain could be addressed and dealt with, mental pain didn't prove as easy to treat.

"Letting your thoughts get away from you, Jane," she warned herself quietly.

She bent down and placed her gardening tools in her basket. She removed her gloves and tossed them in with the tools, then hooked the basket on her arm. She stood once again and turned toward the door to the back of her shop.

"Hi, there," Samantha called out to her, swinging the back door open to join her outside.

Jane realized her problem. She kept no lock on the door to her private quarters behind and above the store. She had every intention of rectifying that problem before the end of the day.

As usual Samantha looked beautiful. Jane didn't think there was a dress style that didn't suit Samantha. No matter what the young woman wore, she looked terrific in it.

"Looking at another dress to have stitched?" Jane asked, hoping this little visit didn't concern her father.

Samantha grinned. "When can a woman not use a new dress?"

"I like your thought. Every woman should feel that way. I'd be much busier, not to mention richer."

Samantha agreed with a nod while her grin faded. When she spoke, it wasn't with a young woman's tone, but that of a daughter concerned with her father's welfare. "My father is completely healed?"

Jane placed her garden basket on the back porch and motioned Samantha to one of the two wooden rockers at the other end of the small porch.

Samantha sat down, relaxing in a gentle sway. Jane joined her in the rocker beside her, her own weight setting it in motion.

"Don't worry about your father," Jane said with a shake of her head and a laugh. "He can look after himself. He has a stubborn enough nature to do so."

Samantha's grin returned. "He does set his mind to

things at times, and Lord knows there's no changing it when he decides on a matter."

Jane sent her a teasing wink. "His mind can be swayed given the right approach."

"You've been good for my father, Jane."

Jane was startled by her declaration and puzzled. "Good for him?"

Samantha shook her head. "I worried about him after my marriage. We always had each other, and then he was suddenly alone. Then you came along and filled his days and nights."

"He needed tending."

"You gave him that and more." Samantha hesitated a moment. "I only wish it had lasted . . ." She stopped as though searching for an appropriate word. "Longer."

Jane sought a response but found herself speechless. She had the distinct feeling Samantha settled for the word *longer*.

Samantha stood, her smile having returned. "Heard you arranged some great games for the Fourth of July celebration."

Jane breathed easier now that the subject was changed. "I've planned games that will delight and challenge."

"Great combination," Samantha said. "A lot like yourself."

Jane thought her remark strange and was about to comment when Samantha gave her a quick peck on the cheek.

"I'm off before my hubby comes hunting me down," she said with a laugh and vanished through the door as fast as she had appeared.

Jane stood staring at the screen door that led to her kitchen. She touched her cheek, wondering over Samantha's display of affection.

"Enough," she told herself. She had supper to make and studies to see to. The past few days' strange events had best be put aside and forgotten.

She entered her kitchen, fresh and spotless from the recent scrubbing she had given it upon her return home. Newly stitched bright yellow curtains trimmed in white lace framed the window while on the sill beneath, lined neatly in a row, were potted herbs.

Fresh-cut daises filled the white ceramic pitcher on the table and were joined by a plate of oatmeal cookies and a tall pitcher of lemonade.

Jane froze and stared wide-eyed at the cookies and lemonade. She tore her gaze away and busied herself preparing supper. She didn't want to remember; remembering hurt too much.

She soon had a pan of biscuits in the cookstove and potatoes and eggs frying in a skillet on top. She added a few slices of onion to flavor the meal and set the table while the food finished up cooking.

In minutes she had the meal transferred to platters and was ready to take her seat at the table. She grabbed her chest, startled by what she had done without even realizing it. Looking over the table, she saw that she had set the meal for two. The food she had prepared was even measured with two in mind.

She dropped into her chair. Was it wishful thinking that caused her to set the table for two and cook for two? Had the last few days of eating alone made her realize she missed sharing a meal with someone?

Disagreeing with her own assumption, she shook her head and rubbed her face with her hand. "Not someone," she corrected herself. "You miss Alex."

She sighed and leaned back in her chair, grabbing a biscuit and picking at the soft dough to pop in her mouth. Admitting her loneliness for him relieved some of her tension. She had been fighting the fact that she had found her solitary life unsatisfying since her return home.

Her thoughts had often drifted back to her days and nights spent with Alex. Whether sharing in a conversation with him or relaxing in silence while he wrote his articles and she studied, they still had the company of each other. Shared and enjoyed company. She hadn't tired of him being around so much of the time. She had looked forward to being with him. She especially liked when she had been called out late at night to tend to a patient that he had insisted on accompanying her.

She had actually thought that he was different and would understand her penchant for medicine. But she supposed she was wrong and had only imagined his tolerance and acceptance of her profession, feeling obliged to her for nursing him in his time of need.

She stiffened her spine and sat forward. This melancholy had to stop. Feeling sorry for herself would get her nowhere. Though her stomach rumbled in protest of the amount of food she spooned onto her plate, she forced herself to eat. She needed to resume her former lifestyle, and the sooner the better.

After supper she would study the book on medicine Jacob had given her and make a list of questions to ask him concerning anything she didn't understand. She also had bolts of material and thread that needed ordering, and there was that unfinished dress she had been sewing for the Fourth of July celebration. She had much to do. Her life was full.

Jane shoved her plate away from her. "If my life is so full," she questioned, "then why do I feel so empty?"

Jacob's office was scrubbed from top to bottom. There wasn't a corner or crevice that hadn't seen Jane's cleaning cloth. The room smelled of fresh pine and fresh air, the windows having been shoved open and the curtains drawn back.

Busy hands made for a busy mind, Jane reminded herself as she wiped the shelves of the medicine cabinet down with hot sudsy water.

"You're going to wear yourself out, gal," Jacob said,

entering his office and taking in a brisk glance of the sparkling clean room.

"You, yourself, spoke to me on the benefits of keeping a sanitary office," Jane reminded him. "I'm only following your advice."

"You got me there. I did comment on recent developments in medicine on sanitary office and hospital conditions."

Jane paused in her work. "I'd love to visit a hospital one day and see for myself how it operates."

"Perhaps as your studies progress, we'll make arrangements to have you tour one so you can see firsthand the latest medical advances."

Jane grew excited. "I'd really like that, Jacob."

"We'll see what arrangements can be made." He nodded as though confirming his own suggestion.

"You know, Jane, I've found your lessons on herbal medicine most interesting. I have a few questions to ask you, and I thought you might be free for supper tonight."

The idea of not eating alone appealed to Jane, and she grinned at the prospect of sharing an informative conversation with Jacob over supper. "I'd like that."

"Wonderful. I'll be by your place around seven, and we can take a leisurely stroll to the hotel for supper."

Jane looked forward to his delightful suggestion. "I'll be waiting," she promised and turned to finish her task.

The afternoon summer breeze grew raucous, and the dry dirt from Main Street soon began to blow in the office. Jane worried that her hours of cleaning would be wasted, and she hurried to shut the windows. Unfortunately a gust of wind slipped in as she closed the last window, and a particle of dirt caught her suddenly in her eye.

Her hand jumped protectively to cover the afflicted area, and Jacob, noticing her distress, hurried over to her.

"Let me have a look," he said, coaxing her hand gently away from her face.

Jane berated her own bad timing. "My fault for not closing the windows sooner."

Jacob's touch was tender and professional. Jane couldn't help but think of the consequences if it had been Alex standing so close to her. His fingers wouldn't have only comforted her eye. His hand would have deftly trailed her face, her neck, her . . .

She chased her tormenting thoughts away.

"Easy now," Jacob said. "I'm going to see if I can wipe that tiny little speck right off your eye. So be still and relax."

Jane couldn't be anything else. Jacob reminded her of her grandfather. Kind and thoughtful and ever so considerate of his patients.

"That's it, nice and easy," he cajoled as his fingers used a piece of folded gauze to probe the area where the speck had adhered to the center of Jane's eye.

Jane stood still, standing directly beside him, their bodies a mere inches apart and his face close to hers as he studied her eye intently.

"That's it, easy. Let me in," he gently persuaded. With a tender and quick swipe Jacob captured the irritating intruder. "Ahh, but that was a sweet capture."

A rough cough from the doorway caused both their heads to turn sharply.

Alex stood, a solid, impregnable form in the doorway, his arms crossed firmly over his chest. His frowning brow and tight-set jaw clearly announced his annoyance, and his biting tone confirmed it. "Am I interrupting something?"

Twenty-one

"Not at all," Jacob assured him. "I was just tending to Jane, and quite successfully may I add."

"Really?" Alex drawled.

Jane wondered over his odd behavior. "I had something in my eye." She didn't understand herself why she offered him an explanation, but she did and her response irritated her.

Alex remained silent, looking from Jane to Jacob.

Jacob broke the tense silence as he walked to the waste bucket by his desk to discard the gauze. "Were you looking for medical advice or looking for Jane?"

The silence grew more tense as Alex stared directly at Jane.

Jane sensed his confusion—or was it her own confusion she sensed? She thought she saw a baffled look centered in his eyes, but she could have been mistaken. It could clearly have been irritation that set him on edge. Only she wasn't certain as to the irritant. Certainly it couldn't have been her? They no longer saw each other on a day-to-day basis, not even on an every now and then basis. In fact, she hadn't seen him at all since last they made love.

Her cheeks heated at the reminder, and she turn away to restore her composure.

Alex finally answered. "I've come to have my arm

looked at. It's been giving me a bit of pain on occasion." He appeared finished, but he had only paused as though in doubt that he should continue. "And I came to talk to Jane."

Jane whirled back around, her blue skirt whipping around her legs. Her cheeks glowed a soft pink, and a hesitant smile captured her face. Hope sprang inside her, and she tucked it back down, locking it away deeply, fearing disappointment.

"Let's have a look," Jacob said, waving his hand toward the examination table.

Alex followed his direction and hopped up on the table, unbuttoning his white shirt and slipping out of it.

Jane cast him an appreciative glance. His chest was just as she had remembered it. Muscled and full of strength, yet soft enough to pillow her head upon. Her cheeks pinkened to a rosy hue, and she turned her head away from the source of her embarrassment.

"Where's it hurt?" Jacob asked.

Alex pointed to his wrist. "Here mostly."

Jacob probed the area, his focus concentrated on his task. "Been doing a lot of work on the printing press?"

Alex answered him with a nod.

"More so than usual?"

"I've had more work than usual," Alex informed him.

"Overdoing it," Jacob announced, releasing Alex's arm. "Your arm needs to gradually accept the work it was accustomed to performing. Take it easy."

"Easier said than done," Alex said, reaching for his shirt beside him and shoving his arm into the sleeve.

Jacob spoke blatantly, though not sharply. "You want to disable yourself again?"

Alex's strong "No!" reverberated in the office. He hadn't cared for being so dependent on someone, though he missed her company, her smile, and the intimacy they had shared. He had decided he wanted her back. The problem being he wasn't certain how to go about getting her back or even if she was as inclined to a relationship as he was.

Jacob shook a finger at Alex, intending authority, yet he resembled a parent warning a naughty child. "Be careful."

Alex grinned. "Sure thing, Doc." His grin faded, and with a serious expression he said, "I'd like to talk to Jane alone."

Jacob looked to Jane, and seeing she made no move to protest, he quietly left the room.

Jane, with as much courage as she could muster, faced him directly.

Alex itched to walk over to her, grab her in a possessive hug, and kiss her soundly. Then, when she was thoroughly saturated by his kiss, he'd ask her why the devil she had left after they had made love.

Jane grew tired and nervous with the silence. "What did you want to see me about?"

Her cheeks were heated with a rosy flush. Was it the warm weather? The heat from the bucket of hot water beside her? Or had her body betrayed her and rushed the flaming patches to stain her cheeks?

The answer didn't matter to him. Her heated cheeks and moist lips were enough to set him in motion. In deliberate slowness he walked over to her. His stride had purpose and strength. His direct approach forced Jane to take several hasty steps back.

His hand moved swiftly, rising up to capture the back of her neck and draw her to him. His lips descended on hers.

Alex felt her body go limp as soon as he tasted her. He circled her waist and caught her up against him, offering his body as support. She melted against him, opening as his kiss grew more intimate, more demanding.

He traveled down to feast along her neck, wishing he could unbutton her blouse and close his fingers around her breast, teasing her nipple until it was a hard bud his mouth could enjoy.

Completely lost to his passion, he whispered, "Come home with me tonight, Jane."

Her body went rigid at his words. He silently cursed himself. He had handled the situation poorly. He had allowed his emotions to rule. Common sense was what he required now. He had repeatedly warned himself to proceed cautiously, and yet he went and jumped right into the thick of passion.

Jane eased back away from him, though she didn't go far. His hold remained firm, allowing her only a mere margin of distance. "Is that what you wished to speak to me about?"

He squeezed his eyes shut a brief second, as if regaining his common sense, then he gave his head a bare shake. "No, it wasn't."

She waited, expecting an explanation.

"There's so much I need to speak to you about." He paused, searching for the right words, fearing he'd repeat his mistake.

Jane intended to hear him out. She was anxious to hear what he had to say. She only hoped his words didn't hurt her. "You can talk to me here."

An adamant head shake informed her of his objection. "This will take time, and you appear to have tasks to finish. Please," he said softly and added a disarming smile. "Come to my place tonight."

She held her tongue, biting it to prevent herself from crying out *yes*! If she agreed and joined him at his place, they would do more than just talk—actually they probably wouldn't talk at all.

"That wouldn't be wise."

He traced her lips with his finger, lingering along the fine line that held them closed. "I promise I'll be a perfect gentleman."

Jane produced a smile so darkly sensual that it

caught Alex by surprise, as did her response. "But I can't promise I'll be a lady."

His passion soared, and with a low growl of desire he lowered his mouth to hers.

"Jane," Jacob called from the other room.

They broke apart instantly like two young kids caught in a naughty act.

Jacob entered the office, remaining in the doorway so as not to intrude. "Just wanted to check on the time I should pick you up tonight before I run off to see a patient."

Alex looked down at her, his brow raised.

She shrugged. The gesture was more for Alex's benefit than for Jacob. "Whatever is comfortable for you."

"Seven?"

"Fine with me," Jane informed him. "I'll be waiting."

Alex didn't care for the sound of her response. Her words were closer to what *he* wanted to hear from her, not what she was saying to another man.

Jacob nodded and left, the outer door closing softly behind him.

"Whose idea was supper?"

"Jacob's, not that it should concern you," she added. "I dine with whomever I choose."

Alex folded his arms across his chest and grinned. "You really think Jacob had a say in inviting you to supper?"

Jane grew irritated. "What are you implying, Alex?"

"You're intelligent, figure it out."

A protest almost slipped from her lips when his implication dawned on her. "Minnie!"

"Knew you had a quick mind," Alex said with what Jane sensed was pride.

Tapping her chin with her finger, Jane thought a moment, then shook her head. "But Jacob asked me, so how did Minnie have a hand in it?"

"Maisie had a hand in me coming here."

Jane shot him a surprised look.

"I complained about a pain in my wrist in her presence, and she got herself all upset saying that something might be wrong and my bones may not be healed after all and that I'd better get myself to *you*, not Jacob, so you could tend to me. She was so insistent that I found myself believing her."

"Was Minnie around when this conversation took place?"

Alex paused in thought and then nodded his head, his grin widening. "She sure was, though she didn't say a word. A mighty strange reaction for her."

"By any chance did this conversation take place this morning?"

"Right again," Alex assured her. "If I had given myself more time to think about the pain, I probably would have ignored it and never bothered to come here."

"Minnie didn't waste time; she was here this morning."

"Doing what?"

Jane threw her hands up in the air. "Can't say for sure. She and Jacob spoke for some time. I was busy scrubbing the office and paid them no mind."

"Bet she convinced Jacob to ask you out to supper."

"I wonder how she ever convinced him to do that?"

Alex cast her a strange look. "Why would Jacob need that much convincing?"

Jane placed her hands on her hips. "Why would Jacob want to take me out to supper?"

"You're intelligent, you're interesting to converse with, and you're attractive to look at."

Her eyes grew wide with each of his compliments until they looked about to burst from their sockets.

"You underestimate your charm and character, Jane."

He was serious. Dead serious. She still found the idea hard to comprehend. She had never received many compliments in her life, and it felt strange to hear them about herself.

Uncomfortable with his flattery, she switched the subject of the conversation. "Do you think Maisie and Minnie will ever give up this matchmaking contest?"

"Not until one of them tastes victory."

Jane shrugged. "Then they both have a long wait."

The finality of her response disturbed him, and he returned to his original reason for wishing to speak to her. "We need to talk."

"I'm really very busy at the moment," she said, not at all eager to speak with him.

Alex once again walked over to her, though his gait was less intense than before. He stopped in front of her, and she looked directly at him. "It's inevitable."

She froze at his words. What exactly did he mean?

"When you're ready, I'll be waiting." He leaned down, dusted her lips with a kiss, and left the office.

Jane stood staring at the empty space he left. Her legs were not solid—they trembled and she sought a nearby chair, collapsing into it.

His scent and that hint of lemon remained and drifted around her. She was reminded of him sitting on the examination table naked to his waist. She recalled their night together and how his hard muscles had pillowed her head comfortably and the warmth of his passion-heated flesh had warmed her to the core. Forever was how long she had wished to remain in his arms.

Whatever was she going to do? She certainly had a few decisions to make, and from the looks of matters it wasn't going to be easy, especially if she allowed her emotions, passion in particular, to rule.

Alex watched Jacob and Jane from a corner table, at the Hutton Hotel, that was partially sheltered by a large potted fern. Earlier in the evening he had pulled the large leafy plant closer to his table, affording him privacy, yet providing him with an overall view of the room.

Spying appeared the appropriate term for what he was about, though he refused to acknowledge the fact. He had convinced himself he was hungry for a decent home-cooked meal, and what better place than the hotel to get one?

Jane laughed, catching his attention. He frowned. Her laugh was musical, tinkling like tiny bells being played in a memorable melody.

"Damn," he muttered. He sounded like a man besotted with a woman. "Lord help me."

He glanced down at his plate and realized he had finished his dessert—fresh apple pie, two helpings, and not as good as Jane's—and he had drunk his fifth cup of coffee. He'd have no choice but to take his leave and soon, or he'd draw attention to himself for sure.

He watched Jacob lower his head nearer to Jane. She bent her head toward him, and they appeared to be whispering. They looked like lovers sharing intimate secrets.

"Damn," he swore again. He threw his white cloth napkin down on the table, added enough money to cover his bill, and stood. He'd had enough. He intended to talk to Jane and clear up this matter once and for all. And he intended to do it tonight.

He brushed the large leaves out of his way and quietly left the hotel so as not to be seen. He glanced up and down Main Street almost as though viewing the main thoroughfare for the first time. His eyes finally located his destination. He took a deep breath, stepped off the boardwalk, and headed toward his intended target. Jane's shop, You Sew and Sew.

"More and more the townsfolk are requesting your services as a doctor, not an assistant. I've heard many comments on your ability and knowledge. You're building a unique reputation," Jacob explained.

His compliments were hard to accept, but then, she had received far too many today to believe all of them. "You exaggerate, Jacob."

Jacob finished a sip of coffee and then shook his head. "Absolutely not. Why, just the other day Lillie Taylor commented on your extensive knowledge of herbs and how blended with modern medical techniques your skills lay far beyond the ordinary doctor."

"That's a mouthful," Jane said with a laugh.

"Not for Lillie Taylor," Jacob teased, and they both laughed together.

"Don't underestimate yourself, Jane."

She felt her heart flutter hearing Alex's statement repeated. "So I've been told."

Jacob cleared his throat, an indication that he was preparing the listener for a lecture. Jane had become aware of his little habits, having worked so closely with him. She was comfortable and familiar with them by now. She sat back in her chair, her teacup in hand, prepared to listen. She wasn't prepared for the subject matter.

"Jane, how do you feel about Alex?"

Jane almost dropped her teacup. She returned the delicate cup to the saucer, afraid her shaking hands would cause her to drop and shatter the china, along with her raw nerves, to pieces. "Whatever do you mean?"

Jacob smiled kindly. His expression reminded her of her grandfather when he had felt it necessary to discuss a delicate matter with her.

"I have the feeling that Alex means more to you than you care to admit."

Jane attempted levity, though her voice quivered. "Changing from physician to matchmaker?"

Jacob smiled and shook his head. "I'll leave matchmaking to the pros like Maisie and Minnie. I'm talking to you as a friend who would like to see you happy."

"I'm happy," Jane defended too quickly.

Jacob reached out and patted her hand like a parent reassuring a child. "Of course you are."

"I am," she reaffirmed, more to convince herself than Jacob.

"You're happy with your chosen work," he confirmed patiently.

"You know I am." Irritated, Jane shifted in her seat.

"You have a thriving business," he continued.

Jane didn't bother to respond, certain Jacob hadn't completely finished.

"How have you felt since returning to your shop?"

She sat forward prepared to deliver an immediate answer when she was suddenly hit with the realization that upon having returned home she had been miserable. The simple truth was that she missed Alex. She ached with loneliness for him, and the pleasurable moments they had shared. Their relationship had begun with a battle of wills and had transformed into one of compatibility.

"You hesitate," Jacob said, intruding on her thoughts. "Is your reluctance to answer because you have finally faced the question you have neglected to ask yourself?"

Jane sighed and her shoulders lumped. "I've been hiding from the truth."

"The truth being?"

This time Jane answered without hesitation, her own confession surprising herself. "I love Alex."

Jacob smiled so broadly that the wrinkles around his eyes deepened. "I was wondering how long it was going to take you to realize that."

She cast him a strange look. "You knew I loved him?"

"For some time. I was waiting, and none too patiently, mind you, for the realization to hit you."

"It hit me all right. I just didn't want to admit it."

"Why?" Jacob asked, concerned by Jane's sorrowful expression.

Jane wondered if she should trust Jacob. She didn't

want her fears making the rounds of the Harmony gossip vine tomorrow.

Jacob reached his hand out to her once again, his touch gentle on her arm. "I care about you, Jane. I want to see you happy, all the time."

Jane understood from the sincere look on Jacob's face that he would never betray her trust. He was a true friend. "I wonder," she began and stopped, unable to finish expressing herself. She worried that upon voicing her own doubts, she'd leave herself vulnerable to further hurt and disappointment.

Jacob patted her arm and in a fatherly tone urged her to continue. "What do you wonder? Tell me."

She wanted badly to tell someone how she felt. The hurt and uncertainty were tearing her apart emotionally. She needed a shoulder to cry on, and at that moment staring at Jacob and him reminding her so much of her grandfather that she allowed her last vestige of armor to slip away. She finally, with a sense of relief, laid bare her emotions. "I don't know if Alex feels toward me as I do toward him."

"Has he given you any indication that his feelings are mutual?"

Jane thought of lying in Alex's arms naked and him whispering how much he wanted her. *Wanting* someone was far different from loving someone. "Not exactly."

"Perhaps you misunderstood his intentions."

She couldn't stop a smile from surfacing. "His intentions were clear."

"Really?"

The impact of that one word jolted her. Had she misinterpreted Alex's intentions? Did he *want* more from her than she had assumed? Could he have wanted a relationship? Could he love her?

Jacob spoke with the wisdom and experience of his years. "Sometimes our misunderstandings or false assumptions prevent us from finding happiness."

"I suppose we stand in the way of ourselves."

Jacob laughed. "That's the truth. I've seen more people create their own obstacles and then complain about them being there."

She had created obstacles, insurmountable obstacles, or so she had thought. Now she had to remove them. The question was how?

Jacob yawned. "Excuse me. My advanced years are catching up to me."

Jane nudged his arm gently. "You just like people to think that, but I know the truth."

"Which is?" Jacob challenged in a teasing tone.

"You're full of more energy than anyone I know. I find it difficult keeping up with you."

Jacob lowered his tone so no one could hear him. "Need to keep up the image of the overworked doctor so I'll keep getting all those invites to dinner from the kind ladies of Harmony."

Jane laughed, having thoroughly enjoyed her evening with Jacob. For the first time in days she felt good, as though tomorrow had a purpose to it, and she looked forward to facing any and all challenges.

Jane stood. "The walk home in this warm night air should to us both good."

"A splendid suggestion." Jacob offered Jane his arm after standing. "Shall we go?"

Jane slipped her arm through his, and they strolled out of the hotel onto the boardwalk. They walked toward the depot, crossing the street just before they reached the building.

"Can't get over these colors," Jacob said. "Near blinded me they did, when I arrived here in Harmony."

"The colors have received mixed reactions."

"I'd say whoever mixed the colors had eye problems."

Jane's laughter rippled along on the warm night air.

They stopped at the back of Jane's sewing shop by the white fence that guarded her herb and flower garden.

"After I learn about the herbs' properties, I'm going to learn how to cultivate them," Jacob said seriously.

"I'll be glad to teach you what I know," Jane offered.

"I was counting on it."

Before Jacob could turn away, Jane leaned over to him and whispered, "Thank you." She followed her appreciation with a kiss to his cheek.

Jacob smiled. "You're welcome," he murmured back and kissed her cheek. With that he waved good night and strolled off across the street toward his office.

Jane swung open the gate, the rusty hinges squeaking in protest. With the walkway being so narrow and it being dark, she took cautious steps, fearing she'd step on and crush one of her plants.

A sudden movement in the darkness up ahead brought her to an abrupt halt. "Who's there?" she demanded with more bravado than she felt.

A rustle of movement caused her to retreat a step. "Who's there?" Her voice quivered, her legs trembled, and she silently cursed her own fear. She thought to turn and run, but her stubbornness took hold, reminding her that she knew almost everyone in Harmony.

Regaining her courage, though her bravery hadn't reached her shaking legs yet, she spoke. "I won't ask again who's there."

A sharp and perturbed voice sounded from the darkness. "You don't have to, but I sure in hell have a few questions for you."

Twenty-two

ALEX stepped out of the night shadows. He approached Jane in rapid strides, stopping only inches in front of her.

Jane stood firm and gave him no opportunity to speak. "What are you doing here at this hour?"

"Me?" Alex said, stunned.

"Yes, you." Jane poked him in his chest to emphasize her remark.

He grabbed her finger, squeezing it firmly. "What were you doing kissing Tanner?"

For a minute Jane seemed confused. She hadn't the slightest idea what he was talking about.

Alex watched her oddly. She couldn't deny that she and Tanner had kissed. He had witnessed it with his own eyes—dark as it was, he had seen them kissing.

Realization dawned on Jane, and she burst out laughing.

Alex moved his grip from her finger to her wrist, pulling her toward him. "You find this amusing?"

"Yes," she answered and laughed harder.

He jerked her up against him, silencing her laughter. "I don't find it the least bit amusing."

Jane found the situation delightfully comical, and his commanding manner failed to dispel her humor. "That's because you lack any sense." She couldn't contain the bubble of laughter that followed her remark.

"*I* lack sense?"

"Are you having a problem hearing, Alex? You keep repeating me." Her grin widened.

"Don't you dare laugh again," he warned, peering down into her face, his nose almost touching hers.

"And if I do?" she challenged, mirth already evident on her trembling lips.

He laughed. Then, low and lazy, he said, "I'll silence you."

She confronted his implied challenge. "How?"

His answer was to lower his lips to hers and capture them quickly in a breath-stealing kiss.

Jane loved the taste of him. His flavor, she was convinced, was a special blend. *Sensually addictive.* Once his essence was savored, no other would do. The taster was hooked, and Jane was definitely addicted.

Her fingers threaded up and into his hair while she sampled him with a hungry appetite.

He moved them both swiftly back into the night shadows. The darkness swallowed them up, surrounded them, and provided anonymity. Their intimate seclusion fired their passion, and Alex ran his hand down her back and over her backside.

She needed no urging; she moved into him.

"I've missed you," he growled like a hungry bear gone too long without his sweet honey. His followed hug was much like a bear's hug. Strong, solid, and entrapping.

Jane tilted her head to rest on his shoulder, providing him easy access to her slim neck. His lips were warm and wet and sent shivers through her.

Her little warning voice urged her to question what it was he missed. Was he only interested in her intimately? Or had his "I've missed you" meant more?

His hand resting on her waist moved to cup beneath her breast. The heat of his touch penetrated her cotton dress and scorched her senses, melting away the last vestiges of her doubts.

"Let me love you, Jane, please let me love you?"

She couldn't deny his plea. She needed to love him as much as he needed to love her. She only wished he meant it emotionally as well as physically. She whispered her consent. "Yes, Alex, I want you to love me."

Alex scooped her up into his arms, and after a couple of fumbled attempts to open the back door, he succeeded. Unfamiliar with Jane's home, he paused inside the kitchen and waited for directions.

"To the right."

Alex took the steps without any difficulty. She continued directing him down the short hallway to the last room on the right.

He entered her bedroom and glanced hastily around. His only light that of the full moon shining through the lace-curtain-covered windows, he spotted the bed. A big, wide brass bed dressed with a rose-flowered quilt that appeared excessly trimmed with ruffles while batches of matching pillows made themselves comfortable against the brass posts.

He dumped her and himself onto the bed and sprawled over her, afraid that if he released her she would flee from him.

He kissed her softly while his fingers worked at the small blue buttons on the front of her dress. "Later we'll talk."

"Yes, Alex," she agreed, her nimble fingers busy at the buttons of his shirt. "We must talk."

Their talk ceased and their hands worked skillfully, divesting each other of their clothing until, panting, they lay together. Alex remained resting on top of her.

Jane cupped Alex's face in her hands, and with a pleading gentleness she said, "Love me."

His whispered response startled her. "Without a doubt." She had no time to question his reply, for he took her nipple into his mouth and caused her to lose all rational thought.

With each touch, taste, stroke, all sane reasoning vanished and left her completely under his control. Her mind, her body, her soul was his. It couldn't be any other way. She loved him.

Exhaustion claimed Jane only minutes after they had made love. She lay with her head on Alex's chest and her left leg sprawled over his legs. Her arm was draped across his waist as though she had him completely captured, and she did.

Alex stroked his hand up and down her arm. He wanted to think that their lovemaking had been so satisfyingly exhausting that Jane couldn't help but sleep. But his common sense told him that her deep slumber had been brought on by a combination of her long day.

He had hoped to speak with her, and he had been pleased that her eagerness to talk matched his. She had attempted a few words, babbled as they were. He had managed to understand her rambling and deciphered it to mean that the kiss she and Tanner had shared had been one of friendship. Alex had been about to argue the point when she had nestled comfortably against him and immediately drifted off to sleep.

Looking back on the episode, he admitted she could have been telling the truth. She and Tanner had shared but a brief exchange, certainly not one long enough for a meaningful kiss. At the time Alex hadn't considered that possibility. His only thoughts had been murderous toward the man who had dared to kiss *his* Jane.

His Jane. She belonged to him, plain and simple. He didn't know exactly when she had become such an important and essential part of his life, but she had, and he couldn't, wouldn't, and had no intentions of living the rest of his life without her beside him. She would have to marry him, and that's all there was to that. He had given the matter thought. He paused in his musings and smiled. Actually the last ten minutes was how long it had taken him to reach his conclusion, but he assured himself it was a valid conclusion and the simplest and most logical.

Jane would respond well to logic, and when he explained that they had no choice but to marry since they had already shared the intimacy of a married couple, she would most certainly agree.

Horse shit!

Alex shut his eyes against the voice that retaliated in his head. Why, when he thought he had everything figured out, did that tormenting little voice intrude?

Think about it, the voice urged, and Alex opened his eyes and gazed at the ceiling above.

All her life Jane had felt different from the other women—and why? Because she had chosen a field of interest that wasn't acceptable for a woman. Even though she owned and operated the seamstress shop, everyone was still aware that she preferred to be stitching up a wound instead of a dress. She had never really conformed to society's standards, so why in heaven's name did he think she would now?

He moaned softly and Jane stirred. He settled her with a tender stroke, and she resumed her peaceful slumber.

Lord, but how he wanted her to be his wife. He liked having her sleep in his arms, and he had missed sharing his meals with her. He just found life too dull and boring without her. He even missed her pots of herbs growing in his kitchen. They had given the room warmth and life. Now his kitchen looked barren, and he hated taking his meals there alone.

He needed to talk with Jane. He needed to tell her how he felt about her and how he felt about her work. She had to understand that he'd be supportive of her no matter what role she chose to take. She had to understand how very much he loved her.

"Jane! Jane!" came the excited voice from downstairs.

Jane jumped up, flying out of Alex's arms.

"Who's there?" she called back, disoriented from being so abruptly wakened from her sleep.

"Jane, it's me—Jacob."

"What's wrong?" she called out, reaching for her cotton robe on the vanity bench and sending Alex a wide-eyed look.

"A couple of cowhands passing through town got into a knife fight. They need some serious stitching."

She hurried over to the bedroom door and took a step out into the hall. "I'll be over to your office in a few minutes."

"Fine, but hurry. One man is hurt bad, and I don't know if we'll be able to save him."

She heard her downstairs door slam shut and rushed back into the room, slipping out of her robe while she picked up her discarded clothes to put back on.

She wasn't certain what to say to the man in her bedroom. She suddenly found herself feeling self-conscious. Why, she wasn't certain. His name quivered off her lips. "Alex?"

Alex slipped out of bed and walked up to her.

His nakedness didn't help matters. It heightened her awareness of his masculinity and all they had shared only a few short hours ago. And her body responded instantly to the sight of him and their recalled lovemaking.

He stopped in front of her and adjusted her blouse on her arm, then began buttoning the small row of buttons that ran down the front. "You'd better hurry. It sounds like Tanner and that man need your skill with a needle."

She stared at him.

He kissed her.

She continued to stare at him as he finished buttoning her buttons. "I'll leave here nice and quiet so no one sees me, then I'll stop by Tanner's office in a couple of hours to see how you're doing."

"Alex?" She questioned again, uncertain how to react

to his strange actions. He was actually being understanding, completely understanding.

"Later," he said more seriously and cupped her chin in his hand. "We'll talk."

"Yes, please," she said softly, nodding her head. "We must talk."

He kissed her again briefly, skimming her lips still swollen and sensitive from his earlier ardent kisses. The reminder that he had possessed her so thoroughly set his passion on edge.

"Go," he ordered. He turned her around and pointed her toward the door. Not wanting her to see his aroused desire for her, he whipped his trousers from the floor and hurried into them just as she reached the door and turned back around.

"I will see you later?" she asked, her voice sounding doubtful.

"Promise," he said.

Jane disappeared down the hall, and in only a few seconds Alex heard the door slam shut. He breathed a sigh of relief and dropped down onto the bed.

He sighed heavily like a man weighted down with problems. He hadn't wanted her to run off. He wanted her there with him, in his arms until morning. But emergencies were common in her profession, and he would have to learn to accept them, no matter how difficult.

Time would also prove another obstacle for them. There either wasn't enough time, or they couldn't coordinate their time satisfactorily. They were in a sense forever running opposite of each other. That was why it was imperative that they marry. At least then there would always be a home base for them both to return to. A place where they could share and love.

He bent over and snatched his shirt off the floor. He'd returned home, wash up, shave, and then get over to Tanner's. He and Jane needed to talk, and it couldn't wait any longer.

Twenty-three

"Jane's busy," Minnie said, standing in the doorway of Tanner's office with her arms folded solidly over her chest. She appeared an immovable force. Nobody but nobody was about to get past her.

"That's what you told me two hours ago," Alex said, trying to remain polite while thinking that nothing would please him more than to wring her neck. "And two hours before that and—"

"She's tending a patient." Her reply was curt and sounded as though she thought an explanation unnecessary.

"She's still with the man who was knifed?" Alex sounded concerned since that was hours ago, and he worried she'd be tired from him keeping her up most of the night. He didn't like to think of her exhausting herself, especially when he was to blame.

Minnie shook her head. "One man's recovering, thanks to Jane's skill with a needle. The other man didn't make it. Knife wound hit a vital organ, Jacob says."

Alex nodded, then looked Minnie straight in the eye. "Then who is she tending?"

"Slew of folks," Minnie said. "Things got backed up while she and Jacob—they work so well together—tended to the two men."

Alex ached to push her aside and march into the of-

236

fice to make certain Jane was all right. All things considered, his actions would prove opposite of what he wanted Jane to realize—that he supported her work. If she were his wife, the situation would be different. He'd have been in there this morning checking on her and then repeatedly throughout the day, and no one would have thought anything of it.

He was more determined than ever to settle this situation between them once and for all.

"Tell Jane I'll see her after supper," he said to Minnie, and not waiting for a response, he turned and walked away.

"Minnie," Jane called from the inside office and peeked her head out. "Has Alex stopped by?"

"Yes, a short time ago," she answered with a sweet smile. "He said he'd see you after supper."

With a wrinkle of her brow being her only response, Jane returned to her duties. She sat in the chair at the desk and proceeded to write the report on both knife wound victims while Jacob saw to a rash on an elderly gentleman's arm who had been passing through town.

Jacob had been adamant about keeping records on all cases. He explained how they provided excellent sources of material for future cases. Jane agreed and saw to it that a file was prepared on anyone who was treated.

She glanced down at the desk, and Alex's file caught her eye. He had told her he would stop by earlier, and yet he hadn't stopped by until later afternoon. She wondered if his work had prevented him from coming by or if he really hadn't been interested enough to do so.

She didn't want to jump to conclusions or assume wrongly about his actions—or, in this case, inaction. She supposed she was measuring all he did on a scale of whether he loved her or not. If he loved her, she reasoned, he would have made a point of coming to the office this morning as he'd said he would. If he didn't love her, then he would have stopped by anytime it was convenient for him.

She doodled circles on the corner of the paper while her mind wandered. She wanted so much to believe he loved her as much as she loved him, but then, that was probably asking too much.

If he loved her a little, that would be all right.

No, it wouldn't.

She rolled her eyes heavenward. She wished that voice would mind its own business. But then, it was.

Who was she kidding? She wanted Alex to love her as deeply as she loved him. Nothing less would do. She had waited far too long to love, and she wanted it all. A man who loved her breathlessly, right down to her very soul. That's what she wanted from Alex.

But could he give her that?

That was the question at large and the one that tormented her on a regular basis.

Tonight. She'd talk with him tonight and finally settle these nagging doubts.

"Jane," Jacob called to her. "Bring me the golden seal powder. It helps to heal sores, right?"

Jane nodded while reaching for the jar of golden seal powder. She brushed her musings aside and set back to work, looking forward to this evening.

Maisie waltzed into the *Sentinel* as Billy hurried out. Alex had to keep his smile in check when Billy hesitated at the window and sent him a sympathetic smile followed by a exaggerated wave goodbye. The young devil was informing Alex that he was glad to have made his escape before Maisie arrived.

Maisie looked her cool, confident self, and as usual, her attire was impeccable. Her pale gray day dress was perfectly pressed and fit her aging figure well. She looked the exemplary lady. She also looked determined.

Alex stood and walked around to the front of his desk. "What can I do for you, Maisie?"

"I want to know what you are doing here," she asked in a no-nonsense tone.

He glanced around the office before focusing a smile on her. "I work here."

"Aren't you the least bit interested in how Jane is faring over at Jacob's?"

He'd had enough problems with one twin today. He had no intentions of dueling with the other. "I've stopped by several times, but she's been busy."

"Who says so?" she demanded, her expression warning him that she had a good idea who it was and wanted verification.

For a brief moment he thought not to answer, but her name slipped out. "Minnie."

Maisie wagged her finger at him. "Minnie's too busy minding everyone else's business."

Alex attempted to calm her down, but Maisie went right on as if she didn't hear.

"When she sets her mind to something, there's no changing it. And when she thinks she's right"—Maisie flung her hands up into the air dramatically—"there's no living with her. I sometimes wonder how we could ever be twins."

Alex's brow shot up.

Maisie paid him no mind and continued talking. "According to her, she does everything right. She's the best cook. The best with a sewing needle. Why, you'd think she was perfect at everything."

Maisie suddenly smiled with glee and clapped her hands together. "But this year I'm going to prove her wrong. I," she said with a thump to her chest, "am going to win the jelly contest at the Fourth of July celebration."

Alex was afraid this tirade of hers would never end and interrupted with a suggestion that he was certain would draw her attention. "Why, then, I'd have to write a special article about you and your prizewinning jelly for the *Sentinel*."

Maisie squared her shoulders and lifted her chin. "I'd be delighted to give you an interview for the paper, Alex."

"My pleasure, ma'am."

"But enough about me," she said, realizing she had veered off track and needed to hop back on. "How are things between you and Jane?"

"Things?"

Maisie lowered her voice to a whisper. "You know what I mean." She searched for the correct choice of words so as not to offend. She hesitated, then shrugged and asked, "Are you and Jane courting?"

Alex smiled. They had never gotten near a courting stage. They had leaped right to intimate. "I don't know about courting."

Maisie looked stricken. "You don't want to court her?"

"I wouldn't mind," he admitted, not wanting the truth to get out and have Jane's reputation ruined.

"Then get busy. What are you waiting for?" she demanded. "Have you asked her to the Fourth of July celebration? It's only a few days away."

Alex had given the idea consideration, but he wanted to talk to her first. Then just maybe he could make an announcement at the celebration. "I've been thinking on it."

"Well, quit thinking and get moving."

Alex bit back his laughing smile. "I'll do that, Maisie."

"Good. I'll be keeping an eye on you." She attempted to sound threatening.

It didn't work on Alex, but he pacified her. "Yes, ma'am."

"Ask her today," Maisie continued. "She may get snatched up before you know it."

She sent his thoughts to churning. The idea that someone else would ask her to the celebration hadn't crossed his mind. Who else would ask her?

PLAYING CUPID

As though reading his thoughts, Maisie answered his unspoken question. "Jacob is new to the area. If he asks her to go, Jane may feel obligated to accept since she works for him."

Damn, but she had a sensible thought there. He'd have to talk with Jane right after supper, and by tonight everything would be settled.

He gave Maisie a wink. "Don't worry. As far as I'm concerned, we've got this matchmaking game won."

She held her hand out to Alex and smiled triumphantly.

"Another piece of blueberry pie, Alex?" Minnie asked, resting the silver server beneath the sliced piece in the pie tin.

Alex glanced at Jane, who appeared so weary her eyes drifted closed from time to time. He had arrived at Jane's house thirty minutes ago to find Minnie enjoying coffee and blueberry pie with Jane. "Couldn't eat another piece."

"Only two pieces?" Minnie asked sweetly. "Why, Jacob polished off three in no time."

Alex sent Jane a questioning look.

Her chin rested in the palm of her hand, her elbow sat propped on the table, and her eyelids were struggling to remain open.

Minnie settled the matter. "I fixed supper for Jane and Jacob. They were both so bone-tired from their long day. Jacob left a few minutes before you arrived. He needs rest, just like Jane does."

Alex could have sworn Minnie was dismissing him and doing so in a way that would make him feel guilty if he didn't leave.

"Alex and I need to talk," Jane said, attempting to fight off her exhaustion.

Alex smiled at her fortitude, though her body announced to all that she was just about out of steam.

"Isn't that right, Alex?" Jane said, seeking his support.

"That's right," Alex said, wondering how Minnie would battle the both of them.

Minnie stood.

For a brief second Alex thought he tasted victory until she spoke.

"You two go right on and talk. I'll just clean these dishes up for Jane so she can get herself right off to bed after you both are finished discussing whatever it is that needs discussing."

Jane for all her weariness took charge of the situation. "That's very thoughtful of you—"

"I don't mind at all," Minnie said, ready to set to work.

"But not necessary."

Minnie stopped in mid-stride, her hand about to snatch away the tin pie plate. "You're tired. You need help."

"I can help her," Alex offered.

Minnie laughed heartily. "You're a man."

"Who raised a little girl all on his own."

Jane slipped her hand over her mouth to hide her smile.

"Don't worry," Alex assured a stunned Minnie. "I can do dishes without breaking a one."

Minnie eyed him critically. "Never met a man that could do a dish and not break one."

Alex patted his chest proudly. "You've just met one."

"You've done more than enough for me, Minnie, and I truly appreciate your generosity." Jane didn't want to hurt Minnie's feelings, but she wanted to be alone with Alex to talk. Her body had already sent her enough signals warning her she wouldn't last long. Soon enough sleep would claim her where she sat, and she didn't want to wait another day to settle things between them.

"Don't your boarders need you?" Alex asked, hoping the idea that someone else required her help would send her home.

"Maisie's seeing to them," she informed him.

He wondered how Maisie felt about Minnie being

here and plying her matchmaking skills. Unless Maisie didn't know.

Alex practically jumped out of his seat. "I'll be right back. I forgot something." He was gone in a flash to the surprise of Minnie and Jane.

Jane yawned wide and long.

"Lord, child, you're plum exhausted," Minnie said sincerely.

That she was. Having had only a couple of hours sleep the night before, the taxing hours of surgery and a heavy patient workload that day had managed to take its toll. As much as she wanted to speak with Alex, she feared she'd never keep her eyes open long enough to do so.

Alex popped back into the kitchen with a wide smile and took his seat. He said nothing, but continued to smile at each woman.

Seconds later Maisie appeared at the screen door, swinging it open and marching in.

Jane leaned back in her chair and returned Alex's smile. She now understood where his hasty errand had taken him.

"Sorry for not knocking, but I have my hands full over at the boardinghouse," Maisie said, directing her annoyance at her sister.

"What in heaven's name is wrong now?" Minnie complained.

"Dumplings like rubber, meat burned to a crisp—"

"I left you specific instructions for that recipe," Minnie argued, sending her sister a chilling look.

"Specific? You call that handwriting of yours specific? I call it worse than chicken scratch."

Minnie retaliated. "It is certainly more legible than your minuscule penmanship."

"My letters may be small, but they're clearly written."

"And who may I remind you won the penmanship award at school two years in a row?"

Maisie shrugged as if the award meant nothing. "You had no difficult competition but me, and if you recall,

I became ill and couldn't participate. Therefore, you had no real competition."

Jane's eyes beseeched Alex to intervene.

He had had enough himself. Never had he known two sisters, twins to boot, who could disagree so much. "Ladies, why don't you both see to your boarders and I'll see to Jane."

"Good idea," Maisie agreed and received a murderous glare from Minnie, as did Alex.

Minnie fought like a trooper bent on victory. "Jane is extremely tired. She may need assistance retiring."

Alex almost blurted out that he'd see to that, too, but he tightened his lips and let Jane handle the response.

"That's gracious of you, Minnie, but I'll be fine. I think your sister requires your help more than I do."

"Maisie always did need my help even when she was little," Minnie complained. "I'm the older, you know, by a full ten minutes, and she always relied on me to take care of things."

"I most certainly did not," Maisie protested.

"She doesn't remember things, either. She's always recalling our childhood differently than it actually was, but then, I suppose a *younger* twin sister is like that."

"Ladies, your boarders are waiting," Alex reminded them before their verbal squabble developed into a full-blown war.

Minnie hesitated until they heard a loud crash from the boardinghouse next door. "You left the kitchen unattended?"

"I came looking for you. The kitchen was just fine and empty when I left," Maisie insisted.

"Well, it isn't now and if anything has happened to . . ."

Minnie's voice trailed off as she and Maisie hurried next door.

Jane sighed in relief. "I thought they'd be here forever."

"Not a chance," Alex said. He stood, walked over to her, and bent down beside her. "You're tired."

"We need to talk," she said, stifling a yawn that fought to surface.

He wanted nothing more than to do just that, but from the fatigued look in her eyes and the droop of her shoulders, she was in no condition to discuss such an important matter. He wanted her wide-eyed and alert and fully conscious when he declared his love for her, not half asleep.

Jane laid her head on his shoulder. He made a perfect pillow. She reasoned she'd rest her head but a few minutes. Once rejuvenated, she would be able to talk with him.

"A few minutes . . ."

Those were the only words Alex heard before Jane's head collapsed on his shoulder. He waited. Her head didn't stir. Her body didn't move, and her breathing took on a low and steady rhythm.

Jane was fast asleep.

Alex felt disappointed, although his concern for Jane outweighed his regret for not being able to conclude matters tonight. There was tomorrow. If the weather held, it would be hot and sunny. A beautiful day to tell a beautiful woman he loved her.

He gently scooped Jane up into his arms and carried her upstairs to her bedroom. In minutes he had her settled, having opened a few buttons of her dress. He didn't think it would be proper if he undressed her, though he itched to do so.

The night was warm, so he refrained from covering her with a blanket. He kissed her lightly on her soft, warm lips. Their taste hinted of sweet and juicy blueberries. A sudden urge swept over him. He couldn't control it. He had waited all day.

Softly he whispered against her lips. "I love you, Jane Carson."

Twenty-four

"WHAT do you mean, Jane's not here?" Alex asked, attempting to keep his temper from exploding.

"She's over at the church. A passel of folks are setting up for the big Fourth of July celebration," Jacob informed him. He rolled his chair back away from his desk and stood, stretching his shoulders back. "Paperwork is boring and time-consuming." Thinking on his remark, Jacob smiled and amended his comment. "Unless you like paperwork."

Alex hadn't taken his remark as an insult. He was too busy being annoyed at Jane. All day he had attempted to speak with her, but she had been too busy either tending a patient, stitching a dress, or preparing an herbal blend, and now she was busy helping set up for the Fourth of July celebration.

"When is she due back here?" Alex asked.

Jacob shook his head, taking time to work the tense muscles from his neck. "She's not due back here today. She has too much work to do for the celebration. Besides, we haven't been that busy. Patient visits have been light today."

Alex fumed silently. *Finally she's not busy with patients, so where is she? Organizing the Fourth of July get-together. What about him?* She had been adamant about them talking—and now? She had practically ignored him all day.

"Thanks, Tanner," he said abruptly and turned, heading out the door and across the street in the direction of the church.

White. The church was painted the only damn sensible color in all of Harmony. He shook his head, though he wasn't sure at what. The white church or his annoyance at Jane.

He approached a large open area just past the right of the church. The grass was thick and smelled fresh from being cut recently. Several large maple trees offered shade from the heat, and a wide-open treeless area invited the perfect setting for games and a place to dance later in the evening.

Everyone in Harmony was filled with anticipation over the approaching event. The whole town was expected to turn out for the games, food, dancing, contests, and excitement. There wasn't a soul in Harmony who didn't plan to attend. Even the weather was expected to remain warm and clear with not a cloud or thunderstorm in sight. A light breeze blowing down from the north added an extra comfort to the outdoors. Everything, but everything appeared perfect for the day ... except ...

Alex stopped, spotting Jane with Billy. They were busy measuring their steps in a squared-off area. Her smile was radiant, her gaze intent on her precise steps. She held her pale blue skirt up, giving a clear view of her ankle-high boots and the white eyelet trim of her petticoat. He immediately recalled her slender calves and how they felt snuggled against his own legs, and his temper flared anew.

He missed her, damn it. With that thought in mind he approached her. "Jane!" he shouted, startling her.

She glanced up, halting in her tracks. Her smile widened, happy to see him. Before she could tell him so, his angry words jumped out at her.

"Where have you been? So busy *tending* to everyone else you don't have time for me?"

Billy took himself off without a word.

Jane stared at Alex as if he had suddenly grown horns and turned into the devil himself.

"Well? I'm waiting for an answer." He folded his arms across his chest and stood in a manner that assured her he intended an immediate explanation.

Jane, having found the long day too busy to be believable, stood speechless.

"I'm waiting," he repeated tersely.

Her own temper flared with his repeated demand. "So you are."

Alex dropped his arms to his sides. "Do I get a reasonable answer?"

Her hands went to her hips. "Only if you ask a reasonable question."

"Reasonable?" he asked in a raised voice. "You call spending all your time taking care of everyone else's business but your own reasonable?"

She couldn't believe her ears. How could she ever think him understanding? "I have obligations."

"To everyone but yourself," he accused.

She attempted to defend herself, but he proceeded to vent his anger.

"We were supposed to talk. *You* had insisted. You made me think it was important. But evidently it wasn't. Your work and"—he paused and made a sweeping gesture with his hand—"all your other commitments appear to hold a higher priority for you."

"I didn't know you kept a list of my activities."

"A necessity if one wants to locate you."

"I'm not hard to find."

He threw his hands up. "Not hard to find? Not only are you difficult to locate, you're difficult to talk to."

"I am not," she insisted, annoyed at his accusing and unfair remarks.

"You either don't have time or you're too tired."

"I'm busy."

"Like now? You must, at this very minute, arrange for the games?"

She had intended to get all her tasks out of the way so they would have time alone together this evening, and then finally they would be able to talk, but she wasn't about to admit that to him now. "Yes," she said with a defiant challenge.

Alex allowed his anger to rule. "Then I suppose we have nothing further to say to each other."

Jane felt a sudden jump of her heart. Had she misjudged him so badly? Where was the understanding and considerate man she had come to know? Her own anger took control. "Not if you intend to be pigheaded about it."

"Pigheaded?"

"There you go with that hearing problem again."

Alex raised a pointed finger at her.

Before he could add words to his chastising action, Jane spoke. "When you come to your senses, then come talk to me." With her ultimatum delivered, she marched off past the church and disappeared from his view before he could gather his senses enough to respond.

Maisie paced back and forth in Jane's kitchen, a jar of jelly in each hand. "Blueberry or raspberry? I'm not sure which one to enter in the contest."

Jane was busy mixing a batch of oatmeal cookie dough. She stilled the wooden spoon thick with dough and cast a glance at the two jars.

Maisie straightened her posture and held the two jars out in front of her for Jane's inspection.

Jane looked from one to the other, took a moment to consider, and announced, "Raspberry. You make the best raspberry jam I've ever tasted, and besides, most of the other women will be entering blueberry jam."

Maisie beamed with pride. "I was thinking the same thing myself. I'll be different and enter my raspberry."

Jane nodded and returned to her mixing. She had set herself to work since arguing with Alex two hours ago. Fresh-laundered clothes hung on the clothesline out back, the gentle breeze drying them. She had weeded her herb garden and had cut a portion of dill to add to her potato-and-ham meal for supper. Then she had set to baking a big batch of cookies to wrap for the celebration.

She had assumed the work would keep her troubled thoughts at bay. It hadn't.

Maisie placed her jam jars on the table. "What's the matter, Jane?"

Jane sighed and released the spoon to fall to the side of the bowl while she wiped her hands on her blue gingham apron. "I've had a disagreement with Alex."

"Yes, dear, I know," she said sympathetically.

"You know?"

"Of course, the whole town heard about it."

Jane was about to ask how when she realized they had argued publicly with enough townsfolk present to hear it. Lord, what must everyone think of them?

Maisie attempted to reassure her. "Most folk are familiar with Alex's rare show of temper. They realize that only a matter of dire importance could set him on edge like that."

Jane looked at her startled. "You feel that he reacted so strongly because the matter was important to him?"

"Naturally." Maisie scooped up her jars of jam. "Alex cares very much for you, Jane. I think you both should settle this matter once and for all and quit behaving like children."

Jane looked even more stunned than before.

"Really, dear, my matchmaking skills are much better than my sister's, and the moment I saw you and Alex together, I knew you both were made for each other. Now, for pity's sake, admit it and let's have another wedding celebration in Harmony."

Jane couldn't find her voice. She sat silently staring at Maisie.

"Do you want my advice?"

Jane nodded, not believing she did so, but then she didn't believe that much of what had been happening to her lately would ever happen.

"Give Alex time to cool down. He'll come to his senses and apologize. Then quick as you can, get him to propose to you."

Jane nodded again, though she didn't know why.

"Wear your prettiest dress and your most charming smile, and he'll melt under your spell," Maisie predicted with a delirious grin. "Romance! It's positively wonderful."

Jane nodded again and continued bobbing her head as she walked Maisie to the door and saw her out. She finally stopped nodding after she had closed the screen door behind her and thought about Maisie's advice.

She wanted Alex to propose to her, but because he loved her and wanted to share the rest of his life with her, not because he was taken in by her charm. She didn't possess any charm anyway. She was straightforward and to the point. She possessed an independent nature and didn't at all like being told what to do. She loved medicine and the crazy hours she kept while looking after people. She wasn't your normal everyday woman. And unless Alex realized that, there was no point in him proposing to her.

She returned to the cookie dough and stabbed the spoon in and out of the thick mixture. Why and how had the matter gotten so complicated? Either Alex loved her or he didn't, and if he didn't love her, then it was time to bring their relationship to an end. She would not steal away to be with him. They would marry or terminate their brief affair. She would not become the talk of Harmony; she imagined enough people were talking about them already.

Above all she would not jeopardize her chance to practice medicine. She had waited too long for the opportunity. As she once thought, the man who loved her would have to be mighty special. She had thought Alex special. She hoped and prayed with all her heart that she hadn't been mistaken.

Alex slammed the pot down on the cookstove. The blackened meat stuck to the charred bottom. "Damn," he mumbled.

He shook his head with disgust at the uneatable food and walked out of the room and upstairs. He entered the parlor and went to the cabinet that held his whiskey and cigars. After pouring himself a full glass of liquor and lighting up a cheroot, he took both and retired to the chair by the window.

The sun had just set, and Harmony was getting ready to settle down for the night. He sipped at the fiery liquid, relishing in the way it slipped smoothly down his throat and heated his belly. He drew deeply on the cigar, closing his eyes and exhaling the smoke. He sat in silence, listening to the sounds of the night outside his window.

He opened his eyes and without thought cast a glance to Jane's shop. A light shone in her upstairs window. He recalled her bedroom at the end of the hall, her large bed, the softness of her mattress, the feel of her legs wrapped with his and the pleasure of her naked body resting comfortably next to his.

"Damn," he muttered and took another gulp of the whiskey.

He'd been more than dumb this afternoon when he had attacked her for ignoring him. He had allowed his jealousy to rule, when he had warned himself repeatedly that Jane was different and needed to be treated differently.

PLAYING CUPID 253

Besides, he liked her just the way she was, independent and stubborn. She was interesting and enjoyable to be with, and he didn't want her any other way. He loved Jane, and his accusations had been stupid and uncalled for, and he had made a complete ass of himself.

"So now what do you do, Evans?"

He didn't receive an answer. That little voice that had so loved to offer advice was silent. He wondered if it had stubbornly remained so, thinking that since Alex had so brilliantly gotten himself into this mess, he could certainly find a way out of it himself.

Serves you right.

"Sure," Alex said. "When I need you, you desert me."

He took another swallow of the whiskey and another puff of the cigar. Leaning his head back, he exhaled the smoke toward the ceiling. Why had he been so utterly stupid?

Love.

No other explanation would do. He acted like a fool because he was helplessly in love. But he hadn't had a chance to declare his love for Jane, and of course that nagging doubt still plagued him. Did she love him?

He shook his head, denying his own query. She loved him. He could feel it. Feel it in the way her body responded to his touch, the way she sought him out to discuss a problem, the way she melted in his arms and comfortably went to sleep, the way she relied on him to tend to her from time to time. No, she loved. He finally had no doubt about that.

Then what doubt nagged at him? Was she prepared to give up her independent ways and settle into married life with him?

Idiot, the little voice berated.

Sudden realization hit him, and he bolted straight up in his seat, reaching over to the crystal ashtray and crushing out his cigar. He gulped down the last of the whiskey, appreciating its potent flavor as it ran down his insides. He set the empty glass next to the ashtray and rubbed his hands together.

"Problem solved," he announced to the silent room.

He stood and looked over at Jane's window. "You're going to marry me, Jane Carson. Why? Because you love me, and I love you just the way you are. You never once suggested I change my ways, and I don't want you to change yours. We're going to make one hell of a husband and wife."

He stood staring across the street. "Now, how do I propose to you after I've made such a mess of things?"

Alex gave his problem thought. A simple apology wouldn't do, especially after he had managed to make a spectacle out of them at the church this afternoon. He'd need to make his proposal more public so people would see exactly how he felt about Jane, and so Jane wouldn't doubt his feelings or intentions for one moment. And of course she'd be less likely to turn his proposal down in front of other people.

He laughed at his assumption. No little voice was necessary to warn him that if Jane didn't want to marry him, she wouldn't care who was around, she'd refuse. But then that was what made his Jane special.

His Jane. He sure liked the sound of that. He'd like it even better when he could introduce her as *his wife*.

He gave her window one last glance and then turned and headed to his bedroom. Tomorrow was the big Fourth of July celebration, and it would be a celebration in more ways than one.

Tomorrow in some unorthodox manner he intended to propose to Jane. How and when he wasn't certain, but when the time was right, he'd know it and then . . .

"You're all mine, Jane Carson."

Twenty-five

JANE sat at her kitchen table waiting. She had expected Alex to arrive at her doorstep last night full of apologies, but he hadn't. She had misjudged his character, and the sooner she accepted that fact, the better off she'd be.

Early this morning she had taken herself off to Jacob's office to do some work and discovered Jacob had the same thoughts. She had found him deep in paperwork at his desk. He had attempted to console her without openly acknowledging her and Alex's public altercation yesterday.

Jane, not wanting to hear any more well-intentioned advice, blurted out, "Would you like to go to the celebration with me Jacob?"

Jacob grinned and rubbed at his chin thoughtfully. "You have your picnic basket all packed?"

She laughed. The man was forever thinking about food. "To the brim."

"Cookies?"

"Oatmeal," she enticed. "Cold lemonade, fried chicken, dill potatoes, green bean salad, blueberry pie—"

"Good Lord, I've died and gone to heaven," he said, beaming.

"Then you'll go?"

Jacob laughed and added with sincerity, "I'll go, but it isn't because I'm after your picnic basket. It's because I enjoy your company."

"The feeling is mutual."

"Jane." His tone turned serious. "Things will work out, you'll see."

Jane understood his reference was directed to the situation between her and Alex. She wanted the *situation* to work out, but she was suffering from painful misgivings as to the outcome.

Minnie burst into the office. "She's entered her raspberry jam. Do you believe she did that to me? Maisie always enters her blueberry jam like all the other women, and this year, when I decide to enter my raspberry, what does she do? She enters her *raspberry!*"

Jane and Jacob stared at the raving woman, both choosing to remain silent. Her usual neat gray hair had strands hanging lose at the sides of her face, and her apron hung haphazardly around her waist, covering her cornflower-blue cotton dress that was trimmed with a delicate white lace collar. Between her tone and her appearance, it was obvious she was agitated.

Minnie paced in front of Jacob and Jane. "Maisie's done this to me on purpose. Yesterday I was busy decorating the covers to my jams with yellow calice material, and what does she do? She comes into the kitchen, her jars already decorated with the identical material. Then she accused me of stealing her idea. Me?"

"Perhaps it was just a coincidence," Jacob suggested calmly.

Minnie shot him a reproachful look. "It was no coincidence. Maisie did it on purpose. I bet she found my material and used it for her own benefit."

"Maybe her tastes run the same as yours," Jane offered.

Minnie grabbed her chest. "Lord, don't even suggest such a horrible thought. Maisie and I are like night and day. Completely opposite from each other."

Jacob turned his head to hide his smile.

Jane didn't even attempt to disguise her smile.

"I don't understand how people can ever mistake our identity. I obviously have a straighter nose and higher cheekbones. I have less wrinkles around my eyes, as well as my mouth. I'm also taller than Maisie and weigh less. The difference is tremendous."

Jacob coughed, hiding his laughter.

Jane's smile grew.

Minnie pushed the fallen strands of her hair up, tucking them neatly into place. "Today people will see once and for all the difference. My jam will win the contest, taking first place, and then the matter will finally be settled as to who is the best cook."

"Jacob, would you like to accompany Maisie and myself to the celebration?" Minnie added a charming smile to her invitation.

"I'm going with Jane." Jacob looked to her for help.

Jane couldn't leave the bickering sisters on their own for the day. She was too afraid of serious repercussions if one should win the jam contest and not the other one. They definitely required a referee. "You and Maisie are welcome to join us. The more the merrier."

"Alex isn't taking you?" Minnie asked, a spark of delight in her eyes.

Jane shook her head, refusing to explain.

"We'd be delighted to join you," she said and grinned from ear to ear. "I'll just run along and tell Maisie. My, but she'll be surprised."

Jacob looked to Jane after Minnie left. "This is going to be an interesting celebration."

Jane agreed with a quick nod.

"Do you know who I feel sorry for the most?"

Curious, she asked, "Who?"

"The judge of the jam contest."

Jane and Jacob's twin laughter could be heard outside his office.

* * *

"It is an absolutely gorgeous day," Maisie said, helping Jane spread the brown blanket under the large maple tree.

Jane looked up at the rustling maple leaves and the patches of sun that peeked through the numerous branches. "It's a perfect day to celebrate the Fourth of July."

She dropped down to the blanket, opening her picnic basket.

"Hello, Samantha, Cord, Alex," Maisie called out and waved.

Jane froze, her hand in the basket. She didn't want to acknowledge Alex's presence, but she had no choice. She looked up and across a few feet to another huge maple tree where all three sat relaxing much the same as her party was doing.

She waved, her eyes scanning the trio quickly. She intended to look away just as quickly, but she couldn't. Alex looked so handsome, her eyes remained fixed on him.

He wore his dark trousers, white shirt, and dark jacket, which she knew from experience he'd remove in no time. His brown hair hung carelessly along his forehead, making him all the more appealing. His blue eyes, she realized with sudden awareness, were concentrated intently on her.

She felt a shiver run through her and heat stain her cheeks.

She turned away, drawing her attention back to her basket. "Lemonade, Jacob?"

"I'd love some," he said.

Maisie arranged her and Minnie's food along with Jane's. "Have one of my biscuits with my prizewinning raspberry jam on it, Jacob?" Maisie asked, spreading a thick layer of jam over a golden-brown biscuit.

Jacob reached out eagerly for it.

"You haven't won yet. You can't call it your prizewinning jam unless you've won," Minnie scolded.

Maisie shrugged. "I'll win. It's my best batch ever."

"I'll say," Jacob agreed between bites.

Maisie sent her sister a smug smile.

"Taste mine," Minnie said, popping open her jar of raspberry jam and spreading a thick layer on her lightly browned biscuit.

Jacob accepted hers. "Good, very good," he said, keeping his mouth full so he wouldn't be questioned further.

"See," Minnie said to her sister.

"We'll see," Maisie corrected her. "Jacob is no judge. He's a good friend who I am sure wouldn't want to hurt anyone's feelings."

Jacob nodded vigorously and reached for one of Jane's perfectly baked biscuits.

Jane found her appetite sluggish and her eyes constantly drifting. She couldn't prevent herself from searching Alex out. She watched the way he talked so easily with people, and the way he played with the children who ran over to him, swinging one little boy up into the air and causing him to burst into giggles. She ached to run over to him and fling herself into his arms, but she had her pride.

"Damn pride," she mumbled.

"Did you say something, Jane?" Jacob asked, having returned from speaking to a group of men from the Double B ranch.

"No, just thinking out loud."

"Day sure is beautiful."

"It certainly is."

"Too beautiful to spend under a maple tree all day."

Jane smiled up at him. "Are you trying to tell me I'm moping."

"Yes," he said and reached his hand down to her to help her stand.

"I suppose I should go see how the games are doing since I organized them."

"You should join in some of them yourself. You'll have some fun, and that's what this day is for—fun."

"Jacob!" Minnie shouted as she approached.

"Jane!" Maisie called out, running behind her sister.

Minnie got to the pair first. "You must come with us. The jam contest is starting."

"Yes, Jane, do join us," Maisie said, almost breathless.

"Ladies," Jacob announced gallantly. "I would love to join you both, but Jane must go off to see how the games and races are going and to have some fun herself."

Maisie glanced toward Alex and then back to Jane. "That's a wonderful idea. Go join in the fun. Minnie, you and Jacob run along—I'll catch up with you."

"Where are you off to?" Minnie demanded.

Maisie's answer was a wave of her hand as she hurried away.

Jane wished Minnie luck and headed in the opposite direction toward the open area where the games were being held.

Jane stopped and enjoyed the sight of Billy Taylor bobbing for apples. His whole head was submerged. He was bound and determined to capture one.

She stood watching his head bob up and down, chasing the elusive apple. Then in a flash his head sprung up, and there in his mouth was an apple, shiny red and dripping wet to match his face. She clapped her hands in appreciation of his accomplishment and moved on. She stood a good distance back as she took in the fun and excitement of the pig-chasing contest. She didn't want her newly stitched lavender dress sprayed with mud.

Against her better judgment, and acting like a woman out to impress a man, she had taken Maisie's advice and worn her prettiest and newest dress. She had even fussed with her hair, something she had rarely worried about.

A squeal from the pig returned her attention to the contest. The kids seemed to be having a grand old time chasing the fat little animal, while the pig delighted in outsmarting them and staying out of their reach. Most of the kids were covered from head to toe with mud, many having just missed from grabbing the animal only to fall face first in the mud. Mothers shook their heads and stood close by with a bucket and towel, ready to tend to their children as soon as the chase was over.

Jane wandered on, pleased by the results of her efforts in organizing the games. She received many waves and appreciative remarks.

Lillie Taylor had stopped her and made a point of telling her how much better the games were this year than last, and how she, Jane, should be appointed chairperson for the games every year.

Jane was certain her praise was related someway to her pleasure of her son doing so well in bobbing for apples.

The sack race had just begun when she approached the starting line, and she found herself jumping up and down and cheering the participants on. Kincaid Hutton won, and his wife, Faith, and his daughter, Amanda, ran over to him to give him congratulatory kisses.

The loving family scene tore at her heart, and she turned her head away, unable to watch such a loving exchange. She had thought this day would be wonderful for her and Alex. She had had visions of them attending the celebration hand in hand and announcing to all their plans of marriage. Instead she was here with Jacob and spending most of the day on her own, though she had to admit her solitude was of her own making.

Many of the townsfolk had asked her to join them for a cool drink or a bite of food as she had passed their blankets, but she had chosen to remain alone. She wasn't at all in the mood to be congenial.

She was feeling despondent and sorry for herself, pitiful emotions and ones she had never expected to equate with herself. The disturbing thought set her into motion. She'd had enough self-pity. If Alexander Evans wanted to make the mistake of his life and walk away from a relationship with her, then it was his loss, not hers. She had a full rewarding life and would continue to have one with or without him.

She marched over to the sign-up sheet for the other games and signed herself up for the three-legged race. Zeke Gallagher was pairing up people and promised her he'd find her a surefire winner to team up with.

Jane moved along to the side while waiting for the race to begin and partners to be called.

"Hi, Jane," Samantha said, walking up to her.

Jane felt awkward at first seeing Samantha, but quelled her misgivings. The daughter had nothing to do with her father's actions.

"Hello, Samantha, enjoying the celebration?"

"The celebration is wonderful as usual. How are you enjoying the day?"

"I'm having a wonderful time," Jane said in an attempt to convince herself she actually was.

Samantha smiled at her though she could have sworn she appeared disappointed. "Have you joined in any games?"

"Just signed up for the three-legged race."

"Who's your partner?" Samantha asked curiously and looked around her to see if she could discover his identity.

"Zeke's promised to find me a winning partner."

Samantha's smile grew wide. "A winner, you say?"

"Surefire winner," Jane repeated his words exactly.

Samantha leaned in close to Jane, placing her hand on her arm and whispering, "You deserve a surefire winner."

Jane looked at her in surprise, feeling she wasn't talking about the race."

"See you later—and good luck."

Jane watched Samantha hurry off, weaving in and

out of the crowd as though in a hurry to reach her destination.

Jane shrugged, wondering what had gotten into the young girl.

She cast a quick glance around the area—she supposed in search of Alex, though she didn't want to admit it. He was nowhere to be seen. It didn't matter, she attempted to convince herself. She intended to have a good time for herself, and that good time was about to begin with this race.

"Three-legged race starting!" Zeke bellowed from the starting line. "When I call out the names, all you three-legged folks hobble on over here."

Laughter rippled through the crowd, and Zeke began calling off names.

Jane wasn't surprised to hear Faith's and Kincaid's names called out or Cord's and Samantha's. It seemed that all the names being announced were married couples, and Jane suddenly wished she hadn't signed up for the race.

"Jane Carson."

Jane stepped forward.

"Alex Evans."

Jane felt her heart drop near to her feet. Alex stepped up beside her. "Looks like we're a team whether we like it or not."

Why did his blue eyes look more appealing than usual, and why did his lemon-scent aftershave balm have to sting her senses and bring back intimate memories? He was minus his jacket, and his shirtsleeves were rolled up, displaying the strength of his arms. Bravely she forced herself to speak. "It doesn't bother me. Your obstinate trait should come in handy for this race."

"Unless your stubbornness interferes and doesn't allow you to follow my lead," he retaliated, glaring down at her with a disarming smile.

Jane recognized a challenge when issued, and she realized at that moment just how much she had missed his willful nature. Due to their combating personalities, they had kept each other on their toes. Facing challenges and discovering solutions, they had worked as a team and had never realized it.

Jane turned a bright smile on him. "I suggest that whoever sets the best rhythm take the lead."

"You're on," he agreed, but added, "We both know it will be me."

Jane laughed as Alex took the sack handed to him by Zeke.

"Doubt me, do you?" he asked, holding the sack down for her to step into.

Before placing her foot in the sack, Jane bent down, grabbed the back hem of her skirt, pulled it up between her legs, hooking the end in her waistband, and forming wide pants that only showed a little of her stocking-covered calf.

She ached to answer that she had never doubted him, that she loved him beyond reason, but it wasn't her love he questioned. "Doubt never entered my head," she said softly.

Alex looked at her strangely as he slipped his leg into the sack and pulled it up both their legs.

"Get ready," Zeke shouted.

Alex circled her waist with his arm, holding her firm. She had no choice but to slip her arm around his back to balance their support.

"Move to the edge of the starting line," Zeke ordered.

Laughter echoed in the air as several couples fell to the ground.

"Guess we know who hasn't worked out who's the boss in their marriages yet," Zeke joked.

While everyone enjoyed a good laugh and the couples that had fallen righted themselves, Jane and Alex moved with ease to the starting line. Their accomplishment was made simple because Alex had practically lifted her off the ground to do so.

"Your arm, be careful," she scolded.

"My arm is healed completely. Quit worrying."

"You have no sense."

Alex looked down into her eyes and seriously and in a soft whisper said, "You're right, sometimes I don't, and you're the reason."

Jane felt her breath catch. His response could be construed in different ways. Jane chose the romantic reason. He loved her and his love mixed up his senses.

"On your mark!" Zeke shouted.

Alex's arm hooked more firmly around her.

"Get set!" Zeke added in a higher pitch.

"Follow me, Jane?" Alex whispered in her ear.

His fresh breath tickled her ear and sent goose bumps running down her arm. "Yes, Alex."

"Go!" Zeke screamed at the top of his lungs.

Twenty-six

ALEX set a perfect rhythm, and Jane followed. They raced as though they were one, a unit, whole, together. Each step was matched by the other. They were a perfect pair.

Jane smiled, pleased by their unity and pleased by the way he held her so possessively to his side. The warm air whipped at their faces, and the sun beat down on their heads. It felt glorious.

Couples began to fall, peels of laughter echoing their descent to the hard ground. Jane laughed and felt an exhilaration stir her senses as she spied the finish line ahead.

"We're going to make it," Alex said, picking up speed.

Jane fell in sync with his pace change while her thoughts challenged her. Did he love her? Would *they* make it?

They crossed the finish line far ahead of any other couple and to the cheers of the surrounding crowd.

Alex hugged her to him.

She hugged him back, her breath rapid, her heart racing and not only from the three-legged sack race, but from the race she and Alex had run for the last six weeks.

He looked down into her face. She looked up. Her

breath locked in her throat. Would he tell her now? Would he tell her he loved her? His expression was anxious and hesitatnt all at once. His own breathing was labored and matched hers. He was getting ready, preparing to speak to her. To say what? To admit what?

Oh, Lord, please let him tell me he loves me, she silently prayed.

"Jane," he said, both of them ignoring the cheers of congratulations that surrounded them. He lowered his head, his lips a fraction from hers.

"Jane!" The scream pierced the air and was followed by an identical yell.

"Jane!"

Alex snapped his head back, glared down at her, shook his head, released her with a slightly reluctant shove, and marched off, disappearing into the crowd.

Maisie and Minnie were on top of her in no time.

"You won't believe what that idiot judge did!" Maisie said, grabbing Jane's arm.

Minnie uncharacteristically agreed with her sister. "Maisie's correct. The judge is an idiot." She grabbed Jane's other arm and the two sisters walked off the race field, forcing Jane to go along with them.

"A tie," Maisie said, shaking her head. "The man actually had the audacity to claim the jam contest a tie."

Jane didn't give a fiddler's damn about the judge, the jam, or anything but Alex. She had thought—no *felt* his need to admit . . .

Her thoughts halted abruptly. What was he about to admit? Was it his love for her? Was it that he didn't desire a permanent relationship with her? Her soaring emotions plummeted like a deflated hot-air balloon. Confusion and despondency overwhelmed her all at once.

"It's not fair," Minnie complained as they neared their blanket under the big maple tree.

Jane cast a quick glance across the way to where Alex had camped with his daughter and her husband.

Their blanket remained empty. She dropped herself onto the blanketed ground, a heavy sigh following her descent.

Jane didn't feel like listening to the twin women arguing and agreed with their every comment, hoping to ease their agitation. "You're right, ladies. It doesn't seem fair to declare a tie." Though she certainly understood the judge's decision. If he had chosen one sister's jam over the others, there'd be a war unleashed in Harmony.

"Maisie," Minnie said, sending her sister a direct look. "We must do something about the judging for the contest next year."

Maisie agreed with a sharp nod. "You're absolutely right. I think we should take on the task ourselves and interview and decide upon the judges for next year."

"Excellent," Minnie said with a clap of her hands. "I have a suggestion for one judge."

"Who?" Maisie asked, her excitement matching her sister's.

"Zeke!"

Maisie smiled with pleasure. "A good choice. A very good choice!"

Jane couldn't for the life of her believe what she was hearing. The two sisters were actually agreeing on something. She had never, in the whole time she had known them, heard them agree on anything important.

Minnie grew bubbly like a young schoolgirl in the throes of excitement about her first date. "Let's go ask him now."

"Good idea," Maisie readily agreed. "And while we're at it, let's ask Fred Winchester, too."

Minnie eyed her sister skeptically. "Any particular reason why?"

"He'd make a good judge, that's why," Maisie defended.

"Possibly," Minnie said.

"Not possibly, he would," Maisie insited, hurrying along after her sister as Minnie walked away.

Jane smiled and shook her head. At least all was well with the world—Maisie and Minnie were disagreeing again.

Jane watched Maisie turn and look at her. Jane waved goodbye, but the woman hesitated a moment and then made a hasty path back to Jane.

"Did you and Alex talk?" she asked anxiously.

"Somewhat."

Maisie shook her head and her finger at Jane. "That man had better get a move on and listen to me. I have no time for his dallying." With that she stomped off.

Jane stared after her and wondered what the devil was going on.

Alex paced the area not far from the race field, but far enough removed for him to be alone. He'd had the moment right before him, the perfect time, and he had let it slip right through his hands.

He wanted, at that very moment, to wring Maisie's and Minnie's necks. The two women had interfered between him and Jane since day one, and he was sick and tired of it.

He should have dragged Jane right off the race field and told her exactly what he had been aching to tell her for some time. He loved her and wanted her to be his wife.

Damn, but this day was trying his patience. He had imagined it so simple. He'd find the appropriate time and propose. So what did he do? He found the appropriate time—well, maybe not appropriate, but it felt right—and he let it slip by him.

He ran his fingers through his hair, its length reminding him he required a haircut. He conjured up images of how delightful it would be to have Jane cut it for him.

She'd stand close to him. He'd be able to clasp her

waist, draw her near, drink in her scent, nestle his head against her belly . . .

He moaned, ran his hand over his face, released several oaths, and stomped off.

Jane sat relaxing under the maple tree, a glass of lemonade beside her. She watched some of the young mothers put their babies down to nap on their blankets while they shared a cool drink and gossip. Children ran playfully around the blanket while others sat and munched on fried chicken and some delighted in large slices of recently baked apple pies.

Races were still going on, excited shouts still being heard, and . . .

Jane stilled her thoughts and her wandering gaze to listen more intently. Claps and loud shouts of encouragement caught her ear.

Billy ran by her, a large dripping ice cream cone in his hand.

"What's all the excitement?" she asked.

"Strength contest," he answered and hurried on so as not to miss a moment of it.

Jane stood and made her way slowly over to the area where the commotion was taking place. A crowd had gathered round the participants. Not being able to see well, Jane stood on her toes to peer over the shoulders of those around her.

She was surprised to see Alex standing in the middle of the clearing, holding a large and heavy sledgehammer clasped in his hands. Several men gave him an encouraging slap on the back with a few passing remarks.

"Show the young bucks a thing or two."

"Give 'em hell, Alex."

Jane wrinkled her brow. That sledgehammer looked mighty heavy. She glanced around the crowd, catching sight of Jacob. She weaved her way in and out of the throng of people until she stood next to him.

"What exactly is going on?"

"Strength contest," he said. "Alex is one of the finalists."

Her eyes widened considerably. "He's been swinging that sledgehammer?"

"Several times," Jacob informed her.

"That tool looks mighty heavy."

Jacob smiled. "It is mighty heavy. A man needs more than a bit of strength to swing that thing. That's why this is called a strength contest."

"His wrist," Jane said without further explanation, since to her those two words said everything.

Jacob raised his brow. "Think the strain may be too much?"

"Don't you?" she questioned incredulously. "His wrist is barely healed. He has no business swinging a sledgehammer."

"You've got a point."

Jane looked stunned. "I've got a point? Don't you think you should stop him?"

"Not my place to interfere. He's a grown man, and besides he's your patient."

"He's right, dear, Alex is your patient and your responsibility," Maisie said, coming up behind Jane. "If you feel he shouldn't be participating in such a strenuous event, then it is your duty as his caretaker to tell him so."

Jane was about to argue, but looking at both of them standing there like comrades in battle, she thought better of it and said, "You're both right. I'll handle this myself." She took off, shoving people out of her way as she walked through the crowd toward Alex.

She pushed and shoved at the herd of people, but they were all bound and determined to watch this ridiculous display of brute strength. She supposed to the men it was proof of manly potency and to the women it was exciting.

Cheers filled the air and sent a shiver through Jane. She saw the sledgehammer rise in the air above the heads of the few men in front of her who blocked her view of Alex. She shoved the brutes who barred her path with her elbows and stepped into the clearing just as Alex swung the sledgehammer.

His arms, thick with strained muscles from their exertion, struggled with the heavy tool, and as it turned sharply to make its descent, so did Alex's wrist.

Jane couldn't tell if the snap she heard was a twig or a bone, but the sound and uncertainty of its origin filled her with dread.

In the next instant the air was pierced by a loud yell, and Alex and the sledgehammer collapsed to the ground.

Jane, for a mere second, found her limbs frozen, and then realizing Alex's plight, she rushed to his side, dropping down on her knees beside him.

"Don't move. Don't you dare move!" Her fear made her voice sound stern.

Alex was on his knees himself, doubled over with his one arm tucked over his other arm. The cursed sledgehammer lay to the side.

"Brainless," she reprimanded, her hand running over his back, attempting to comfort while scolding him at the same time.

He mumbled, but she couldn't understand him. "What did you say?" She leaned down closer to him.

He mumbled again.

"I can't understand you. Give me your wrist," she commanded, slipping her hand beneath his cradled arm while reaching for his injured arm.

He relinquished his limb without a fight, and she hastily examined it, not taking the time to look up into his face.

She ran her hand down his arm and over his wrist, testing carefully and gently for breaks. She repeated her examination, surprised by what she felt, and then her fingers stilled.

Nothing. There was absolutely nothing wrong with his wrist.

His fingers sneaked beneath her chin and slowly lifted it up. She was met with a smile.

"I needed your attention. We needed to talk. Neither happened and I found myself a desperate man. The one surefire way I knew I'd have your undivided attention was to appear injured."

"Well, you got my attention," she said softly, still clinging to his wrist.

"Actually I got near the whole town's attention."

They both cast a quick glance around them. Near everyone in Harmony surrounded them with anxious expressions.

He spoke low, his attention fixed on Jane and Jane alone. "But then I suppose the whole town will know soon enough."

"Know what?" she whispered, feeling as though this moment was theirs to share alone.

He brushed a kiss across her lips. "That I love you . . . just the way you are."

Her heart soared. She had been right about him, oh, had she been right! She wasted no time in confirming her own feelings. "I love you, Alex."

He smiled and wrapped his arms around her. "Good, then you'll marry me?"

She threw herself against him, her arms going around his neck as they tumbled to the dry dusty ground. "Yes, most definitely yes!"

Epilogue

POTTED herbs lined the windowsill and overflowed the basket in the center of the table. A cool fall breeze drifted in through the open window, stirring the cornflower-blue curtains. Hot apple muffins only minutes from the oven and still in the muffin tin sat hastily discarded on a crocheted pot holder. And laughter, softly teasing, trickled down from the upstairs bedroom.

"It isn't even dark," Jane whispered in a giggle.

Alex hugged his naked wife closer to him beneath the blanket. "Time is irrelevant when you're in love. And I do love you, Mrs. Evans."

Jane slipped her arm across her husband's slim waist and squeezed. "And I love you, Mr. Evans."

Alex caught her chin and turned her face up to look at him. Her look of utter contentment and satisfaction nearly took his breath away. Still, he worried that she might have harbored some regrets. "You're not sorry we married so soon and had only a small wedding?"

Jane delivered a quick kiss to his lips and then laughed. "I'm glad we married on July fifth. I couldn't have waited a moment longer, and you call having the whole town of Harmony attend our wedding small?"

Alex laughed with her. "I suppose we couldn't have kept them all away if we'd wanted to."

"They're our friends and neighbors, they care about us, and it felt good to have them join in the celebration."

"And everyone certainly celebrated," Alex agreed.

"Even Minnie and Maisie did, to everyone's amazement."

"Ha, their minds were busy scheming their next matchmaking plan."

"Well, Maisie was the victor in ours," Jane said, snuggling up contentedly against her husband.

Alex ran his hand down his wife's soft naked backside. "And I'm damn glad she was."

"Alex! Your language," she teased.

Alex gently moved his wife onto her back, then slipped over her and whispered, "I'm damn, damn glad you're my wife."

Jane smiled. "And I'm damn glad you love me."

"I'll always love you, Jane Evans. Always." He lowered his head, captured her lips, and showed her just how much he loved her.

Come take a walk down Harmony's Main Street in 1874, and meet a different resident of this colorful Kansas town each month.

A TOWN CALLED HARMONY

__PLAYING CUPID   by Donna Fletcher
0-7865-0056-5/$4.99

When Harmony's newspaperman needs some neighborly help after an accident, he gets more than he bargained for. Maisie and Minnie Parker are going to help him mend his broken heart–and match him with a very special love.

__COMING HOME   by Kathleen Kane
0-7865-0060-3/$4.99 *(Coming in December)*

There's no place like home for a new beginning. But when young widow Libby Taylor comes back to Harmony, she turns it into a town divided. Sheriff Travis Miller must lay down the law with this lady–even as he's falling in love with her.

Don't miss the rest of the Harmony series...

__KEEPING FAITH   by Kathleen Kane
0-7865-0016-6/$4.99

__TAKING CHANCES   by Rebecca Hagan Lee
0-7865-0022-2/$4.99

__CHASING RAINBOWS
0-7865-0041-7/$4.99   by Linda Shertzer

__PASSING FANCY   by Lydia Browne
0-7865-0046-8/$4.99

Payable in U.S. funds. No cash orders accepted. Postage & handling: $1.75 for one book, 75¢ for each additional. Maximum postage $5.50. Prices, postage and handling charges may change without notice. Visa, Amex, MasterCard call 1-800-788-6262, ext. 1, refer to ad # 489

Or, check above books   Bill my: ☐ Visa ☐ MasterCard ☐ Amex
and send this order form to:
The Berkley Publishing Group   Card#_____ (expires)
390 Murray Hill Pkwy., Dept. B   ($15 minimum)
East Rutherford, NJ 07073   Signature_____
Please allow 6 weeks for delivery.   Or enclosed is my: ☐ check ☐ money order

Name_____   Book Total $_____

Address_____   Postage & Handling $_____

City_____   Applicable Sales Tax $_____
                                      (NY, NJ, PA, CA, GST Can.)
State/ZIP_____   Total Amount Due $_____

ROMANCE FROM THE HEART OF AMERICA
Diamond Homespun Romance

Homespun novels are touching, captivating romances from the heartland of America that combine the laughter and tears of family life with the tender warmth of true love.

__YOURS TRULY 0-7865-0001-8/$4.99
  by Sharon Harlow
__SUMMER'S GIFT 0-7865-0006-9/$4.99
  by Deborah Wood
__FAMILY REUNION 0-7865-0011-0/$4.99
  by Jill Metcalf
__PICKETT'S FENCE 0-7865-0017-4/$4.99
  by Linda Shertzer
__COURTING SEASON 0-7865-0023-9/$4.99
  by Jo Anne Cassity
__COUNTRY SUNSHINE 0-7865-0042-5/$4.99
  by Teresa Warfield
__FORGIVING HEARTS 0-7865-0047-6/$4.99
  by Christina Cordaire
__OUR HOUSE 0-7865-0057-3/$4.99
  by Debra S. Cowan
__PARTING GIFTS 0-7865-0061-1/$4.99
  by Lorraine Heath (December)

Payable in U.S. funds. No cash orders accepted. Postage & handling: $1.75 for one book, 75¢ for each additional. Maximum postage $5.50. Prices, postage and handling charges may change without notice. Visa, Amex, MasterCard call 1-800-788-6262, ext. 1, refer to ad # 411

Or, check above books Bill my: ☐ Visa ☐ MasterCard ☐ Amex	(expires)
and send this order form to:	
The Berkley Publishing Group Card#_____	
390 Murray Hill Pkwy., Dept. B	($15 minimum)
East Rutherford, NJ 07073 Signature_____	
Please allow 6 weeks for delivery. Or enclosed is my: ☐ check ☐ money order	
Name_____	Book Total $_____
Address_____	Postage & Handling $_____
City_____	Applicable Sales Tax $_____ (NY, NJ, PA, CA, GST Can.)
State/ZIP_____	Total Amount Due $_____

If you enjoyed this book, take advantage of this special offer. Subscribe now and get a

FREE
Historical Romance

No Obligation (a $4.50 value)

Each month the editors of True Value select the four *very best* novels from America's leading publishers of romantic fiction. Preview them in your home *Free* for 10 days. With the first four books you receive, we'll send you a FREE book as our introductory gift. No Obligation!

If for any reason you decide not to keep them, just return them and owe nothing. If you like them as much as we think you will, you'll pay just $4.00 each and save at *least* $.50 each off the cover price. (Your savings are *guaranteed* to be at least $2.00 each month.) There is NO postage and handling – or other hidden charges. There are no minimum number of books to buy and you may cancel at any time.

Send in the Coupon Below

To get your FREE historical romance fill out the coupon below and mail it today. As soon as we receive it we'll send you your FREE Book along with your first month's selections.

Mail To: **True Value Home Subscription Services, Inc., P.O. Box 5235
120 Brighton Road, Clifton, New Jersey 07015-5235**

YES! I want to start previewing the very best historical romances being published today. Send me my FREE book along with the first month's selections. I understand that I may look them over FREE for 10 days. If I'm not absolutely delighted I may return them and owe nothing. Otherwise I will pay the low price of just $4.00 each: a total $16.00 (at least an $18.00 value) and save at least $2.00. Then each month I will receive four brand new novels to preview as soon as they are published for the same low price. I can always return a shipment and I may cancel this subscription at any time with no obligation to buy even a single book. In any event the FREE book is mine to keep regardless.

Name

Street Address _____ Apt. No.

City _____ State _____ Zip

Telephone

Signature
(if under 18 parent or guardian must sign)

Terms and prices subject to change. Orders subject to acceptance by True Value Home Subscription Services, Inc.

0056-5